THE STAR SOULS N

THE WISH FULF
LIFE/DEATH

JAY CLIFFIX

Book cover designed by Jay Cliffix with Canva.com
Map designed by Jay Cliffix with Map Effects Fantasy Map Builder

This book is a comprehensive English adaptation of 生死還願,
originally written by Jay Cliffix but never published in any form.

CONTENTS

MAP

PARALLOY TEDDIX W.D. 471

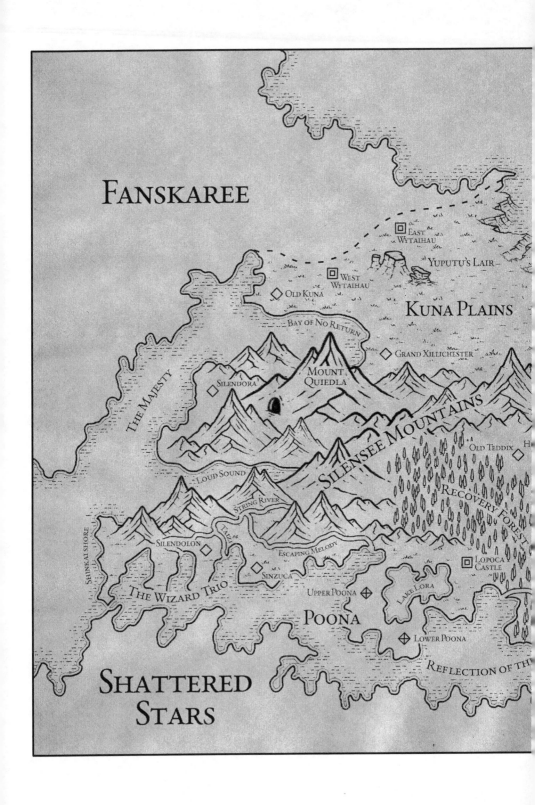

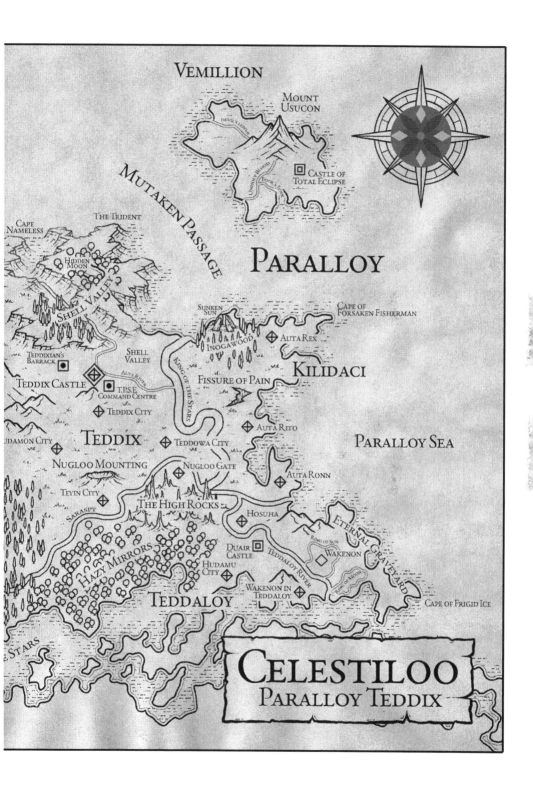

THE STAR OF DILEMMA

AWAKEN THE SOUL STANDING AT
THE CROSSROADS OF DILEMMA

CHAPTER 20

THE LOSS OF A CLEAR BOUNDARY BETWEEN GOOD AND EVIL
WILL LEAD THE COMMON PEOPLE
ASTRAY FROM THE RIGHT PATH

9 Aqual, W.D. 471
Wakenon in Teddaloy, Teddaloy

He once left the place he called home, but now he had returned with a new purpose.

The warm sunlight gently caressed the surface of the water, each ripple reflecting a myriad of colours as if the sea channel held an ethereal treasure within its depths. This majestic sight was known as the Reflection of the Stars, a natural phenomenon that marked the division between Shattered Stars and Paralloy, two distinct continents on Celestiloo. The unparalleled beauty of it left everyone spellbound, even the Auras themselves were once again stunned by its celestial iridescence.

Approaching the shore of Teddaloy aboard a modest boat, Rafaelzo and Gloria, both wearing attire befitting warriors, were seemingly guided by the unseen force of Elementro as it glided effortlessly over the waves. Their journey felt like sailing through a dream, where the line between reality and fantasy blurred, mirroring the Auras' perception of time—nebulous and inconsequential in the face of their ambitions and destinies.

Standing at the boat's edge, Gloria's eyes scanned the horizon, her features resembling her younger sister Miria but bearing the weight of more experiences etched into her countenance. Despite their similarities, the two hailed from different clans—Miria, a master of mind Elementro, and Gloria, a formidable wielder of lightning and electricity whose temperament often betrayed her prowess.

"Chief Elder Rafaelzo, what things do you still remember about this place?" Gloria asked, her voice slicing through the tranquility of the scene. "Paralloy... It was meant to be the heart of the Auras."

Rafaelzo paused for a moment before answering. "We were supposed to forget, not remember. Our goal is to find your sister, to deal with the Umbras, and to negotiate with the Son of Chaos. We have to focus on the present."

"True," Gloria conceded, "but sometimes, memories can be stubborn."

"I am fully aware of that," Rafaelzo smiled with his usual kindness and affinity. "Life is not easy for people who have lived countless days like us."

As the boat reached the shore, Rafaelzo looked around, trying to find something familiar in the landscape. But everything had changed—the air felt heavy, the natural world seemed subdued, and even the sky bore invisible scars and streaks that hinted at a darker history. Feeling the weight of the past, Gloria grumbled, "Ugh, the Auras really did a great job eliminating the Binaries back then... or our journey now would have been much shorter."

Rafaelzo simply kept smiling, not offering a response. As they approached a city called Wakenon in Teddaloy near the shore, he observed the bustling human activities around the city gate. This was a new experience for him, as he had never witnessed the prosperity of human beings in person like this before. He stopped in his tracks, considering their next move.

"Are you suggesting we should disguise ourselves?" Gloria asked.

Rafaelzo pondered for a moment before shaking his head. "No... I think we shouldn't fear so much. Let's just walk past them."

"Are you sure about that?" Gloria challenged, her eyes narrowing in suspicion. "We could easily attract unwanted attention."

"Maybe not," Rafaelzo replied confidently, his eyes meeting hers. "Let's give it a try and see."

Together, they walked towards the city gate. Ignoring the whispers and stares of the city's inhabitants, he led Gloria to a vegetable stall manned by a middle-aged woman who seemed unfazed by their unusual appearance.

"Excuse me." Rafaelzo started his very first conversation with the human beings since he left Celestiloo hundreds of years ago in the human calendar. "Could you show us the way to Teddix Castle?"

The woman looked annoyed at being interrupted but

begrudgingly pulled out a map of Paralloy from behind a stack of crates. She spread it across the table of the stall and pointed to the north side of the continent. "It'll take you about two full days to get there, not counting any time for rest," she explained. "That's where those nasty Teddixians reside."

Gloria raised an eyebrow. "Huh? I thought you were a Teddixian yourself," she remarked.

The woman ignored her comment, hastily rolling up the map and shooing them away. "Now be on your way," she said gruffly.

As they departed from the stall, Gloria's confusion was apparent, while Rafaelzo appeared to grasp the situation well. They proceeded to stroll through the city, with the clamour of bustling life gradually receding into the background as they delved into discussions about the politics prevailing on the continent.

"Seems like the Son of Chaos isn't such a great king after all," Gloria mused, frowning.

Intrigued, Rafaelzo glanced at her. "How did you come to such a conclusion?"

"Because the people here don't seem happy," Gloria replied. "Isn't ruling supposed to improve the lives of your subjects? Just look at us. We have exceptional leaders like you, like Novaubri, and we have been thriving so remarkably."

"Am I an exceptional leader?"

"I wouldn't dare to say you are not."

"Hah, well, judging the state of an entire kingdom based on a single person's opinion is hardly fair. Beliefs run deep, and people will cling to them no matter what. Changing a person's beliefs is often the most difficult task anyone can face."

"Fine," Gloria relented, her rebellious nature briefly surfacing before being tempered by her trust in her chief elder. "I'll reserve judgment until I meet the Son of Chaos myself. Now, do you remember the way to the castle from that sketchy map?"

Rafaelzo pointed to his head, reassuring her. "I always remember the way."

"So what's the purpose of requesting a map?"

"I just wanted to observe the actual changes for a brief record."

4

"You truly have a penchant for creating dramas, don't you?"

"I won't deny it," Rafaelzo laughed again. "Anyway, hopefully, we'll reunite with the others very soon. Let's keep going. Just two more days until our arrival at Teddix Castle and our encounter with the Son of Chaos. I'm looking forward to that."

10 Aqual, W.D. 471
Boundless Ocean

With his so-called new purpose, his destiny hung in the balance, uncertain of whether it would lead to life or death, unlike those who claimed to have all the answers for what he should have become.

At the northeastern edge of Paralloy, beyond the Mutaken Passage and even further, past the massive island known as Vemillion, the Boundless Ocean extended across a vast expanse of water on Celestiloo. Standing on the deck of the dilapidated fishing vessel, Mu Mann experienced a momentary respite from her usual worries. The ocean around her lay eerily calm, its surface smooth and unbroken like a mirrored glass. She inhaled deeply, taking in the mixture of salty air and the faint, decaying odour that lingered beneath. Aware that the deceptive tranquility concealed a world of chaos and destruction beneath the waves, she allowed herself to savour the fleeting peace, if only for a while.

She loosened the strands of her hair, allowing them to flow freely and breathe in the fresh air. A sigh escaped her lips as she reminisced about the last time she had been on the ocean—it had been another life, it seemed. She tightened her military uniform jacket around her waist, the fabric serving as a reminder of the battles she had fought and the ones yet to come. Then, she turned her head, her gaze settling on the eleven light pillars jutting out of the water in the distance. Yet one pillar was conspicuously absent, and no one seemed willing —or able—to explain its disappearance.

The mystery gnawed at Mann, but she pushed it aside as the sound of footsteps approached. A burly fisherman appeared on the deck, his tall frame and dark green outfit making him an imposing figure. His black hair was short and unkempt, while the sides of his facial hair extended to his cheeks, framing a grin that showcased the gap between his two upper incisors. As the fisherman hooked a fishing net to the edge of the fishing vessel and cast it into the sea, he glanced at Mann and joked, "You know, standing there might attract sea monsters. They might just snatch you up and keep you forever."

Mann rolled her eyes and forced a weird smile, stepping away from the edge.

"That's not funny," she criticised, but her curiosity got the better of her as she studied the fisherman's face, tracing the shallow scars that crisscrossed his muscular arms like a tapestry of his past struggles against sea creatures. "So… how's the fishing been since we set out?"

The fisherman chuckled, his laughter energetically booming across the deck. "To be honest, I haven't caught a single fish. But then again, this is my first time fishing in these waters. Who knows what's down there?"

"Are you just enjoying the act of fishing, knowing that the chances of catching anything are slim to none?"

He laughed loudly once more. "You've seen right through me," he admitted, his face lighting up with amusement.

"I guess we're not so different, then," Mann couldn't help but sighed again, her eyes scanning the fishing vessel before she made her way to the left side of the deck, resting her arms on the edge. "Always trying, even when the outcome is uncertain… Maybe we're not enjoying it, but we're just getting used to it."

As she spoke, her thoughts shifted to the unseen presence that had driven the fish away, leaving the fishing net empty. It compelled her to recount the details of every destruction that had occurred in the past two weeks. Shaking her head, she redirected her focus to the present. "It's quite nice to have the chance to sail on the ocean like this, but really, what's the point? We have a battleship that can get us to our destination in no time."

"Can't say I know either," the fisherman replied, shrugging his broad shoulders. "Maybe you should ask the one who arranged this little boat trip?"

With another hearty laugh, he walked away from the deck, leaving Mann alone with her thoughts. No sooner had the fisherman disappeared than Huxtin, clad in his signature black cloak, approached Mann.

"Autaming mentioned that you were grumbling about me wasting time on this journey," Huxtin said, his voice deliberately soft as he spoke to the woman who had always fought alongside him. "And he claimed that you were very angry—angry to the point where you wanted to throw me off the ship."

"Whoa, really? It's not that serious," Mann replied without turning to face Huxtin, her tone dismissive. "Don't listen to that crazy guy; he always blows things out of proportion."

"He is a friend," Huxtin gently reminded Mann. "I made a promise to him that one day I would take him out on the ocean to the north, on a fishing vessel like this, and not by any other means."

His words carried an unspoken tenderness, and for a moment, Mann felt her defences slip. She resisted the urge to expose her vulnerabilities, determined to safeguard the fragile side of herself that she had always strived to conceal from Huxtin.

Then, surprisingly, Huxtin's fingers wrapped around a pair of black binoculars, and he raised them to his eyes.

"I thought you didn't need those to see things from afar." Mann glanced at him, her face displaying disbelief. "Using them doesn't quite align with your typical image."

"Why not?" Huxtin adjusted the focus. "With this gadget, I can see even farther."

He scanned the horizon intently. After a while, his eyes narrowed as he caught sight of something unusual. Lowering the binoculars, a look of mild surprise crossed his face. Curious, Mann snatched the binoculars from his hands and peered through them herself. "Hmph? I don't see anything special," she muttered.

Huxtin retrieved the binoculars from Mann and took another careful look. "There are ships on the water. Two metal ships with firepower, to be precise."

The vessels were strikingly different, though—one was sky blue and designed for practicality, while the other was blood red and ghastly black, adorned with extravagant decoration.

"Metal ships? And with firepower?" Mann exclaimed. "That's impossible!"

"Actually, it's quite possible." Huxtin handed the binoculars to Mann, who accepted them mostly out of reflex. "It's the exact same reason why you and your fellow Earthlings are here on this planet."

"Then it's either soldiers from the Earth Alliance or thieves."

"Let's find out." Huxtin then pressed the button on his earpiece. "Sheung Oren, deep scan the ocean ahead for any signs of danger."

The voice of Sheung Oren, the ace pilot of T.P.S.E., transmitted to his ear. "Roger that. Please hold on for a moment... What? That's... Hostile factions detected. Two spaceships belonging to the Cosmo Scavengers—Blue Justice and Nightmare Crimson—are ahead of us."

"Spaceships? Blue Justice and Nightmare Crimson? Got it."

"Oh dear, the thieves," Mann whispered. She remembered hearing about the notorious Blue Justice, though its connection to any notion of justice remained unclear to her. She also envisioned the Cosmo Scavengers pillaging Celestiloo's resources, selling them on the black markets, or worse— employing them for some nefarious purpose.

When Huxtin turned to leave the deck, Mann caught his arm. "What do you plan to do about them?" she asked, her voice edged with concern. "If they find a way back to Earth, who knows what they might do with what they steal from Celestiloo?"

"We will question them," Huxtin suggested, his tone neutral. "And then we can figure out a way to get you and the rest of the Earthlings back home."

He gently pulled his arm away and strode off, leaving Mann to follow in his wake. As she trailed behind him, her heart ached with uncertainty as well as helplessness. "You know," she murmured under her breath, "I don't really need to go back."

Before Huxtin and his companions arrived at the scene, the battle between the spaceships had concluded: the blue one, battered and broken, sank beneath the unforgiving waters, leaving only the victorious faction to celebrate their survival. Aboard Nightmare Crimson, an atmosphere of intensity and desperation hung in the air, suffocating the three captured men from the sunken blue spaceship as they huddled on the metallic surface.

Soon after, the ruthless captain of Nightmare Crimson, a man with eyes as cold as ice, closed in on the hostages. He seized one of them by the collar, pressing the blade of his machete against the captive's neck with deadly intent. Another subordinate grabbed a second hostage, while the remaining one knelt on the deck, anguish evident on his face as he mourned the loss of his fallen comrades.

"Tell me where to find the treasure," the captain demanded, his voice laced with malice. "Tell me now, Lokiata Kee, or your remaining men will die before your eyes."

Lokiata Kee, the kneeling hostage, maintained a countenance akin to a dying prey that refused to surrender its dignity as he locked eyes with his captor. "I know nothing about the treasure you're referring to," he declared, his voice infused with defiance, further fuelling the captain's anger.

"Fine… Kill his lapdog!"

With an unbearable scream, the lifeless body of the captive was callously hurled into the turbulent sea, prompting a torrent of tears to stream down Kee's face. The captain, displaying his cruelty, then pressed his machete even closer to the throat of his next target, drawing blood. "I'm giving you one more chance," he snarled.

"You'll be disappointed," Kee whispered, his voice cracking under the weight of his grief. "I cannot give you what I do not have."

"Pathetic!" the captain spat. "You hide behind ignorance, hoping to save your skin. I'm gonna have what I want, and if you can't give it to me, you're gonna pay the price."

Kee's heart raced beneath his chest, but he remained resolute. "You don't scare me. I've faced worse than you."

"Is that so?" The captain's eyes glinted with dark amusement. "Very Well. Let's see how much more suffering you can endure before you break."

Kee looked at his last man, and despite the fear coursing through him, the man managed to subtly shake his head.

"I will uphold the creed of Gathiv until my dying breath,"

Kee looked up and declared, his voice strong and his expression hardening. "Even if I knew where your precious treasure was, not a single word would escape my lips!"

"The creed? Oh, nah, the creed... The creed also teaches me to stop at nothing to seize what I desire, and this is my justice!"

"Justice is not something that can be bent or twisted to suit one's needs! Those who do so, like yourself, will ultimately meet their doom!"

"Time will reveal which side is truly righteous, but before that comes to pass, I will ask you once more: where is the treasure?"

Kee's eyes bore into the captain's soul, steadfast and unyielding. They spoke volumes even as he remained silent, communicating an answer that both men understood all too well. The ruthless captain's face twisted into a snarl, and with a swift motion, he brought his weapon down upon the unfortunate man's neck, severing it cleanly from the body. Unwilling to witness the horrific bloodshed, Kee clenched his eyes shut. He knew that he was being humiliated, and that death's cold embrace would come for him soon.

"Your justice will not save you today," the captain continued. "For it is I who truly understand the creed. Only with blood, with hatred, and without mercy can we claim the treasures of the universe for ourselves!"

Suddenly, the air above Nightmare Crimson filled with chaos as two smoke grenades exploded, releasing thick white gas that quickly engulfed the scene. Everyone aboard the vessel exchanged panicked glances, their faces a canvas of confusion as they struggled to discern the cause of the disruption. Their vision blurred by the smoke, none could see the figure in a black cloak running at astonishing speed on the surface of the water, a silver-white sword firmly in hand.

In a flash, Huxtin leapt onto Nightmare Crimson. Caught off guard, the crew members were no match for his skills; one by one, they found themselves knocked overboard into the sea. Some attempted to fight back, but their efforts proved futile against Huxtin's prowess. Even the ruthless captain, once full of confidence and bravado, found his blood-stained machete disarmed, and himself captured. It seemed as though the cycle of fate had turned against him.

When the easy fight ended, Huxtin turned to the Earthling stranger whom he hadn't met before but gave him a strong sense of familiarity. "Tell me what you want. Do you wish this man alive or dead?"

Kee hesitated, his eyes widening as he assessed the mysterious man in the cloak. "I don't know who you are, but I have no intention of killing him, or the others," he replied. Although it could be a lie, he had already made his wish clear.

The captain scoffed, bitterness lacing his tone, "Hah… I didn't realise you had friends on this planet… I must admit, I underestimated you, Lokiata Kee."

Upon hearing Kee's name, Huxtin became exceptionally cautious. "I personally know two individuals with the surname Lokiata: Lokiata Edwin, the current president of the Earth Alliance, and his only son, Lokiata Zen. And you… I have heard your name before."

The mention of those names sent a jolt through Kee, his entire demeanour shifting as if a dormant part of him had been awakened, a spark reignited by the revelation of his family connections.

With that, the captain seized the opportunity to sow discord. "The Lokiata bloodline is nothing but trouble!"

"Who are you really?" Huxtin interrupted. "I don't need to listen to your comments or insults about anyone. You have no place here."

With a forceful shove, he sent the captain tumbling off the spaceship and into the waves below. Next, he established a connection with the colossal bird lurking beneath the ocean. "We're in the clear. Bring the Hokan in."

As if on cue, Autaming's fishing vessel sailed towards them, the hidden form of the Hokan rising from the depths below. The sleek design of the battleship, now adorned in energetic reds and blues, seemed to hum with untold power as it emerged.

"Your choice is simple, Lokiata," Huxtin continued, fixing his eagle eyes on the Earthling before him. "Join me, or share the fate of your enemies."

"What do you know about me?"

"Something, everything, or nothing at all," Huxtin replied cryptically. "It depends."

Before Kee could respond, the front head of the Hokan came to life, its impulse blade vibrating with jade light. The impulse blade pierced Nightmare Crimson, effortlessly slicing through the spaceship as if it were butter. Reacting quickly, Huxtin grabbed Kee and leaped onto the ocean, escaping the doomed vessel.

All around them, the crew members swam frantically away from the wreckage, fearing injury from the fire and metal debris. The impulse blade continued its upward trajectory, leaving a deep gash in the body of the spaceship. When it returned to its horizontal position, the Hokan charged forward, cleaving the spaceship in two with a violent crunch.

As the falling water ceased its fierce cascade, the Hokan's camouflage system reactivated, rendering the battleship invisible once more. The aftermath of their confrontation disappeared as if it had never happened—the ocean was adept at concealing secrets.

"It's the XC302 Series…"

Inside the Hokan, Lokiata Kee studied the corridor's design, a flicker of recognition playing across his features. It was uncanny—the battleship's layout echoed one of his own prototype designs from years ago. Memories resurfaced like air bubbles breaking through calm water, reminding him of the time he had spent with a team that shared his goals. But now, he found himself alone once more.

"Uncle Kee!"

It had been thirteen years since Kee had last heard someone address him so familiarly. Turning towards the voice, he saw a woman who had grown into maturity from the small lady he once knew. Her eyes held a hint of recognition as they scanned him—the older face, the small ponytail he now wore despite his previous aversion to long hair. Most striking of all was the deep, angled scar stretching from his lower lip to his cheek.

"Kid?" Kee managed to break out from his momentary speechlessness. "Are you… Are you the kid from the Geoka

Orphanage? Mu Mann?"

Mu Mann grinned widely and nodded, her eyes welling up with tears. "Yes, I am! You remember me!"

He marvelled at the coincidence. "I... I can't believe this! After I left the Earth Alliance, I tried to find information about you. I heard you joined the army and became the commander of a special force, but I hadn't heard anything about you in years... I never thought we'd meet again like this!"

"It's a long story... Well, I'm not the commander of that special force anymore." Mann paused, curiosity sparking in her blurry eyes. From her observation, the benefactor in her life was wearing a long-sleeve red shirt and brown trousers laden with pockets, an outfit more reminiscent of typical Earthling attire than the extravagant clothing she would have expected from a Cosmo Scavenger. "I never thought I'd find you on a spaceship belonging to the Cosmo Scavengers, though..."

"Life has a funny way of bringing people together," Kee exclaimed, a touch of sadness in his voice, "I faced demons and chose my destiny... I'll explain to you later."

After a brief silence, Huxtin stepped out of the shadows like a spectre, his cold blue eyes piercing through the corridor. He spoke in an unfriendly tone, recounting the story of Kee's failure, "Your demons? Your destiny? You attempted to overthrow your brother, thirteen years ago. You went from hero to villain overnight. The facilities you supported were investigated, and innocent people became collateral damage."

As Huxtin continued speaking, Kee's eyes grew distant, the memories of his past and the weight of his actions visibly burdening him.

"Lokiata Kee, your nephew shared your story with me just days ago. Quite the coincidence that we meet now, and I have questions for you. Why did you join the Cosmo Scavengers? To repay your sins? Or do you simply seek something to compensate for your losses after losing everything?"

"Huxtin! That's enough!" Mann cut in, her face flushed with anger. "Don't speak to him like that!"

Unperturbed, Huxtin shot back calmly, "He must confront his nightmares sooner or later. He has to acknowledge what he has done before he can embark on the path of redemption."

Mann clenched her fists, struggling to find the right words. Her gaze shifted between Huxtin and her long-lost uncle figure, torn between defending Kee and agreeing with Huxtin's perspective. Upon their return from Cape Nameless, Huxtin became even more challenging to engage in reasoning, and Mann hadn't anticipated having to attend another lesson to uncover what lay beyond the recently constructed high wall.

"That's alright." A faint smile appearing on Kee's lips. "I actually respect him, not to mention he just saved me from, well, never mind. It's true that I need to confront my past in order to progress. His words may be harsh, but they hold more value than empty platitudes."

"Then hopefully, you can choose the right path and become the person you want to be." Huxtin's expression softened slightly. "Otherwise, you'll end up like me, unsure if living or dying is the better choice."

"Live," Mann interjected forcefully. "For the sake of the future of this universe and for those who care about you, you must choose to live. No more arguments.

Huxtin briefly glanced at Mann and Kee before departing down the corridor, leaving them grappling with their own thoughts. Kee appeared unusually calm and optimistic, despite having just lost all his comrades moments ago. Perhaps this was his way of coping as someone who had endured immense pain and saw through the complexities of the universe.

In contrast, Mann was still haunted by Huxtin's unexpected changes. She always held onto hope for a brighter future, but it seemed that circumstances continued to unfold in the opposite direction. Aware that this was just the start of a series of mysterious events, she had countless questions in her mind that required answers from Kee. However, in this moment, she chose to channel her energy into repressing her negative emotions and saving the nostalgic conversation for a more opportune time.

As for the man who cloaked himself in darkness, he sat isolated in the pitch-black rest zone of the Hokan. His eyes tightly shut, as if attempting to shut out the entire world. His fingers dug into the armrests, and his breath came in shallow puffs.

It was only in darkness that the beast's soul within Huxtin found solace. Although Mu Mann's words were like daggers that plunged deep into his heart, the turmoil within him seemed to quiet down, and for fleeting moments, it felt as if he could fly freely without flapping his wings.

"Still struggling, aren't you? Trying to mask your wounds with empty gestures."

"I thought you wouldn't bother persuading me anymore."

"Only describing what I see: a broken heart and a shattered mind."

"I didn't ask for your meddling."

"Lonely, aren't you? You need someone to talk to, to reach the depths of your heart."

"Like you care."

"Actually it's you who cares about me."

At that moment, Huxtin opened his eyes. Autaming stood before him, arms crossed, and leaning against the wall with a concerned expression. The lights flickered back on, and Huxtin felt the intense weight of his emotions return with a suffocating force, as if he were drowning in a sea before finally gasping for air.

"Who were you talking to?" Autaming asked.

"No one, and there's nothing of importance," Huxtin lied.

Autaming chuckled, trying to lighten the mood. "Just came here to check on my old friend, that's all. It's been years since we last saw each other, and I can't help but wonder what you've been going through." He flashed a grin at Huxtin, who remained stoic.

"Enough with the fake laughter, Autaming. Drop it. We're alone here. No need for pretence." Although Huxtin's words were harsh, there was no visible sign of annoyance on his face.

Autaming's smile faded. "Old habits die hard, I suppose." He paused, staring at the silver streaks in Huxtin's hair and considering his next words carefully. "What's wrong, Huxtin? I'm worried about you."

"Nothing's... wrong with me."

But Autaming continued, undeterred, "You've changed, Huxtin. I don't mean your appearance, though I admit that's puzzling too. No... It's something deeper."

"So, what's that?"

This was the first time Autaming had ever seen Huxtin avoid eye contact so deliberately, and it was unsettling.

"Remember how we used to talk? How you used to teach me about life and battle? I thought you'd forgotten me these past few years, and it made me hurt. But now that you're back, I'm scared of what I see. What really happened to you? You told me not to pretend, but I think it's you who should stop pretending. We both know something's definitely off. That woman mentioned something similar about you changing. If she's noticed too, then maybe—"

"Which woman?" Huxtin asked, even though he was well aware of exactly whom Autaming was referring to.

"Uhh, Mann Mu? Or was it Wu Mann?" Autaming hesitated for a moment, recalling the correct name. "Oh, Mu Mann! That's it. Mu Mann... Anyway, my point is, if she's expressing concern, you should take it seriously. Please, think about it, my friend, my only friend in my goddamn life."

CHAPTER 21

IN THE DEPTHS OF EVERY SOUL RESIDES A TREASURE,
WORTH SACRIFICING EVEN ONE'S OWN ESSENCE TO RECLAIM

7 Aqual, W.D. 471
T.P.S.E. Command Centre, Teddix

After their return from Cape Nameless, Huxtin and Mu Mann wasted no time heading straight to the command centre of T.P.S.E. Huxtin had long harboured suspicions, but had been lacking the concrete evidence or justification to address the matter directly. However, the time had come for him to take bold and definitive action.

Shadows enveloped the dark corner of the command centre as Kayley Mien, the chief communicator of T.P.S.E., hid herself in a cabinet. Her heart pounded against her chest, each beat echoing through the silent room like a ticking clock. Peeking through the slits on the cabinet door, Mien's breath hitched as she saw a figure pass by, his footsteps soft but menacing. She held her breath, a survival instinct kicking in, and waited for the figure to disappear from view.

Once the figure was gone, Mien exhaled—a shaky breath that did little to quell her fear. As she prepared to step out from her hiding spot, the figure reappeared, his eyes with dark purple pupils visible through the slits, cold and unblinking. The atmosphere thickened with dread. The unsuspecting victim was trapped, akin to being in a horror story, knowing her fate yet powerless to change it. Then, the violent man attempted to open the cabinet door but encountered resistance from within. With brute force, he tore the door open, splintering the metal and sending Mien sprawling onto the floor. A scream ripped through her throat, only to be smothered by the man's hand as he yanked her up by her long hair.

"Run if you can," he snarled, revealing himself to be Poco Talam, the main analyst of T.P.S.E. His grip remained firm on her hair, rendering escape impossible. "Or we can have a little chat about what you need to do next if you want to survive."

As Talam's venomous words slithered into her ear, Mien could sense a malevolent energy emanating from him, utterly inhuman in nature. Fear gripped her like icy talons, and she knew that whatever stood next to her was something far more sinister than a mere human. Soon, the darkness that cloaked the room swallowed her whole as she lost consciousness, with Talam's mocking laughter echoing in her ears. "Poor human being… too weak and fragile to withstand even a moment of fear."

At that very moment, Huxtin burst into the room, clad in his combat outfit with an Earthling laser gun gripped tightly in his right hand. He aimed it directly at Talam, his expression stone-cold. Upon recognising the intruder who had disrupted the scene, Talam's lips curled into a twisted smile. "Aha, My King," he said sardonically, "I'm truly impressed you managed to track me down… Are you here to request that I set her free?"

"It's not my concern if she's alive or dead." Huxtin shook his head, feigning disappointment. "I just feel ashamed for taking so long to finally deal with you."

"Hmm, to be honest, it's not quite what I had anticipated. I expected a bit more of a struggle between you and me for the survival of this unfortunate girl."

"What do you propose instead?"

"Return with me to the Umbras," Talam boldly suggested. "Rule over us as you were meant to, and no longer burden yourself with these insignificant humans, Earthlings, Teddixians, or whosoever."

"Too many fools have made that same offer lately," Huxtin replied, his voice remaining icy. "If I hear it again, I swear I'll kill the one who dares to repeat it."

Despite Huxtin's unfriendly demeanour, Talam appeared unfazed, even amused.

"Although you said you're not concerned for this girl, but I doubt you'd shoot with her in my grasp," he added tauntingly, "Besides, do you even know how to use that Earthling weapon?"

As a matter of fact, Huxtin's finger hovered over the trigger, but he never unlocked the safety pin.

"Being with the Earthlings hasn't made you one of them," Talam continued, a big cruel grin spreading across his face. "You're our king. You shouldn't think like a human because you're not one—"

His sentence was abruptly cut short by the piercing sound of a gunshot. In an instant, Talam vanished like smoke on the wind, leaving Mien collapsed. Emerging from the shadows, Mu Mann held an antiquated model pistol in her hand.

"I told you," she chided Huxtin. "You don't know how it works."

Huxtin lowered the laser gun. "Thanks to your interference, the target has escaped," he grumbled, his words betraying more concern for Talam's escape than for Mien's well-being.

Mann ignored him, rushing to Mien's side and kneeling down, then let out a long sigh of relief upon confirming that Mien was unharmed, albeit unconscious. "She needs medical attention immediately," she urged.

Huxtin barely seemed to register her words, his focus elsewhere. He strode purposefully towards the silver bullet shell lying on the ground, adjacent to Mann and Mien. As he picked it up for further investigation, his eyes caught sight of several tiny scratches on the metallic floor, like those left by claws. Turning his attention back to the bullet shell, he found similar markings on its surface. He didn't bother counting them; something about the scratches resonated within him, a connection that sent chills through his body.

"How is this even possible?" Mann demanded, struggling to understand the situation. "Is he... no longer human?"

"There is no living being by the name of Poco Talam," Huxtin revealed. "He has been dead in Bagoland."

"We were all fools..." Mann muttered, bitterness creeping into her tone. "We believed that after that explosion, there could still be survivors. But there never are, are there?"

Huxtin remained silent, his cryptic expression unreadable. Mann knew that the truth about Talam hinted at an even more dire crisis looming over them all. The dark memories of Bagoland resurfaced in her mind, a painful reminder that the Earthlings would soon have to confront their past in order to survive on this planet. And that day was drawing closer, ever so ominously.

Desperate for some semblance of hope, Mann looked to

Huxtin, seeking reassurance in his face. But as her eyes met his, she found only dark shadows, a reflection of the secrets he still kept hidden deep within.

10 Aqual, W.D. 471
Boundless Ocean

"So, is this also connected to the disappearance of my nephew?" Lokiata Kee asked immediately upon hearing the story narrated by Huxtin and Mu Mann. "The Auras and the Umbras... What are they?"

"Umm, somewhat connected?" Mann attempted to provide further explanation while realising she was at a loss for words. "Anyway, simply put, the Umbras are the bad guys, and the Auras are... the good guys."

The group selected by fate now gathered around the working desk of the Hokan's cockpit. Huxtin, Mann and Kee carried the weight of their conversation, while Autaming leaned against the wall, arms crossed, silently absorbing the shared information. On the other hand, Sheung Oren was completely occupied with piloting, although her hands were actually free from the controls since the Hokan was primarily in auto mode for underwater navigation.

The abyssal depths outside the battleship concealed unknown dangers lurking just beyond their vision. An undercurrent of power seemed to ripple through the water, as if waiting for a chance to ensnare an unwary soul. Huxtin granted Oren permission to become involved in matters concerning the Auras and the Umbras, knowing that his need for her unparalleled piloting abilities left him no choice. Oren, however, chose to divert her attention to the reflections in the glass window of the cockpit. She keenly observed the charged interactions between Huxtin and the rest, particularly her closest friend, Mann.

"The more important question is: where is my nephew now?" Kee continued the conversation, setting aside the complexities that eluded his comprehension. "Who has him?"

"Curious," Huxtin mused, eyeing Kee skeptically. "You seem to care greatly for the son of your archenemy."

While Kee was pondering the question, Mann's face tensed

up, her eyes beseeching for a more compassionate response from the man who held her utmost attention. She desperately wished that she could somehow control Huxtin's choice of words with just a look, but knew it was futile. With a heavy sigh, she averted her gaze, turning to focus on something—anything—else in the room.

"Family is family," Kee finally replied, his voice sharp, meeting Huxtin's eagle eyes. "I would go to any lengths to ensure their safety."

"You don't seem to exhibit much concern for your family," Huxtin argued, "given all the secrets you are harbouring."

"I may be hiding secrets." Kee dared to fight back with his brave words. "But I'm sure you're hiding even more than I am."

Huxtin crossed his arms, unflinching. "I won't deny that," he admitted, "but you should forget about Lokiata Zen, focus on our mission, and follow my orders without question."

Kee glanced around at the others assembled in the cockpit, taking in their expressions and postures. Oren, the pilot, exuded the demeanour of a steadfast soldier, displaying self-discipline and a willingness to obey superiors without hesitation. Autaming, the fisherman, appeared to be a loyal attendant of Huxtin's, readily accepting whatever instructions or beliefs the influential figure presented to him. And Mann, whose concern for Huxtin was evident, seemed torn between her feelings and her duty.

"Everyone seems so eager to circle around you, Huxtin," Kee mused aloud, admitting that an aura of authority surrounded Huxtin. "But are you a great leader or a great dictator? I don't usually enjoy taking orders. I am just having no choice in this situation."

"Call me what you will—leader, dictator, whatever suits your fancy. Regardless, even if the world were destroyed, I wouldn't feel good or bad about it. I'll do whatever it takes to achieve my own goals."

Mann's irritation flared once more upon hearing Huxtin's chilling declaration. "Do you care to explain what it is you truly want, Huxtin?"

Ignoring her, Huxtin addressed Kee instead. "People like us

have a tendency to layer one mask upon another, each more intricate than the last. It grants us the ability to assume new identities while concealing our hidden wounds that lie beneath. So, I must ask, how many masks have you worn up until this very moment?"

"Hey! That's enough!" Mann angrily rose to her feet, as if about to dash toward Huxtin and give him a slap on his face. "I told you to behave yourself!"

But Autaming quickly stepped in, trying to grasp her arms. To his surprise, she resisted with considerable force, her muscles tensing as she fought against his grip. Amidst the embarrassing atmosphere, he let out a boisterous laugh. "You two are just like a lovely couple, you know? Bickering and all. You should keep those little arguments inside the house instead of exposing them to the public."

Mann's face flushed with a combination of anger and embarrassment as she forcefully stepped on Autaming's left foot, freeing herself from his grasp. Autaming winced, hiding his pain behind an uncomfortable giggle while Mann glowered at him disapprovingly. Meanwhile, Oren called Huxtin over, removing him from the conversation that had taken a different turn. Sensing a self-conceited opportunity to lighten the mood, Autaming whispered to Mann, "Looks like you've got some competition."

"Shut up," Mann warned, her embarrassment unabated. "Or your right foot will suffer the same fate."

Autaming laughed heartily, causing Mann to offer Kee a helpless smile. As she walked away, she caught sight of Autaming following her through the reflection in the glass window. She felt annoyed by his constant attempts to inject humour into the situation, though she recognised that he was genuinely a good and reliable person, and she couldn't deprive the privilege of him having such happy-go-lucky attitude.

"Sorry for my jokes," Autaming apologised, catching up to Mann. "Please don't be mad at me."

"Well, it's not a big deal." Mann turned around, summoning her well-trained tolerance. "But it would be appreciated if you could keep your senseless jokes to yourself."

"Listen, I talked to Huxtin earlier. He's not acting normal, you know. It's like he's in a great trouble, but even he doesn't know what the trouble is."

"Really? This is what you want to tell me?"

"Yep. After this mission, you should talk to him in peace. Try to figure out what's going on with him."

"I'll do my best," Mann stressed. "But he... he's truly a challenging individual to handle."

"That's why we're friends." Autaming patted her left shoulder before leaving for the rest zone. "The horrible boss and his annoying myrmidon, hahaha!"

Mann watched as Huxtin and Oren became engrossed in their discussion, feeling the fatigue of constantly worrying about him and his mysterious plans. She then cast a quick look at Autaming's retreating figure, and she found herself impressed by his optimistic heart, wishing she could embody such resilience herself.

10 Aqual, W.D. 471
Isle of Sealina

Standing alone on the deck of Autaming's fishing vessel, Huxtin gazed out at the expansive Boundless Ocean. In his right hand, he summoned Shuuen, the gleaming Star Soul of Imortalli, its silvery luminous glow casting beautiful reflections. He felt an uncanny connection to the vastness and solitude of the sea, perceiving it as a mirror of his own spirit. With each discovery about his abilities, he grew increasingly apprehensive about the true nature of his being. His personal struggle had intensified more than ever before. It was a dilemma, a burden he couldn't evade.

As the light from the core of the Star Soul grew brighter, a unique symbol appeared, heralding their imminent arrival at their destination. Huxtin pointed Shuuen in the direction where its brilliance shone the brightest, and at last, the elusive Isle of Sealina came into view. Empowered by Shuuen, the isle's camouflage gave way like substances being corroded, exposing its rocky beaches, grasslands, trees, small streams as well as jagged stones.

The most remarkable feature of the Isle of Sealina was a grand marking of Configuration of Twelfianity etched into its centre. This sacred place held a fascinating history, for there had once been an identical isle called the Isle of Imortalli. Imortalli had created her isle in an ambitious attempt to rival her sister, but fate had other plans. The Isle of Imortalli, along with a vast continent on Celestiloo, now lay submerged beneath the ocean's depths. In its place, the remaining Isle of Sealina had been transformed into a Starfall Tomb for the Children of God, an eternal resting place for these celestial beings.

Stepping onto the isle, Huxtin led the group along a well-trodden path, the radiant power of Shuuen still emanating from his right hand. Autaming followed closely behind, his fishing rod, crafted from a rare bronze-coloured metal, swaying with each step. Mu Mann and Lokiata Kee trailed a few paces behind. As they walked, Mann couldn't help but think back to her previous missions with Huxtin, Lokiata Zen, and Miria. A mix of nostalgia and concern brewed within her as she hoped this time would be different—that no one would vanish by the end.

"Uncle Kee," Mann called out casually, trying to distract herself from her thoughts. "In fact... how long have you been stranded here on Celestiloo?"

"About half a year," Kee replied with a bittersweet smile.

Mann pressed on, "Have you found a way to go back home yet?"

Kee shook his head. "No. The engine of my spaceship isn't capable of overcoming Celestiloo's gravity. It simply wasn't designed for that."

Mann nodded, a wave of relief washing over her at the knowledge that Kee, too, was bound to this strange world. Yet, deep down, she knew part of her should be actively seeking a way to help her fellow Earthlings return home. But for now, those thoughts were buried beneath more immediate concerns.

Changing the topic, she inquired, "Then why did you decide to join the Cosmo Scavengers?"

Instead of responding to her question, Kee counter-questioned, "Do you think I'm a bad guy because of it?"

"No! I mean... I never thought that—"

"The government has twisted our true nature. Not all members of the Cosmo Scavengers are evil—many of us steal to help the poor and needy. But going against the government makes us enemies. Unfortunately, some among us have used that label to justify truly terrible actions."

Mann frowned, feeling shame for her ignorance. "I'm sorry... I didn't know any of that."

"It's perfectly alright. I chose to join my team voluntarily, and I believe I made the right decision," Kee expressed, his eyes searching Mann's. "Does it alter your beliefs about the government and the military?"

Mann hesitated for a moment before responding. "Everyone understands that doing what is right holds greater significance than blindly following orders, but as a commander... I mean, as a former commander of the army, I had to adhere to my organisation's beliefs, regardless."

As she spoke, memories of her time on Celestiloo flooded her mind, forcing her to confront the choices she had made— both righteous and questionable, virtuous and flawed.

"Indeed. Above all, do the right thing, make the right choice. Don't overthink it. It can be challenging, but I am striving to embody that throughout my life. I genuinely mean it," Kee concluded before changing the subject. "What about the fisherman up there? How well do you know him?"

Mann looked at Autaming's tall and broad back as they walked. "He's Huxtin's bestie, but I've only heard of him prior to this mission. Never met him in person until now."

As if sensing their gaze, Autaming turned his head around and flashed a bizarre grin. "I can hear you two talking about me, you know."

Kee chuckled, unfazed by the sudden attention. "You seem like an interesting guy, Autaming. Maybe we could make a strong team."

"Sure, we could be a good team," Autaming agreed.

"Then we should be friends too, right?" Kee ventured, hopeful.

"Hah, nope, thanks."

Kee was dumbstruck, feeling a sharp sting of rejection. "Why not?"

"Because being teammates and being friends are two distinct concepts," Autaming explained, sharing his personal philosophy on life. "We can work together just fine, but I don't need any more friends. That's the end of the deal."

"Fine..." Kee replied, his face falling into a resigned expression.

"This is so awkward..." Mann sighed, noticing that the atmosphere among the group was tense. Nevertheless, it was a vast improvement compared to the strained dynamic among the quartet in her previous mission.

Eventually, they reached the exact centre of the Isle of Sealina, coming to a halt at the edge of the marking of Configuration of Twelfianity. Huxtin's communicator beeped, and he attentively listened to Sheung Oren's message.

"Huxtin, unusual activities have been detected nearby, possibly related to Elementro particles."

"Monitor the situation," Huxtin instructed. "Inform me immediately if anything goes awry. I will concentrate on my mission for now."

"What's wrong?" Mann inquired when Huxtin ended the call, not expecting to receive the answer she desired.

"Nothing special." Huxtin's face was a blank mask. He glanced at Mann briefly, and the orchestra of silence continued for a few seconds.

Mann correctly surmised the situation, yet she also recognised her lack of authority to intervene in whatever plan Huxtin had in mind. "Okay. Do whatever you want."

"Obtaining the Star Soul is our top priority. We can discuss other matters afterward."

"If you say so."

Afterwards, Huxtin channeled the Elementro particles within Shuuen. The isle began to fade from view, as if gradually being erased. The colours around them seemed to drain away like watercolours in the rain, leaving behind only a golden swirl of dust surrounding the marking. Kee stared wide-eyed at the scene unfolding before him, feeling as though he was standing on thin air above a vast sea.

Autaming, however, didn't hesitate for a moment. He strode confidently into the golden vortex. Mann reassured Kee with a nod and followed suit. "It's safe. He opened this portal for us," she said before disappearing from Kee's sight.

"What happened to your adventurous spirit?" Huxtin challenged Kee, who squinted uncertainly at him.

"Usually, I know what I'm after." Kee rubbed the scar on his cheek. "But this time, it's your treasure hunt, not mine."

"There should be an artefact resembling a book inside. Consider it your objective," Huxtin suggested cryptically.

"Am I being hired as a treasure hunter? And what will be my reward?" Kee demanded, seeking clarification on Huxtin's intentions and what he stood to gain from this endeavour.

"Your reward will come in due time. Trust me," Huxtin

promised, a rarity for him. "You will obtain the truth at the end of everything."

Kee pondered for a moment, then smirked. "Fine. Fate has a funny way of arranging things, doesn't it?"

With that, he closed his eyes tightly and stepped into the golden vortex. When he emerged, he found himself in a small stone chamber, accompanied by Mu Mann and Autaming. Ancient symbols glowed with the same mesmerising golden dust that had enveloped them moments before.

Finally, Huxtin emerged from the vortex, and it dissipated behind him. Mann's frustration got the better of her. "Why did it take you so long?"

The question lingered in the air as two beams of light, resembling lightning, abruptly streaked across the ground in a perpendicular pattern. From Huxtin's vantage point, the horizontal beam traveled from left to right, while the vertical one surged directly towards him, converging at the point where the two beams intersected.

"Thunderites!" Kee and Mann exclaimed in unison. Autaming reacted instantly, grabbing Mann's arm and yanking her to safety on the right side of the chamber, while Kee scrambled leftward. In the blink of an eye, a large portion of the ground crumbled away along the path of the Thunderite beams. The stones on Huxtin's side tumbled into the abyss, dragging him down with them. Panic surged through the group as they realised their leader had vanished, leaving them stranded in the mysterious chamber.

"Huxtin!" Mann peered into the abyss, her voice trembling with urgency. The sound of her voice echoed back to her after a few tense seconds, turning out that the depth wasn't as great as she had feared, but that did little to ease her concern.

"Uncle Kee! Are you alright?" Mann shouted across the wide chasm that now separated her from her ally.

"I'm fine!" Kee waved his arms above his head. "Don't worry about me!"

Autaming interjected, eyeing the gap between them, "Do you think you can jump over?"

However, Kee smirked at the question. "Thanks for the

invitation! I'm afraid I lack the magical prowess required for such a feat!"

"Aha, me either!"

"But what do we do now?" Kee asked while soothing his scar. "Do we wait for him to magically rise from the bottomless pit?"

As if answering their unspoken prayers, two stone doors silently opened on either side of the chamber, revealing shadowy corridors that beckoned them forward. Kee looked at the doorways, then back at his allies. "It seems fate leads us once more!" he shouted again. "We should go our separate ways, and if fortune favours us, we'll find the exits, reunite, and perhaps even find Huxtin waiting for us!"

"Agreed!" Autaming nodded solemnly and waved Kee goodbye. "I'll see you on the other side, teammate!"

"Be careful!" Mann shouted after Kee as well. In response, Kee raised his left hand in acknowledgement before turning away and vanishing into the secret doorway.

"Come on, lady," Autaming urged, gesturing towards the remaining open door. "We should proceed before we stumble and end up with our bones shattered."

"You're really great at relieving tension," Mann said, sarcasm dripping from her words. "Just like your best friend."

He chuckled, a warm smile spreading across his face. "I'll take that as an important compliment."

Mann found herself struggling to catch her breath as she conversed with Autaming, so she made the decision to ignore him and walked away on her own. Meanwhile, the fisherman's eyes lingered on her, captivated by an unexpected connection that stirred introspection within him. She seemed to embody contrasting aspects of life that he had never before considered, prompting him to contemplate his own existence and the unexplored depths within himself.

10 Aqual, W.D. 471
Starfall Tomb of Sealina, Isle of Sealina

As Huxtin plummeted through the abyss, his body twisted and turned, free-falling towards a seemingly inevitable fate. Yet, even in this dire situation, he remained calm, focusing on the power within him—the very essence of the wind Elementro energy coursing through his body. At the last possible moment, Huxtin stretched out his arms, splaying his fingers wide as he summoned a whirlwind of orange turbulence. The powerful gusts created an air cushion beneath him, slowing his descent. His body flipped into a somersault, and he landed gracefully on the stone ground below, though his footing was less stable than he had hoped since it was his very first few times using such a technique.

Looking upward, Huxtin could see nothing but darkness above, leaving him unable to estimate the distance he had fallen. He surveyed the area around him, noting the broken stones that littered the ground. Bending his upper body, he squeezed through a narrow opening in the wall and found himself in a vast, circular chamber. The lofty ceiling dissolved into the shadows above, while the walls were adorned with Configurations of Twelfianity in diverse shapes and sizes. Some featured circles of varying dimensions, while others displayed slightly altered formations.

As he gazed upon these ancient carvings, he felt a surge of energy emanating from them. It was as if the very walls themselves were imbued with power, and he could feel his own strength growing, fuelled by the mystical symbols.

"From the moment of your birth, the Son of Chaos, I knew there would come a day when our paths would cross, and you would seek to collect all twelve of us for a sacred purpose."

Suddenly, a female voice with a warm and serious tone resonated within the chamber.

"And how can you be so certain that my intentions are virtuous?" Huxtin demanded, scanning the chamber for the source of the voice. "What if I were to employ the Star Souls for malicious purposes? Especially considering that I have been betrayed by the Auras, manipulated as a pawn. They even have a plan to eliminate me and wipe out my lineage."

"I cannot state with absolute certainty, but observing you here, in this moment and place, I can perceive your sincerity. Furthermore, despite the actions of the Auras, there are those among them who still believe in your inherent goodness and have made significant sacrifices to support you."

At these words, Huxtin's memories of his first encounter with the Auras surged forward like a volcanic eruption, threatening to overwhelm him with complicated emotions. He fought to maintain control, aware that surrendering to rage or sorrow would only fuel the uncontrollable power within him.

"What is your stance then? As an observer of the universe," he asked, his voice strained. "Will you support me? Will you grant me what I am pursuing?"

"Your soul is stirring, the Son of Chaos. That is what you must learn to control."

"How can I possibly do that?" Huxtin urged, his emotions slightly ignited. "The Auras, the Umbras, the whole universe is constantly pushing me to the brink, wanting to squeeze me until there's nothing left. They never give me a chance to breathe."

"Pass my trial, and then we can speak further. But remember, you mustn't use the power of the Star Souls for this trial."

Upon the completion of the voice's statement, Shuuen was summoned, despite being locked within Huxtin's concealed personal inventory. It floated away, shining brightly with its unique symbol glowing at its core. Then, four pale-coloured illusions of the Children of God materialised before him: Flammando, Windalia, Aqual, and Eawe, ready to test his strength and resilience.

This was the first time Huxtin saw their forms, except for Flammando, noting Windalia's orange streamlined combat outfit and flute-like weapon, Aqual's blue wavy extravagant robe and jewel-encrusted vase, and Eawe, whose entire body was obscured by floating rocks. He tightened his fists, realising that the illusions were primed, leaving him no time to prepare.

Without warning, the illusion of Flammando lunged towards Huxtin, raising his fiery axe high. With a powerful swing, Flammando sent countless fireballs hurtling towards him. Huxtin darted across the ground, narrowly evading each fiery projectile, while his eyes locked onto a transparent orb embedded in the stone wall on the far end, nestled within the centre circle of a standard Configuration of Twelfianity.

As the barrage of fireballs ceased and Flammando vanished, Huxtin understood that he had to either evade or defeat each of the Children of God, one by one. No sooner had this realisation dawned on him than spike rods erupted from the ground, forcing him to nimbly dodge them. The illusions of Aqual and Eawe chose this moment to launch a combined attack. Water poured from the vase, rapidly forming a sea on the ground that hampered Huxtin's movements. Reacting swiftly, he summoned a shield, blocking the water from entering his protected space. Yet, as he navigated the spike rods and passed Aqual, he failed to see the razor-sharp wind blades unleashed by Windalia.

"Tsk!"

The wind blades cut through Huxtin's shield with ease, leaving him exposed. However, he chose not to replenish his shield or even attempt to dodge. The blades struck him directly, yet they seemed to have no effect on him whatsoever. It wasn't that the wind itself had chosen to spare him from harm, but rather he appeared to be completely immune to this specific manifestation of Elementro.

"Something has changed within you. I can see that.

The illusion of Windalia faded away. Huxtin didn't respond to the voice, his focus fixed solely on the transparent orb nestled at the far end. He took slow, determined steps, his heart swelling with the conviction that he couldn't fail in obtaining the Star Soul of Sealina. Every fibre of his being burned with the desire to succeed, to prove himself worthy of the power he sought.

But just as Huxtin's resolve strengthened, a new wave of illusions appeared before him, halting his progress. Litorio materialised first, unleashing a torrent of lightning bolts at

Huxtin with unstoppable force. He quickly released his shield, struggling against the overwhelming power of the attacks. His face contorted in effort as he strained to hold the shield, pushing it to expand further and cover more ground.

However, in his desperation to block the onslaught of lightning, Huxtin missed a critical detail: the larger he made the shield, the weaker its defences became. When he noticed purple crystalline formations spreading across the inner surface of his shield, he realised that Kristalanna must be active somewhere out of sight.

Desperate to counter her influence, he used his left arm to create turbulence inside the shield, shattering the crystals before they could solidify. The commotion he stirred up caused the shield to rupture, granting passage to vine-like tendrils that entwined around his arms, constricting their hold and solidifying into wooden restraints, ultimately rendering him immobilised and vulnerable in the face of Grential, dressed in a combat attire fashioned from foliage and timber.

"The trial ends now."

As the wood entangling Huxtin's arms retreated and reverted back to tentacles, they slithered away, dissipating into nothingness, carrying the illusion of Grential with them. Huxtin's expression didn't hold relief, but instead, a burning anger as his burden seemed to multiply in weight. His navy blue eyes started to flare crimson while his face twisted into a snarl.

"Your power of Chaos is difficult to control because you desire something deeply, and you've never considered why you can't obtain it or what stands in your way."

Upon hearing those words, the rage in Huxtin's eyes vanished, and his pupils returned to their normal hue. Confused, he questioned the unseen speaker, "What do you want me to do? If I have already exerted my utmost effort but still failed to attain the desired outcome, what must I do?"

"Living beings are sometimes ignorant, and that's perfectly acceptable. Despite your immense power, you still possess a soul—fragile and susceptible to the influences of the universe"

The words resonated within Huxtin, prompting him to search inward for the unstable core of his being. He delved deep into himself, endeavouring to grasp the evils within, yet they remained elusive as he struggled to attain the desired fulfilment.

As he immersed himself in contemplation, he witnessed the manifestation of the voice's owner appearing before him. Sealina floated effortlessly in mid-air, her long silvery hair cascading down like ribbons to her feet. She wore a shimmering golden gown adorned with countless glass shards that reflected light from every angle. Her golden eyes held angelic wisdom, and the golden dust sparkling and swirling around her fingertips was as brilliant as all the great minds and wonderful ideas combined.

Looking at the leader of the Children of God, Huxtin felt a pang of sympathy as he recognised that Sealina's ethereal form was bound to her Star Soul. Knowing she was the self-sacrificing eldest among her kin, he wondered if she truly understood his heart—or even his soul.

"Sealina," he asked hesitantly, "what happens now that I've failed your trial?"

"You haven't failed, my dear." Her response surprised him. "You arrived here with a purpose and never wavered from it. Your success has always been ensured, the Son of Chaos."

CHAPTER 22

THOSE WHO ARE UNWILLING TO BE BOUND
BY THE DICTATES OF DESTINY
WILL CREATE A NEW PATH OF THEIR OWN

10 Aqual, W.D. 471
Starfall Tomb of Sealina, Isle of Sealina

"But I still need to warn you: your choice is inevitable, and the wheel of fate will not stop until you have made your decision and chosen your path."

The glass shards encircling Sealina seemed to hold specific stories that she didn't want to view again in her life. Her eyes, which could strike fear into the hearts of many at first sight, held a deep sorrow that was only visible to those who dared to look closer.

"The war between 'Good Deeds' and 'Bad Deeds' may never end, even if you make the choice," Sealina continued. "The vicious cycle could persist regardless. You must make the choice, not because you are destined to become anything, but because you have the responsibility to decide for yourself."

"I know you're not like the others who would force me against my will..." Huxtin averted his gaze, as though afraid that Sealina might unearth the hidden depths of his heart, where more secrets lay buried. "But it seems I have no other option than to choose between being the King of the Umbras or the Lord of the Auras, and that fills me with great pain."

Sealina succeeded in delving into Huxtin's soul, as deep and vast as the ocean itself. She sensed his spirit sinking into an abyss, and it stirred within her a desperate need to pull him back from the edge.

"Answer me. If you were in my place, what would you do?" Huxtin's head gradually lifted, pointing towards Sealina as he posed the question. "Although I don't expect anything from the Children of God. You have all become outsiders, unable to understand and feel the emotions of this universe."

Sealina paused for a moment before speaking again. "I understand that your trust in the Auras has waned, and they might not accept you as their lord. Besides, your ability to resist the Umbras may weaken over time. I know that you fear losing yourself and becoming unrecognisable. You hesitate to ask for help because you also fear involuntarily hurting others if anything goes wrong. If I were you…"

As Huxtin watched, Sealina vanished into thin air. His heart raced as she reappeared before him in a blink of an eye, catching him off guard. She embraced him, and for a moment, he was too stunned to react. He never expected this from a stranger, let alone from the very first living being born on Celestiloo.

"If I were in your position," Sealina whispered with a strong sense of righteousness, "I might only need a hug… or someone willing to share my burdens."

Huxtin's body tensed, then slowly relaxed into the embrace. He could feel Sealina's warmth seeping through his body, soothing his weary soul. It felt as if she had pierced through the veil that shrouded his heart, effortlessly breaking through the layers of defences guarding the box of secrets within, offering solace in a moment of vulnerability.

"Huxtin," the Children of God murmured, "do not convince yourself that you are alone. There are good people around you who support you, and love you as well, remember."

Upon hearing Sealina address him by his true name, rather than the title he always struggled with, Huxtin was eager to put down his ultimate layer of defence, showing atypical emotions on his face and a phantom light in his eyes. With those parting words, Sealina disappeared, returning to her Star Soul embedded on the wall. The golden light of Sujou, Sealina's Star Soul, filled the chamber as it detached from the wall, joining Shuuen's silvery glow in mid-air. The two Star Souls circled around Huxtin, the legacies they held—both beautiful and tragic— enveloping him.

As he reached out to retrieve the Star Souls, he reminisced about the days when he made the choice to conceal his true emotions, always believing that he should eventually reverse that decision. However, he found himself unable to do so, puzzled by the inexplicable reason behind his inability to change.

With Sujou and Shuuen safely in hand, Huxtin's thoughts shifted to the story of Sealina and Imortalli. As the eldest sisters among the Children of God, Imortalli and Sealina held a long-standing rivalry, constantly seeking to outdo each another. Imortalli cherished Sealina deeply, but their hierarchical roles prevented her from yielding and being defeated by Sealina in any circumstance, at any time. There came a moment when Imortalli found herself in grave peril during one of their competitions, yet Sealina was willing to sacrifice her own life to protect Imortalli. Overwhelmed with shame, Imortalli vowed to avoid meeting Sealina in person from that day forward, except during significant incidents. Even as they ascended to become the Star Souls, Imortalli steadfastly clung to the rules she had set long ago.

Huxtin began to grasp the dynamics of their relationship. Perhaps Imortalli's desire wasn't to surpass Sealina in strength, but rather to gain recognition from her sister. She loved Sealina deeply, and that was why she still yearned to be summoned by her. It all boiled down to love, albeit in a complex and distorted manner. Even Sealina displayed excessive tolerance towards Imortalli. Yet, who could truly judge what was right or wrong within a family?

Even the most powerful beings weren't immune to such struggles. In that moment, as Huxtin stood amidst the swirling light of the Star Souls, he felt an unbreakable connection to their story—a bond forged by shared blood, pain, love, and sacrifice.

10 Aqual, W.D. 471
Boundless Ocean

As Autaming and Mu Mann navigated the stone corridors of the mysterious maze, Mann, a naturally talkative person, found herself strangely silent around Autaming. She was afraid that their conversation would inevitably circle back to Huxtin, and she wasn't ready to discuss her thoughts or feelings about him just yet.

The air between them was thick with unspoken words, until Autaming stopped in his tracks and sniffed the air. "I feel a different air movement," he announced. "The exit must be near!"

Mann was impressed by his keen senses. "You've got pretty good survival skills for a fisherman," she remarked.

He laughed. "Well, I've been well trained for it. By the way, are you thinking the same thing I'm thinking?"

"Umm… Maybe you should tell me what's on your mind first?" Mann questioned.

"About meeting Huxtin at the exit, waiting for us," he said frankly, his eyes searching hers. "I think you're hoping for the same."

She didn't answer, but in her mind, she admitted that it was the truth. Besides, she was increasingly curious about the friendship between Autaming and Huxtin. There had to be more to this seemingly simple fisherman.

"You know, Huxtin told me about this mythical isle before we departed Kilidaci," the fisherman continued. "He said that if one wished sincerely enough in this place, their wish would be granted eventually."

"That's an interesting idea, but… Magical things might happen on this planet. Wish granting seems a bit far-fetched."

"Is it?" Autaming challenged Mann playfully. "I am gonna wish for a big fish right now, and my intention is pure. I just might get one very soon."

Mann rolled her eyes but couldn't hide a smile at Autaming's enthusiasm. Suddenly, Autaming's nostrils flared as if he had caught a strange scent. "Wait, I smell something… not right."

Puzzled, Mann turned back to him, straining her senses for anything out of the ordinary but found nothing. "What is it? I don't sense anything…"

Autaming shook his head, his eyes narrowed in concentration. "No, it's like… I wanted to catch a fish, not to become one and get caught myself."

In an instant, he drew his fishing rod out and flung the line forward with incredible speed. As he did so, a flurry of white feathers, which weren't visible to human beings' naked eyes, emerged from the corner of the corridor ahead. The fishing line and the feathers danced around each other, evading each other. Mann couldn't see what was happening, but she could feel the frenetic energy in the air. Realising that they were under attack by some unseen force, she pulled out her laser gun and fired randomly, missing every shot.

"It must be Poet!" Autaming shouted amidst the battle against the invisible foe, expertly manoeuvring his fishing rod as if it were an extension of his own body. The feathers proved too quick, however, and swiftly formed into two giant claws that closed around their preys, rendering them unable to use their weapons.

"You know her too?" Mann attempted to free herself from the invisible grasp as she was lifted from the ground, being drawn towards the source of the feathers. She wondered whether Autaming could perceive the unseen presence of the Fallen, but she doubted it.

"I know her, and I have witnessed her true form—"

"Can't you just take a moment to rest?" Suddenly, Poet's voice interrupted. "You two are making quite a racket."

"Hey! Why are you here? What do you want from us?" Mann immediately confronted Poet, confirming her as the attacker. "Are you stupid enough to think that you can bait Huxtin out with us?"

"Clever lady!" Autaming exclaimed and laughed, despite being in a perilous situation. "You're correct about her being foolish, and you're also correct about what she's doing because she strongly believes Huxtin won't kill her!"

"Silence! Both of you!" Poet howled. "Grr... especially you, murderer of Hazza Village! My relationship with Huxtin is none of your business!"

Upon hearing the mention of Hazza Village and the accusation of being a murderer, Mann noticed a drastic change in Autaming's facial expression. His signature laughter vanished, and his energy seemed to be stripped away. Mann was confused because she had heard from Huxtin that the fisherman came from Kilidaci, not Hazza Village. As far as she knew, based on her brief study of places and events on Celestiloo, Hazza Village was a taboo that no local people in Fanskaree dared to speak of.

As they were pulled towards what appeared to be a dead end, Mann braced herself for impact. But instead of colliding with the wall, they passed right through it and found themselves back on the invisible isle. From this vantage point, Mann could see Autaming's fishing vessel still out at sea, but she also spotted a jet-like vehicle flying in their direction, carrying two men dressed predominantly in white attire. Astonished, she exclaimed, "Are those... Auras?"

Autaming's passion reignited, and his eyes gleamed with excitement. "Whoa! Never seen one before, and now I get to see two! What a day!"

His nonchalance nearly made Mann question her earlier admiration for his capabilities, wondering why Huxtin had formed a friendship with such an eccentric fisherman. As the mysterious Auras drew nearer, Mann once again pondered her place in this terrifying universe. Who was she, really, amidst all these celestial beings and mighty warriors? And how could she possibly contribute to the chain of events that lay ahead?

10 Aqual, W.D. 471
Isle of Sealina

Just moments ago, the silver-white jet sliced through the waves with ferocity, its speed enhanced by the Elementro energy emanating from an Aura named Jeramia. Remezo, Jeramia's companion, gripped the controls tightly, quickening the craft as it approached the invisible Isle of Sealina. The wind whipped at his white outfit, adorned with an assortment of vibrant colours, yet his expression remained stoic and serious.

"Really, Remezo, not even a 'thank you'?" Jeramia questioned, grinning from his position in the back seat. "You ought to be more appreciative. I'm helping you out here."

Remezo tried to ignore Jeramia's incessant chatter. His companion's unassuming appearance belied a talkative nature that had a tendency to distract him.

"I need you to be quiet," he urged. "Can you please stay silent for once? We must focus our attention on finding our target."

"Okay, okay," Jeramia relented. "But you know, if you'd let me ride this thing, we might be even faster." He couldn't resist getting in one last jab.

"Ugh... I wish I were partnered with Sarukan or Gloria," Remezo muttered under his breath. "At least they know the best time to shut up." Inwardly, he knew Jeramia was simply trying to get a rise out of him, but his patience was wearing thin.

"I suggest bringing Anari with you," Jeramia countered, unfazed. "He can guide you to walk directly on the ocean, eliminating the need for your lousy illusion."

As the jet rapidly approached its destination and Autaming's fishing vessel became visible, gently swaying on the ocean's surface not far from the isle, Remezo unleashed a surge of his Illusion Elementro energy. The silvery Elementro particles turned into golden energy, enveloping the entire isle, forcefully revealing its true form and simultaneously deactivating the Hokan's camouflage system.

Right at that moment, a flock of white feathers in the form of two giant claws emerged from a blink of golden light near the marking of the ancient symbol on the ground.

"There she is!" Jeramia exclaimed in surprise, glancing at Remezo. "And she's captured two humans! Should we save them or let them be collateral damage?"

"Did Rafaelzo order us not to save anyone on Celestiloo?" Remezo inquired, his tone sincere.

"No?"

"Then we'll save them."

Remezo's sense of justice shone through, leaving Jeramia impressed by his companion's resolute spirit. As their jet touched down on the beach, it disintegrated into Elementro particles. Remezo, transforming into pieces of black and white paper, gracefully floated towards the centre of the isle. Jeramia, on the other hand, morphed into a swarm of glistening stone shards, mirroring Remezo's path.

The scene that greeted Mu Mann and Autaming was one of utter chaos. Though they couldn't perceive it with their eyes, the clash among the paper, stones, and feathers created a fierce and intricate battle of celestial artistry. With expert precision, the paper and stones broke through the feathered defences, catching Mann and Autaming separately. Jeramia briefly returned to his human form, unceremoniously dumping Autaming onto the ground before resuming his disguise and rejoining the fray. In stark contrast, Remezo carefully set Mann down, appearing as a caring guardian angel.

Mann couldn't conceal her astonishment at witnessing the Auras willingly unveil their true forms before the human onlookers. It contradicted everything she had been taught about these mysterious beings.

"I know you're an Aura," she stared into Remezo's silvery eyes and spoke firmly. "Why are you giving up your disguise?"

"What do you know about us and the Son of Chaos?" Remezo's defensive question conveyed his evident shock. "Have you encountered others like us before?"

"Yes, I have… Did the Auras come back to Celestiloo solely to confront Huxtin?" Mann replied with a serious question, her voice unwavering despite the uncertainty she felt within. She didn't dare to tell him that they were with Huxtin, and that he was also on the isle.

Remezo briefly glanced at the stones and the feathers, then turned back to Mann. "I'll come back and talk to you after dealing with my enemy," he said before leaving for the battle, a hint of reluctance in his tone.

As he redirected his attention towards Poet, he urgently ordered Jeramia to get away while preparing to unleash his Elementro energies. After Jeramia's stone shards deftly evaded the feathers, Remezo conjured independent shields around each feather, compelling Poet to react preemptively. Frantically dodging the silvery sparkles, Poet's anger seethed beneath her surface like a boiling cauldron as she returned to her human form. Her green eyes fixed upon the Auras with ferocious intensity. It seemed she wanted to engulf them alive with a tornado of pure wrath.

"You should have never followed me here!" Poet shouted, her smoky makeup on her face jumping with her exaggerated movement. "You ruined everything!"

Jeramia returned to his human form and mockingly retorted, "What? Are you afraid of my good brother's attacking shields?"

The taunt only served to further enrage Poet, who snapped, "Try again, young boy, and I'll go crazy!"

"Careful, Jeramia," Remezo warned, stepping forward to stand beside his companion. "Don't underestimate her. She's experienced, and she's from the Chasing Howl."

"So what? She was a level ten wind Elementro user in the past, not in the present." Jeramia shrugged his shoulders and spread open his hands. "We could be faster than her. I bet she missed her supersonic speed."

With that, he channeled his Elementro energies, creating two long wooden sticks in his hands that ultimately transformed into two olive green metal rods. They then began the second round of the breathtaking dance of celestial powers.

It was at this moment that Autaming approached Mann and sat down beside her. Side by side, they looked on as the Auras fought with the Fallen. Brilliant lights of various colours illuminated their faces, and there were instances where nothing could be seen at all. Bound by their humanity, they could only serve as witnesses to this extraordinary display, unable to actively participate in the fray themselves.

What place did they hold in this colossal, otherworldly struggle? And how would their choices shape not just their own destinies but also the fates of those around them?

Meanwhile, the narrow corridors Lokiata Kee traversed in the maze led him to a small chamber, its walls and ceiling glittering with an array of crystal shards. As he cautiously stepped into the room, taking extra care to minimise the horrifying cracking noise, his eyes fell upon an unusual book lying on the ground amongst the sparkling fragments. He picked up the artefact gently, noting how the book cover was embedded with a piece of glass that reflected his languishing face. The front and back covers seemed to be made from an incredibly thin denim metal, while the creamy white pages were crafted from an unknown material. It was surprisingly light in weight, carrying a smell of ancientness that resembled the scent of thousand-year-old tree bark.

Try as he might, he couldn't pry open the book; the pages appeared to be stuck together.

"Don't tell me that this book has the power to summon ghosts or unleash evil..." he mused, details of past treasures he had stolen flooding his mind, yet none of them compared to the peculiarity of this particular one.

Exiting the chamber from the opposite side, Kee continued down another set of corridors until he reached a fork in the path. Without hesitation, he chose the left path, only to find himself trapped in what felt like a never-ending loop. Relying on his strong memory, he retraced his steps to the fork and tried the right path, but the result was the same: endless circles with no way out at the end.

Frustrated, he stood before the first wall he had encountered, rubbing the scar on his cheek absentmindedly. After a minute or so, a sudden burst of black and white light erupted behind him, and Huxtin materialised before the lights vanished. Kee spun around in shock. "Huxtin? Is it really you?"

"Are you lost?" Huxtin asked, ignoring Kee's question.

"I… I am," Kee stammered, cursing himself for being too quick to reveal his vulnerability. Despite having completed the treasure hunt as requested by the man before him, the mythical yet tangible book now clutched in his hand, he couldn't shake the feeling that something was still missing within his soul. This sense of inadequacy was eating his confidence, causing him to question whether he could ever truly find satisfaction with what he had obtained.

"Do you not see the exit?" Huxtin questioned again with his cold words.

Kee's demeanour reflected a mix of nervousness and attentiveness as he made an attempt to sound confident. "So… you know how to get out of this maze?"

"Who said this was a maze? You're only trapped here because you lack the faith to leave. The exit is just behind you. You can walk right through it if you truly believe." Huxtin gestured toward the wall behind the one who thought the path of departure didn't exist. "Is it your desire to remain trapped here indefinitely, Lokiata?"

Skeptical, Kee glanced over his shoulder at the seemingly solid stone wall, then back at Huxtin, who showed no sign of lying.

"Now what?" He mustered a forced carefree attitude. "Are you going to give me another life or death lecture?"

However, Huxtin's solemn expression carried a weight that couldn't be easily disregarded. "I am thinking, everyone around you is gone, and you've lost your sense of purpose in life. Therefore, I want to offer you a chance to decide if you would like to embrace a new purpose."

Kee scrutinised Huxtin's face, deep in thought, noticing the telltale signs of redness in his eyes, evidence of recent tears shed. Eventually, he came to the realisation that beneath the harsh words, there was true fragility—they shared similarities, had both experienced the same trauma and degradation.

"Lokiata Zen and Mu Mann both told me you were a philanthropist. Although your nephew stressed that you were doing charity as a cover-up, I preferred the version I heard from

Mann," Huxtin said. Before they left, he explained another request to Kee. "You used to help people without expecting anything in return. I want you to try again, just once more, and perhaps in doing so, you will rediscover your lost purpose, and we both will."

CHAPTER 23

THE MOST VULNERABLE MOMENTS
BREED REVELATIONS OF SECRETS

10 Aqual, W.D. 471
Isle of Sealina

The battle between the Auras and the Fallen remained unresolved, with the outcome still hanging in the balance, while Mu Mann and Autaming settled on rocky ground, taking on the role of observers. They remained silent for a while, but eventually, it was Autaming who took on the ultimate responsibility.

"Isn't it funny? We're sitting here, watching that fight like it's some sort of bizarre dream." His cheerful voice sliced through the tension like the moment a big fish was caught. "Everything seems so fake!"

Mann had regarded Autaming as a good person, even though she had suspicions about the dark secrets he might be hiding. However, his artificial and feeble laughter now unsettled her.

"We should be thinking about how to escape if the Auras are defeated by Poet," she said with a long sigh, raising her arms and stretching them out.

"I'm placing my bets on the Auras," Autaming declared confidently, a grin forming on his face. "Those two seem formidable. And besides, Huxtin will come and rescue us. I'm certain you believe that too, don't you?"

"Absolutely," Mann replied firmly, noticing that every time he mentioned Huxtin, a radiant warmth seemed to emanate from him. It was as if the mere thought of his friend granted him the strength to persevere.

"Huxtin would never leave us behind. But..." Autaming continued, his tone growing more serious. "I think, since Hurain's death, he's changed. Sometimes I feel... I hardly recognise him."

Mann had been reluctant to learn more about Autaming's past and Huxtin's life before his wife's death. But now, her curiosity got the better of her. Turning to face Autaming, she asked carefully, "Why did Poet say... you came from Hazza Village? I thought you came from Kilidaci..."

To her surprise, the fisherman's usual smile remained in place. With a carefree air, he asked, "Are you sure you want to hear my story? Don't say I didn't warn you. It's something of a horror tale."

Understanding that the fisherman needed to unburden himself, Mann nodded. "If you're willing to share it, I'll listen."

As Autaming recounted his story in his mind, the ocean waves echoed the sadness and pain of his past. It was as though the ever-churning waters were a reminder that even the darkest memories could never be fully washed away. With a deep breath, he began his so-called horror tale.

"Fifteen years ago, I was... living in a kingdom in Fanskaree..."

23:2

18 Litorio, W.D. 456
Hazza Village, Waluwon

"But the kingdom was attacked, the king was murdered, and everything fell apart in just one day. I was captured, then sent to prison with the others. The prison turned out to be an underground village. Rumours circulated that the villagers residing there were either mentally unstable or physically impaired. Well, they were not.

Nobody chose to move to Hazza village voluntarily; they were all forced into it. It was purposefully built to entirely isolate individuals deemed mad from the rest of the sane world. In the local folklore, 'hazza' symbolised complete darkness. The village was named Hazza Village precisely because it lacked any source of light, be it day or night, regardless of the season. The sealed environment prevented even a trace of sunlight from entering. The guards stationed at the entrance gave it a more fitting name: 'The Paradise of Living Burial.' It is truly something I despise yet cannot deny.

In Hazza Village, there was water, air, plants that grew in the darkness, serving as the only source of sustenance. Not everyone could endure such conditions. Numerous innocent individuals perished within a matter of days, and others were driven to real madness upon their arrival in the village. If they were to end their lives through suicide, perhaps it would provide them with a release from their unbearable suffering. However, in the end, they might not even possess a clear understanding of the true nature of death.

Day after day, they laughed and joked, despite crying out in pain, despite crying out in distress, their expressions distorted, their senses confined to the realm of nothingness. It was truly an unending hellish existence.

Who built Hazza Village? I repeatedly ask myself this foolish question throughout my life. Truly foolish. Who among the sane would confess to creating a twisted amusement park for their own entertainment when consumed by boredom? Perhaps

I have always been a madman, or perhaps I was once perfectly normal, but my memories remain a tangled mess to this day. How can those who have endured life in that hell truly fathom the depths of what they have become? Who has the authority to determine who is deemed sane or insane?

The only vivid memory I have about the village is being forcefully pushed through a massive black gate, which slammed shut with a deafening sound that nearly ruptured my eardrums. Subsequently, the overpowering stench of decay overwhelmed my senses, as if all life had been drained from the surroundings. The lingering remains emitted an aura of death, accompanied by a putrid odour that permeated the air. I immediately threw up, my stomach turning, even though it had been days since any food had entered my belly. What I expelled was merely remnants of bodily fluids. Soon, my sense of smell diminished, and I could no longer detect any scent.

Enveloped in total darkness, my hearing naturally became extraordinarily acute. When I caught the faint sound of a chisel striking against the ground above, I instinctively crawled towards it, extending my parched tongue. The droplets of water that fell from the stalactite moistened my dry and hoarse throat, providing relief to the pain of my cracked and bleeding skin.

In that precise moment, the sensation of pain transformed into a comforting elixir. Something within my dying nerves was triggered. It conveyed to me that remaining trapped, awaiting my demise, would be a great mistake. I yearned to escape. I craved to breathe in fresh air. And all of a sudden, I had been granted night vision by some higher power. I started to comprehended the psyche of everyone around me, understanding their grievances. Their souls cried out in mournful agony. They clutched their heads in torment, proclaiming to the world that their physical bodies were nothing more than feeble restraints on their souls.

I remembered each and every one of the 143 people, including the guards. The final expressions on their faces, as they met their end by my hand, were etched deeply into my mind and my life. Almost every night, I am haunted by dreams of their mutilated visages. I am uncertain if I regret my actions or if I believe myself to be a liberator. What am I? Who has the authority to define whether I am merely a murderer or an unsung hero? Who am I, truly?

The blood on my body had not yet completely dried when I stumbled upon a narrow crevice, allowing me to remove some stones and cautiously poke my head out. The air outside was surprisedly thick with murkiness, perhaps a consequence of my damaged sense of smell. Summoning every ounce of strength, I managed to overturn the remaining stones, realising that when the will to survive burns fiercely, nothing is insurmountable.

I didn't want to die; I wanted to live.

For days on end, I ran, dragging my blood-soaked body through the harsh terrain. Along the way, I sustained myself solely on water, defying the odds to stay alive. Just as I was on the verge of surrender, on that fateful night, I arrived at a location known as Yuputu's Lair. Little did I know the stroke of luck that awaited me—a remarkable encounter that would irreversibly change the trajectory of my existence."

23:3

"Wars were rampant. Paralloy was engulfed in a civil war during that time, and Yuputu's Lair, situated in Kuna, had fallen back into the hands of the Teddixians from the Kunans. Soldier camps were established in its vicinity. As I ventured into the area, whispers of the mass slaughter in Hazza Village reached my ears, spreading faster than my bare feet could carry me. Then, someone rushed past me, their panicked shouts filling the air. I had neither the capacity nor the mental space to spare attention for all the terrified souls around me. Survival became a matter of kill or be killed, a fate determined by forces beyond my control.

The world could never accommodate a murderer saturated in the foul odour of blood like me. Could it even be conceivable? In my wretched state, I had depleted all strength to resist, my body and mind so shattered that I couldn't even let out a cry towards the heavens. That night, the moon bore an uncommon hue of blue, resembling a coagulated blood clot, yet also akin to an eye that had gathered icy blue tears over countless millennia. It stared at me with a vacant, murky gaze.

Soon after, a stone struck my right temple. I was unaware of the size of the stone, and I didn't even feel the fresh blood flowing from the wound before I collapsed to the ground. A commotion erupted among the Teddixian soldiers as their king arrived. With my head resting in a pool of blood, I couldn't clearly see the king's face, but I sensed, albeit vaguely, his subjects kneeling in reverence. My contorted body was lifted up. The blue moon, partly obscured, cast a dim light upon the king's cheeks. He appeared as a saviour, a saint sent to redeem me. I'm not joking, and I can't explain the drastic change in my mindset at that exact moment.

'You cannot casually discard your life. I have saved you today, but it is now your responsibility to find a way to survive and seek redemption for your past sins. Even if the world despises you, insults you, or humiliates you, you must persevere. Let the bloodstains on your body serve as a reminder of the mark you carry. Regardless of who may seek to punish you, you must first hold yourself accountable. Never surrender your life, for even in death, your soul will forever carry the debt it owes to you.'

Had someone else spoken those very words to me, I might not have been able to recite them word for word. Huxtin was the first stranger who showed a genuine willingness to be my friend, unafraid of the madman I appeared to be, a madman dwelling in a distinct realm through the eyes of commoners.

This warrior, so deeply connected to life, rekindled my spirit, infusing an indescribable vitality that gently soothed the multitude of festering wounds adorning my body, penetrating all the dying cells, reanimating the frozen nerves with warmth. Tears flowed like an unending spring, until the blue moon and the morning sun met, only to part once more. It was then that I finally comprehended—I was still a living, breathing human being.

Following that fateful night, news of the pardon granted to the perpetrator of the Hazza Village massacre spread throughout the land. No one dared to pursue me for my heinous acts, granting me the freedom to roam without hindrance. Perhaps they assumed that I would be condemned to a life of insignificance, anticipating my demise within days, weeks, or months. However, Huxtin orchestrated a fresh start for me in the coastal city of Auta Rex, located in Kilidaci. There, I embraced the life of an ordinary, nameless fisherman, finding solace in self-sufficiency and the simplicity.

Occasionally, people passing through Auta Rex recognised me, insulted me, but most of them dared not approach within my usual range. My mind has already intertwined with the lives of those 143 individuals; there is no need for me to remember everyone's unfriendly eyes, ears, mouth, and nose. All I desired was to live a serene existence, disconnected from the world, diligently atoning for my sins as instructed by Huxtin.

Prior to his abrupt vanishing, Huxtin would make regular visits to me, appearing several times each year. During certain seasons, he would arrive accompanied by his wife, and later, their son would join them. Eventually, another son completed their joyful family of four, and their presence slowly thawed my hardened heart.

Years ago, much like the rest of Paralloy Teddix, I had heard that Hurain and Huringo departed to meet their ancestors from the royal lineage, and Huxtin never returned to Kilidaci to visit me again."

10 Aqual, W.D. 471
Isle of Sealina

As the story drew to a close, tears glistened in Mu Mann's eyes, which she held back, and she finally understood why Autaming had such a deep connection with Huxtin, accompanied by a subtle hint of jealousy.

"Are you afraid now because of my story?" Autaming chuckled, attempting to lighten the mood. "For knowing that I have killed a lot of people in the past?"

Mann blinked away her tears. "Why should I be afraid? I... I've been around weird people like you for quite some time," she said, her voice trembling ever so slightly.

"Can you believe it has been twenty years since I first met him?" Autaming pondered. "Time just... slips away, more elusive than the fish in the seas."

"But the Huxtin I knew was always..." Mann trailed off, her voice fading. "Sorrowful, distant, and uninterested in everything around him."

The conversation drifted toward memories of the Bagoland incident—the explosion at the T.P.S.E. transport dock that had forever altered Mann's life. She recalled encountering Huxtin in the aftermath and bearing witness to the unspeakable horrors that had transpired. To her, the past clung to Huxtin like a dark shroud, with each memory acting as a drop of blood staining his very soul. It was a burden they often shared, causing her heart to fracture under its weight whenever the recollection of those dreadful hours resurfaced.

"Autaming, there's something I must tell you," Mann confessed, her hand instinctively covering her chest as if her heart were about to explode. "Huxtin attempted... He has tried to take his own life before."

"Wh-what? He..." Autaming couldn't fathom the scenarios in which his best and only friend had attempted to stab in the heart with a sword, and he could feel the same pain piercing his own heart. "I can't imagine... what he must have gone through these past few years... I'm... I think..."

"I'm terrified it will happen again." Mann took a deep breath before continuing. "You told me to... talk to him, but I don't even know where to start."

"Maybe you could tell him that..." Autaming's suggestion was abruptly cut short as Huxtin and Lokiata Kee seemed to materialise out of thin air. He pointed eagerly in their direction, exclaiming, "Look, there he is!"

Relief washed over Mann's face immediately as she saw Huxtin and Kee emerge unscathed from the enchanting maze. Their safety was a beacon of hope in the darkness that had kept attacking her weakening thoughts.

"Kid! Are you okay?" Kee rushed over to Mann, offering a helping hand to assist her to her feet, while also noticing her gaze fixed upon Huxtin, who was steadily advancing towards the battlefield. "I suppose you're doing alright?"

With Kee's aid, she stood up, her focus momentarily shifting to the peculiar book he held in his other hand. "Yeah... I'm, uhh... perfectly fine," she stammered.

Kee then turned to Autaming and emphasised, "And my good teammate, how about you?"

"Hey, won't you lend me a hand too?" the fisherman playfully requested, but Kee didn't respond to his jest.

As the reunited group exchanged words, an overwhelming sense of unity settled over them. On one side stood the humans, observing the clash between beings of unfathomable power. It was a striking juxtaposition—the fragility of humanity pitted against the might of celestial beings.

Poet, still engaged in combat against the Auras, caught a glimpse of Huxtin's arrival. Her patience wore thin, a desperate need to capture Mu Mann and Autaming as a means to threaten Huxtin fuelling her movements. In her haste, she unwittingly left herself vulnerable, giving Remezo the opportunity to summon razor-sharp wooden sticks from his Elementro energies, which swiftly pursued her.

Anticipating the danger, Poet transformed into her white feathers form, attempting to evade the deadly projectiles. But Jeramia had predicted her manoeuvre; the sticks sprouted metallic spikes that punctured some of her pristine feathers, eliciting a cry of agony. She quickly reverted to her human form and crumpled to the ground, moaning as deep scratches marred her skin, oozing purple-blue blood. Sensing an opportunity, Jeramia moved to deliver the final blow but found himself halted by an invisible barrier. It felt as if a flow of air, following a specific pattern, stood between him and his intended target, creating an impassable divide. He clutched his head, cursing at the unexpected obstacle in his heart.

"Be extra careful," Remezo warned, placing a hand on his companion's shoulder. "The Son of Chaos is here."

An uneasy hush fell over the battlefield as they had never expected to face their ultimate mission target here, yet Huxtin seemed almost unaffected by the presence of the two Auras. One of them possessed a towering, rugged physique akin to Autaming, with his silvery hair intricately braided. The other individual appeared noticeably younger, radiating an abundance of energy and agility, though lacking the same captivating allure.

With deliberate steps, Huxtin approached the Fallen first, his imposing figure casting a shadow over her crumpled form. His calculating gaze swept over the Auras as he assessed his available choices, his mind operating at an astonishing pace, comparable to that of an advanced computing machine. Lying on the ground in unbearable pain, Poet summoned her dwindling strength to implore Huxtin. "Huxtin! I beg you, listen to me! We must unite and flee from the pursuit of the Auras!"

"Firstly, there is no chance of me being captured," he responded icily, refusing to even glance at her. "And secondly, I suggest you cease testing my patience. I am not here to rescue you or align myself with the Umbras."

"The Son of Chaos," Remezo interjected, "or should I address you as Huxtin? It is unwise of you to shield a Fallen. As an Aura, it is my duty to eradicate any source of wickedness, so I request that you refrain from interfering."

Fixing his icy gaze upon Remezo's steely stare, Huxtin responded in a detached tone, "You need not know the reason. Identify yourself."

"I am Remezo, and this is Jeramia," Remezo clarified. "We

have been dispatched by our chief elder, Rafaelzo. He desires a meeting with you on Celestiloo.

"A meeting?" Huxtin questioned skeptically. "I assumed you are here to capture me, dispose of me to other dimensions, or even eliminate me together with my bloodline."

Remezo sincerely shook his head. "I do not speak for all Auras, and I have no instructions to detain you. You need not concern yourself with that."

Huxtin's surprise was evident, but he remained guarded, unwilling to accept their words at face value. "I don't have any interest in meeting your chief elder, but if he or she insisted on a meeting, it will result in a fight." He made it crystal clear.

Understanding the folly of engaging Huxtin in battle, Remezo quickly reassured him, "We won't force the issue. However, we cannot simply leave the Fallen behind. She is posing a threat to our kind."

While Huxtin processed this information, Remezo noticed Jeramia's timid silence, relieved that his companion hadn't said anything to jeopardise their delicate negotiations. The balance of power between the two factions hung precariously in the balance, and one wrong move could tip the scales irrevocably.

"You cannot kill her," Huxtin stated firmly after considering the options. "But you may accompany me back to Paralloy and keep an eye on her until matters between me and your bellwether are resolved."

Upon hearing Huxtin's decision, Poet immediately protested, "Huxtin, you cannot ally yourself with the Auras again! It would be a grave mistake!"

As Poet continued to implore Huxtin for help, Remezo began weaving a shield around her. Hexagons with silvery edges materialised one after another, forming a protective barrier that eventually turned golden in colour. The shield morphed into a large cell that completely isolated Poet from the outside world. As Remezo exerted his control over the suspended cell, causing it to condense into a small golden sphere and draw nearer to him, Huxtin became acutely aware of his special ability—he was capable of harnessing both mind and illusion Elementro particles.

"She needs to be imprisoned because she is too dangerous," Remezo asked Huxtin, his tone cautious yet firm. "Is this deal acceptable to you?"

"Just ensure she remains alive. I may still need her in an emergency."

Remezo nodded in agreement, honouring their promise. With the matter temporarily settled, Huxtin turned and walked away, heading toward his fellows. Remarkably, the air barrier he had created earlier still stood before Jeremia. Tentatively reaching out to touch it, Jeremia marvelled at the dense concentration of air Elementro particles within. "Is it breakable?" he doubted.

"Not you or I can break through it," Remezo confirmed. "This is a high-density formation, at least level eight in air Elementro."

Jeramia stood in awe, his voice filled with admiration. "That's... brilliant. Just how damn powerful is the Son of Chaos?" he mused, awestruck by the power displayed right before his eyes. His hands still felt the structure of the wall, as if he wanted to be fused with the same kind of power.

While Remezo observed the reunion between Huxtin and his fellows, recognising that confronting Huxtin at this moment would be ill-advised, he also realised that he alone wasn't equipped to handle the situation at hand. He silently hoped for Rafaelzo's swift arrival, knowing that their combined strength would be crucial in navigating the treacherous path ahead.

CHAPTER 24

THE NUMEROUS ILLUSIONS THAT MANIFEST IN OUR LIVES EVENTUALLY GIVE RISE TO INGRAINED PATTERNS THAT ARE DIFFICULT TO BREAK

10 Aqual, W.D. 471
Boundless Ocean

On the journey back to Paralloy, the serene white-yellow full moon bestowed its blessing upon the Boundless Ocean, its calm waters barely making a sound as they lapped against Autaming's fishing vessel. Hidden beneath it, within the rest zone of the Hokan, Mu Mann lay with her head on the table, drifting through a sweet dream. Exhausted from the recent chain of events, she desperately needed to recharge and restore her dwindling spirit.

Dreams were a curious phenomenon—sometimes offering solace for unfulfilled desires in reality, while other times morphing into draining nightmares.

In Mann's dream, she was an elegant high-society woman, sitting inside a black sports car, preparing to attend a date. She opened the car door and extended a pair of long legs accentuated by bright red high heels, stepping onto a red carpet with graceful and dignified movements. Her hands, with nails painted in pearl white, delicately held an exquisitely designed invitation card. The location was inconsequential; it could be Earth, Celestiloo, or some unknown world.

Mann wore a grand, vibrant red evening gown for the date, much more dazzling than the mundane outfit she had worn to Huricane's birthday banquet. The gown had a tailored fit, subtle patterns embellished with gold thread, and a layered skirt with beautiful folds of different shades. She let her hair down, styled in cascading curls, and adorned her ears with large black pearl earrings, complemented by a darker shade of lipstick. Every single detail emitted an abundance of self-assured confidence, transfiguring her from an ordinary individual into an emanation of radiance.

Next to the revolving doors of the restaurant, bathed in the glow of neon lights, stood a tall gentleman robot, patiently awaiting. The robot's whimsical finger movements, facilitated by its articulated joints, were intriguing. It accepted the invitation card, placing it into what seemed to be a recessed mouth-like compartment. Once the information was verified, its round eyes illuminated, and with a polite gesture, the robot took Mann's hand as they walked together through the revolving doors and entered the upscale restaurant.

As they strolled, she heard a jazz band playing beautiful melodies, creating a romantic and idyllic atmosphere. She recognised the tune as one that someone often hummed, indicating that the band had rehearsed the performance specifically for this occasion. Finding it delightful, she couldn't help but join in humming along, smiling warmly from the depths of her heart.

Upon arriving at her reserved seat, the clumsy robot awkwardly moved the chair aside, its swaying movements causing amusement. However, Mann's smile remained immersed in the repetitive melodies. She sat down, and the robot attentively placed a napkin on her lap and filled her wine glass with aged red wine before returning to the kitchen to continue its work.

Awaiting the arrival of someone important, Mann leisurely admired the meticulous arrangement of the silverware, the spacing and direction on the square table. As someone who usually neglected such etiquette details, she believed that they were indispensable today. The candle flames on the table slowly melting white wax acted as a measure, calculating when the owner of the seat opposite her would arrive to claim it. The wax smoothly and gradually consumed the prearranged lifespan. The candle holders were beautiful, but as the candles' life neared their end, no matter how beautiful they were, they would lose their qualification as mere accompaniments.

Hours passed. The place became empty. The accumulated white wax turned into a disgusting mess. The band stopped playing, and hearts even emptier. Mann supported her cheeks with both hands, feeling the warmth on her skin as if steam was rising. Her eyelids grew tired, longing to relax and close, unwilling to persist. The carefully applied colours on her face began to blur, and all the good mood vanished. Across from her, the empty seat remained cold, destined to remain untouched by warmth throughout her lifetime.

"Mann!"

It was him, the man who had invited her to this date. Despite scolding him for his tardiness to such a crucial meeting, her delight overwhelmed her, and she burst into laughter. She laughed at her own foolishness, knowing full well that her beloved would never break a promise and stand her up. Surely, he had encountered indescribable obstacles on his way. She firmly believed that.

Then, a massive explosion occurred in the restaurant, engulfing everything in fierce flames, all at once.

As the beep of the microwave pierced the quiet rest zone, Mu Mann awoke with a start. Blinking away the remnants of sleep, she saw Huxtin, sans his intimidating black cloak, retrieving a hamburger from the microwave. She couldn't believe in her sight of Huxtin attempting to taste Earthlings' artificial food, something he had staunchly refused before.

With a jolt, she hastily gathered her unruly hair and secured it with a hairband. "You're like a silent ghost, sneaking up without a sound," she grumbled, while inwardly feeling quite happy to see him, but also felt taken aback, unsure what to say to him.

"Is there anything that can make the Great Detective frightened in the world?" Huxtin jokingly asked.

"It's you I'm most afraid of," Mann admitted, "you big Wood."

Huxtin merely ignored her response, closing the microwave door and sitting down. He unwrapped the wax paper around the hamburger but didn't take a bite, his gaze locked on Mann with an unreadable expression. The silence between them was unnerving, and even though they were used to it, tonight it felt different.

Swallowing hard, Mann mustered up her courage and reminded herself to be brave, as she usually was. "What's the point of staring at me like this? Do you have something to tell me?" She tried to maintain an air of confidence, but her heart raced nervously.

"No, I don't think so."

"Oh, really? In that case… just leave me here. I feel like

70

taking a break."

When their conversation briefly paused, Huxtin hesitated momentarily before finally taking a bite of the artificial hamburger. As he chewed, an unfamiliar sensation washed over him—the taste of meat that had never contained a soul before. He slowly consumed the entire hamburger, its synthetic flavours and textures evoking a sudden pang of loneliness within him, while also prompting him to involuntarily discern the distinct Elementro particles present in the food, marvelling at the Earthlings' ingenuity in extracting various substances from metal and lightning Elementro.

Having finished the hamburger, he picked up the wax paper it had been wrapped in, squeezing it tightly in his hand. He stood up, preparing to leave, but Mann had a change of heart.

"Hey... Just stay for a while, okay?" She had reached her breaking point, summoning her ultimate courage to confront the obstacles that had been festering within her mind. "Can we talk?"

Huxtin resumed his seat, casting glances at Mann while making an effort to maintain a certain emotional distance from her. "You just told me to leave," he pointed out.

"I actually have a lot to say."

"What is it about?"

"I think you've changed, but in a weird way."

"How so?"

"You've been talking a lot more recently, but your words are... difficult for me, and the others like Uncle Kee and the fisherman, to process. It's just—"

"I thought you were the one who wanted me to open up more. You always complained that I hid too much from you. And that it affected your emotions."

"Yes! Yes... I wanted you to speak more because..." Mann responded with her cheeks flushed. "You know I'm a talkative person. I need someone like me to exchange feelings and thoughts with, to... make myself comfortable? And maybe to understand what's going on in each other's lives."

She suddenly remembered their very first missions when she had desperately wanted to punch him and force him to open up.

It was a time she really treasured, despite the initial animosity.

"Maybe you got me wrong," she continued hesitantly, her chest tightening with those memories and fluctuating emotions. "I wanted you to be more open and honest, but not by exposing the truths of others with difficult words and cruel manners... I would rather have the quieter version of you than the new... present you... who isn't quite lovable. Although I must say, even the previous version of you wasn't exactly lovable either."

Huxtin stared at the table for a moment before opening his hand, releasing the wax paper which slowly unraveled. His spirit seemed to lift somewhat. In his mind, he deeply appreciated Mann's honesty, and it made him reflect on how his actions had caused hurt to those around him, all in an attempt to pinpoint himself. He knew he had grown weary of it. He knew he needed to stop, to change his ways, once again.

"I understand," he said quietly. "I know what to do."

Mann's heartbeat was as fast as a galloping ox, uncertain of what he meant by saying he understood. Before she could ask, Huxtin made a motion to leave, but she stopped him the second time. "Wait," she demanded.

"Anything else?"

"You mentioned in Cape Nameless that you asked someone... or something, or a god-like figure, a question, and you said you received an answer. Can you... tell me what you asked? And what the answer was?"

Huxtin's heart was filled with shock, caught off guard by Mann's question, yet he saw no harm in being honest with her this time. "At first, I asked about the true purpose of my existence in this universe. I was given an answer that my birth was intended to fulfil the desire of an entity, yet I was granted another opportunity to ask an additional question."

Mann's breath caught in her throat as she asked, "What was it?"

"I said, 'I yearn to leave everything behind, to lead a simple life devoid of any power. I desire to peacefully dwell in a secluded place, savouring each day, crafting my own dreams, and then bringing them to fruition. I no longer wish to be entangled in the ceaseless conflict between the Auras and the Umbras.' My question was: is it possible for me to have dreams of my own?"

"Dreams? So what was the answer?"

"We both know what the answer was."

As Huxtin finally walked away, Mann felt squeezed like the wax paper which returned to Huxtin's hand. She was unable to avert her gaze from the empty seat, her heart heavy with an even deeper sorrow. "You know you don't have to take all the responsibilities on you alone... Why do you insist of it?"

With Mu Mann's words in mind, atop the deck of the fishing vessel, Huxtin stood at the front edge, deep in contemplation as he gazed out at the dark and somewhat terrifying sea. The waves of the Boundless Ocean ironically mirrored his own life; constantly moving, never knowing whether to go forward or backward.

His eyes ascended towards the ebony sky, immersing himself in the twinkling stars. He wondered how The Creator had decided upon the placement and formation of each celestial body, and if his own existence was similarly destined by the same force. If his life wasn't controlled by The Creator, then who was the wish seeker, and who was the wish fulfiller?

He reminisced about a time when he had considered two radically divergent paths for his life: either obliterating every star himself or perishing like a shooting star, reduced to ashes in the process. The gravity of this decision had eventually compelled him to abdicate his role as the king of Paralloy Teddix, entrusting the throne to Huricane, his cherished but increasingly distant son. However, now he harboured doubts about his choice and found himself wearied by the burdens it had imposed upon him. "Is this truly the path I am destined to tread?" he questioned internally, his mind filled with mirky clouds and dying stars.

"Do you feel a sense of relief when you express, not all, but at least some of your emotions?"

Annoyed, Huxtin snapped, "I don't want to be bothered."

"Ahh, but you do. I told you so. You want someone to

listen, understand, care for you, and soothe your broken soul."

"Wasn't there someone who said that my soul would never be broken?"

"Metaphorically, it will. Everyone is the same. I understand everyone very well. You indulge too much in your own wonderland, wishing to ignore the mortal world's emotions and become the king of an empty kingdom. But you're meant to connect with all life forms in this universe, and that's why you cannot isolate yourself from reality."

Suddenly, an unsettling sensation crept over the deck. Huxtin turned to behold a familiar dark purple fog materialising out of thin air, billowing and spreading across the wooden planks. Emerging from the fog, Hurain manifested, her bare skin vaguely visible.
"You are here again, Hurain."
Huxtin was drawn towards his deceased wife like a moth to flame. The fog enveloping them both as he embraced her, running his fingers through her smooth black hair. The warmth of her skin brought back memories that felt both comforting and distant.
"I'm sorry..." he whispered, his voice choked with emotion, his eyes filling with love and sadness at the same time. "I don't know what to do."

"No, I should be the one to apologise, for I am now a deep scar in your soul."

"Don't worry... Remembering you is all I want."

"Promise me. Protect our child no matter what."

"The Stars of Teddix never set."
As the fog dissipated, Huxtin's body trembled, aching with

the desire for his soul to shatter and merge with Hurain in the dance of unison in a selfless dream. But he knew he had a purpose to fulfil— not just for his own wish fulfilment, but also for the sake of those who cared about him and whom he deeply cared for. There was no turning back.

11 Aqual, W.D. 471
Auta Rex, Kilidaci

Dawn cast a golden sheen over the fishermen's city of Auta
Rex, its rays glinting off the gentle waves that caressed the
eastern shores of Paralloy Teddix. The city was waking to the
rhythmic chant of the sea as Autaming's fishing vessel made its
return. Kilidaci, with its network of docks and fishing cottages
that sprawled along the coastline, teemed with vibrant activity.
Fishermen mended their nets with deft fingers, fishmongers
hawked their fresh goods, and seagulls cawed overhead and
cried out, their songs intertwined with the sounds of the
harbour.

This serene tableau belied the fierce loyalty of Kilidaci to
Teddix. It was an alliance forged in the furnace of war, never
once wavering even as others sought to claim the Teddix
Empire's throne during the Parallian Civil War. Despite having
achieved independence through a clause in an old treaty,
Kilidaci remained a steadfast brother-in-arms—a sanctuary for
the empire's weary soul. Many years later, Auta Rex became the
second-largest city in the kingdom of Paralloy Teddix, serving
as a testament to the gratitude for the assistance received from
Kilidaci during the royal's darkest times.

On deck, Huxtin stood cloaked in silence. His presence was a
tempest contained, his eyes holding storms within their depths.
Beside him, Mu Mann, whose spirit had dimmed in the wake of
tragedy and change, watched as Autaming gathered his empty
fishing nets with his most iconic laughter. Hidden beneath the
fishing vessel, Lokiata Kee, the Cosmo Scavenger, troubled by
his own secrets, lingered in the Hokan. He offered no farewell,
no acknowledgment of the camaraderie they had shared. It
remained uncertain whether their brief acquaintance of only
three days lacked genuine friendship or if he simply despised
the act of bidding farewell because of his aversion to it.

"Need to put more effort into it next time," Autaming
chortled, his gaze flickering between Huxtin and Mann. "Maybe

then, one of those legendary big fish will decide to grace my net!"

The optimism should have been contagious, but Mann couldn't summon a smile or a teasing remark—not after learning of the unspoken stories that lay beneath the bulky fisherman's mirth. Her gaze then shifted to Huxtin, whose aura of negativity seemed to poison the air around him. She worried for him, this king among men, now lost in the shadow of his own chaos.

"Autaming, your heart is larger than anything you can imagine capturing," Mann remarked, aware that she needed to say something to bring their brief journey, filled with both laughter and pain, to a close. "I believe in you."

"Aye aye, Commander Mu! Haha!" Autaming slapped his chest with a broad hand. "I have faith in you too. You will figure it out and eventually attain what you desire."

From the corner of Mann's eye, she caught the slight twitch in Huxtin's expression, a fleeting sign that he wasn't impervious to their banter. But he said nothing, his countenance returning to its inscrutable mask as he observed the interaction with a distance that seemed to stretch further than the ocean itself. Mann wanted to draw him out, to bridge the gulf of blackness that threatened to swallow him whole. She knew Autaming felt it too—the urge to pull their mutual friend back into the light, to anchor him against the tide of despair. Yet, there were no words strong enough to penetrate the fortifications erected by a mind in pandemonium.

With a final well-wish in her heart, Mann addressed Autaming, saying, "Keep at it, and someday that fish will be yours, but don't talk about dying in storms anymore, okay?"

Autaming's eyes, bright as the ocean on a sunny day, widened in surprise when Mann stepped closer and wrapped her arms around his large frame. His laughter, warm and rich, rumbled like distant thunder. "You'll smell like fish too, you know," he joked, yet there was a tremor of something else—a poignant gratitude.

"Better than the stench of fear and suffering we've been steeped in," Mann replied, pulling back. "I'll miss your ridiculous tales and stubborn optimism."

"Don't let Huxtin do anything stupid. Speaking of stubbornness, he is the worst." The burly fisherman's usually jovial face softened, an earnest undertone weaving through his words. "Take care of him for me."

"Always," she assured, her voice laced with an uncharacteristic gentleness, her own heart aching with the weight of unspoken promises. "Live well, Autaming. Live bravely, and blissfully."

"Wouldn't dream of anything less," he responded, his trademark grin returning.

After a moment that stretched between heartbeats, Mann turned to leave, brushing past Huxtin, who stood like a lighthouse among the swaying masts, with a meaningful glance. "I'll leave you two for a bit," she murmured before disappearing down the gangplank.

The two men exchanged a look, brimming with words unvoiced, emotions locked away behind stoic fronts.

"Come on, what about a hug for me, huh?" Autaming teased, aiming to breach the chasm between them with levity.

But Huxtin, enshrouded in his black cloak, remained still, a statue carved from night itself. "I don't think you need one," he replied, his voice devoid of warmth yet not unkind.

"Who said anything about needing?" Autaming's smile didn't waver, a sunbeam piercing through storm clouds. "I'm happy, truly, to have seen you once again."

Huxtin felt a tug at something within him, a flicker of desire to reach out, to reciprocate in some way. Yet, the shadow within recoiled, sealing away the impulse. It was a battle, an internal skirmish that left no room for outward gestures.

"Then be content with that happiness," he finally said, turning his back on the possibility of connection.

The fisherman watched his friend retreat, the longing for that simple embrace lingering like the salt on the sea air. He understood the barriers Huxtin erected, knowing them as intimately as the grooves on his cherished fishing rod. And though the ache for understanding was sharp, he wasn't quite satisfied with the distance Huxtin chose to maintain.

"Huxtin!" He cleared his throat, wrestling with the courage that threatened to slip through his fingers like the elusive fish from his nets. "I have... one more word for you."

Huxtin paused but didn't turn, his silhouette a dark smudge against the dawn-streaked sky.

"What is it?" His words were sparse, each syllable slicing the air with precision.

"Thank you... for keeping your promise... You came back for me."

"Promises are the currency of trust. I spend mine wisely."

"No, Huxtin, you are genuinely a good person, kind and gentle. You are staying true to the essence of your being."

"Is that so?"

As Huxtin walked away, the finality of his departure hung heavy on the salty breeze. Autaming, now enlightened by the truth, comprehended the magnitude of Huxtin's mission and the underlying motive for their encounter amidst its unfolding —he had come to bid his old friend farewell for one last time.

Inside the Hokan, Mu Mann navigated the narrow corridor, the hum of the battleship's core a comforting constant. She cast a quick look at the rest zone, where the Auras sat with the golden sphere cell. Its current compact form, resembling the size of a human head, was a remarkable display of mystical compression. How the prisoner endured within its confines was a mystery that teased Mann's curious mind.

Noticing the perplexity on Mann's face, Jeramia greeted, offering a playful wink and a mischievous hand gesture, "Hey there."

"Uhh... hi," Mann replied with an awkward smile, observing the serene composure of Jeramia's companion, Remezo. Sensing the potential entanglement of a conversation, she quickly took a step back, seeking to extricate herself from its grasp.

Finding her seat behind the pilot of the Hokan, she mustered what little energy she had left. "Thanks for waiting, Oren."

"Umm." Sheung Oren's response was blunt, a verbal wall erected between them, urging Mann to study her best friend's cold shoulder, the frost of their strained friendship seeping into the bones of the battleship. Mann knew the cause, felt the burden of unspoken grievances, yet exhaustion restrained her resolve to confront the issue head-on. For now, silence became her chosen defence.

24:3

Nestled within the secluded embrace of the Shell Valley, where myths breathed life into the very air, there rested a lake known as Hidden Moon. It was cradled by The Trident, a triad of stone sentinels that had weathered the ages. Tales abounded of the valley's mystical nature, whispering of a domain accessible only to those untainted by malice or deceit. Many ventured toward its heart, but the dense foliage would consume all but the purest.

Enveloped within an ever-present fog, a modest greenhouse stood defiant against the elements, its existence revealed solely to those well-versed in the mystical language of Elementro. The garden that surrounded it was a mosaic of flora; each pot a testament to the dual nature of life—some containing deadly toxins, while others nurturing the essence of rebirth. In the corner stood a tall and spacious wooden cabinet, embellished with rows and columns of drawers. It appeared to house a collection of rare herbs and ingredients gathered from across Celestiloo. The atmosphere within the greenhouse resonated with a palpable, yet unspoken energy, a silent guardian warding off the unworthy.

Resting upon a humble bed crafted from the bounties of the forest and securely tethered to the earth, lay a young man. He existed on the edge of awareness, cocooned within bandages that bore witness to recent battles fought, with his chest rising and falling with the rhythm of the living. It might have been the soft caress of morning sunlight that beckoned him from slumber, filtering through the glass panes to waltz upon his closed eyelids. Or perhaps it was the echo of a presence felt deeper than dreams.

His breath hitched as he stirred, eyes fluttering open to gaze upon the canopy above—a lattice of shadows and light. He ached with a dull persistence as he pushed himself upright. With measured movements, he swung his legs over the edge of the makeshift bed and reached for his jacket, hanging loosely on his frame, unzipped.

Next, his hands found the white boots by the chair, pulling them on, feeling the familiar pressure around his ankles—anchors to this world. Stepping out of the greenhouse, he approached an older man who shared his attire in hue but not in wear. The older man's garments remained pristine, untouched by the signs of combat or escape. Standing beside a babbling stream that whispered carelessly of existence, he scattered handfuls of feed to the fish eagerly awaiting their meal.

"Good morning. You return to the land of the waking," the older man said without looking up, his voice rich with the timbre of lived years.

Coming close to the murmuring stream, the young man caught sight of his reflection—Huringo, the mad prince of the troubled kingdom Paralloy Teddix. His once flowing locks were now shorn close to the scalp, exposing more of the grief and anger that clawed at his features.

"Morning," Huringo replied, his voice a low rumble. "And as much as I'd like to claim otherwise, it seems I owe you my gratitude once more."

"Think nothing of it. There's no need for gratitude," the older man dismissed the notion with a wave of his hand. "You are free to leave at any time. Your path is your own to tread."

"Is it now?" Huringo's tone took on an iron edge, his gaze hardening. "I don't think so."

"As far as I recall, I never coerced you into anything. I merely provided you with advice." The older man only paid attention to the fish gracefully swimming in the stream while speaking, as if they were the ones conversing. "You owe me nothing, Huringo. Go whenever you wish, to pursue whatever vendetta fuels your spirit."

"Hmph... Regardless of what you say, I remain your pawn," Huringo uttered bitterly, the taste of irony lingering on his tongue like bitter bile. "I am well aware of it."

The older man admonished, his gaze finally meeting Huringo's. "Your thoughts are clouded. You are too quick to assume the worst in others," he retorted. "You despise being controlled, yet you speak of pawns and games? Look deeper, Huringo."

"Perhaps, but what does it matter when one's days are numbered?" Huringo's hands clenched into fists, nails digging crescents into his palms. "The only ruler that reigns over everything is power."

Within his mind, a tempest raged—a struggle against time, against destiny. There was no room for failure, not again. His desires burned, a furnace that no amount of Elementro could quench. He knew what he needed to do; he would carve his path with or without consent.

"Every moment is borrowed," he continued, murmuring under his breath, his eyes still locked on his fractured reflection, a man pieced together by another's magic. "I will not squander them."

"Nor should you. But remember, power can uplift or obliterate."

"Let it obliterate," came Huringo's answer, swift and sure, his voice laced with a hunger that went beyond the physical. "I need power... More power. I demand the power to shape my fate— to never kneel before destiny again."

In the midst of their charged silence, the Elementro particles in the air began to drift and shift erratically, an unseen portent that put the older man on high alert. The once refreshing atmosphere within the garden took on a faint scent of charred remnants, perceptible to his keen senses. A course of action had to be taken, he pondered, for if delayed, it might be too late to nurture the seeds he had painstakingly planted and tended for an extended period of time.

After careful consideration, he arrived at a decision and said, "Somehow, an idea has illuminated my mind. You understand the strength of your Elementro affinity, but without Elementro transformability, you will be unable to harness Wings of Sunlight."

"Wings of Sunlight?" Huringo exclaimed, his surprise evident in his voice. "What do you want to—"

"You will require me. Listen carefully, young man. Supporting your cause and joining it are two different beasts.

Your path has already garnered enough attention. My presence at your side would only serve to escalate matters, awakening sleepers best left undisturbed."

"Let it burn," Huringo challenged, stepping closer. "I am beyond fear now. Time is slipping through my fingers, and if I do not act quickly, the Auras will make certain my plan unravel before they can even begin."

"Very well. I suppose I must find someone capable of taking good care of my garden and greenhouse, then," the older man conceded, a sigh escaping him as if he were finally releasing a burden long carried. "But for now, hide yourself."

Huringo blinked, momentarily lost, his mind grappling with the significance of what had been left unsaid. Suddenly, he was cocooned by energies, being transported to somewhere pinpointed a location identified by the older man as a place of safety. The next second, a volley of intangible daggers, blazing with celestial light, sliced through the air where Huringo once stood.

The older man's reflexes, honed over eons, saved him as he danced back gracefully, the lethal light grazing the hem of his white garments. With a thought, he flickered from existence— only to reappear across the babbling stream. The world resettled around him, but the reprieve was short-lived; water tentacles surged up from the stream, wrapping around his ankles with deceptive strength. They sought to bind him, to anchor him in place for their unseen master's next strike.

"A proper challenge at last," the older man mused internally, his heart quickening with a warrior's delight. It had been long since he tasted the thrill of combat, the rush of his blood singing the old songs of war.

"Running away?" Rafaelzo's voice pierced his reverie, the chief elder of the Auras materialising with a faint pop behind the older man who was in fact one of the most powerful Auras in the universe. "You know I can track you as easily as the wind chases leaves, Solarades."

"Rafaelzo." Solarades turned, revealing an expression of amused curiosity rather than concern. "I merely wished to gauge if time has dulled your edge—or sharpened it."

With an effortless command, Solarades called upon the soil to rise in defence, wooden tendrils bursting forth to drink deeply from the water tentacles, siphoning their life away. Leaves sprouted rapidly from the interwoven tendrils, showcasing his mastery over the natural elements. Soon, he stepped free, teleporting once more, leaving behind the burgeoning grove as undeniable proof of his might.

Rafaelzo's eyes traced the rapid growth of the woods, his lips curling into a respectful smile. "Impressive as always, old friend. But do you not tire of these games?"

"Games?" Solarades let out a low chuckle, his voice resonating with the depth of ancient mountains. "This is no game. This is the prelude to the symphony of our people's fate."

Though not visible to the naked eye, the older man could feel Rafaelzo's aura pulsing—a vibrant force field that distinguished him as a formidable presence. However, within Solarades, an eagerness that had long lain dormant now stirred, awakened by the prospect of engaging in a battle of wits and powers against such a worthy adversary.

Before Solarades could even draw his next breath after teleporting again, the air above him crackled with an electric fury. The sky darkened as if night had descended in haste before sunset, and from this ominous canopy, lightning cascaded like a torrential downpour, aiming to destroy the greenhouse beneath. But Solarades was agile; his hands wove an intricate tapestry of commands, coaxing the earth to rise. Wooden beams spiralled skyward, knitting together into a lattice that crowned the fragile glass structure below, shielding it from the sparkling onslaught.

"Never!" Solarades roared, his voice resonating through the garden as the tempest relented. "You shall not lay waste to my sanctuary, little Aura! The sin would be too great, for here lies the culmination of my life's devotion—a true heaven on Celestiloo!"

Gloria, her form outlined against the dispersing storm clouds, ceased her attack. She scrutinised the older man before her, his age-worn visage betraying the countless seasons he had endured. Yet, those eyes—piercingly silvery—betrayed no hint of frailty. A flicker of doubt crossed her features; she had heard tales of Solarades's ability to shift his appearance at will. Was this truly his face, or just another facade?

On the other side of the watery divide, Rafaelzo refrained from his usual method of arrival. His body unraveled into a kaleidoscope of marbles, each reflecting a myriad of colours as they danced across the stream. They reassembled on dry land, regaining his stately form as he floated before Solarades.

"Ugh... Show off again," Gloria muttered with an exasperated sigh, her words barely audible.

"Rafaelzo," Solarades addressed the leader of the Auras, redirecting his attention after securing the safety of his cherished possessions and extinguishing his flames. "Your return to Celestiloo was bound to happen. Pray tell, how have the winds of fortune treated you?"

"Fortune has little to do with it," Rafaelzo replied grimly. "The Auras are embroiled in upheaval; we've identified a traitor among us. I am tasked with his elimination, though I wish to unearth his motives first."

"Aha, and why has it taken the Auras so long to act?" Solarades mused, stroking his chin thoughtfully. "Surely such treachery did not escape your notice until now—or is this tied to that archaic decree that forbids the Auras from intervening in Celestiloo's affairs?"

Gloria, who had approached during their exchange, couldn't help but sense the undercurrents of tension between the two. There was something deeply personal in the way they addressed one another—an emotional kindling ready to ignite at the slightest provocation.

"Times do change, Solarades. I know it. I know that change is inevitable," Rafaelzo countered, "but some oaths remain sacred."

"Even when they blind you to the rot within?"

"I think you are just going too far."

"No, no... Have you ever contemplated the reason behind the three of us, Lunarcaria, Novaubri, and myself, arriving as a trio? In moments of conflicting opinions, the presence of a third can tip the scales and serve as a judge, determining whose logic holds superior. And I... I am always the judge."

Rafaelzo's jaw tightened, the edges of his ethereal form shimmering with suppressed energies. "You are venturing down a treacherous path," he retorted, his voice thick with reproach. "This was never Lunarcaria's intended vision."

"And I recall your support for Novaubri," Solarades countered smoothly, though the smirk on his lips did little to mask the growing fire in his eyes. "The punishment of the humankind... the abandonment of Celestiloo... Or have you forgotten? Rafaelzo, blinded by rituals so ancient they've turned to dust!"

Rafaelzo had no defence against the accusation, and he was acutely aware of it. The air around them seemed to thrum with Solarades's rising ire—a silent warning that the seemingly older looking man's patience was fraying.

"Updating the ways of the Auras is one thing," Rafaelzo conceded, his form solidifying and growing more imposing. "But consorting with the Umbras, those creatures of darkness? That is where we draw the line."

"Your line, perhaps. I dare to venture where none of you will."

"The Auras exist to safeguard the cosmos, not to court its destruction."

"Too late," Solarades replied with a surge of his unique Elementro energies, his silvery eyes reflecting a resolute certainty. "The Son of Chaos is approaching his crossroads, and trust me, he won't cast his lot with the likes of you."

Gloria, positioned off to the side, shifted her weight impatiently. The endless circling of words, as fruitless as trying to catch the wind, coupled with Solarades's cryptic allusions— they wearied her. His face, whether illusion or reality, mattered naught; it was the twisted sincerity behind his gaze that eroded her composure.

With a swift gesture, born of resolve and impatience, she summoned a torrent of electric wrath from the very ground itself. Rising bolts of lightning, like vengeful serpents, struck where Solarades had stood mere moments before. Solarades, ever-nimble, had anticipated the assault, vanishing in a shimmer of light that left an afterimage floating in the charged air.

"Must we always leap to violence, Gloria?" Rafaelzo's gaze lingered on the spot Solarades had vacated. "We are here to talk. Fighting is the last resort."

"Have you forgotten our purpose?" Gloria argued, her lips a tight line. "There is no reasoning with those who choose darkness over brightness."

He sighed, a sound that seemed to carry the burdens of all the Auras. "You have your point. Just don't underestimate the enemy in front of you."

In an instant, he too disappeared, leaving only the echo of his departure. Time seemed to bend, and from a tear in the sky, a Binary of Teleportation unfurled like a celestial ribbon. Rafaelzo reemerged, his hand clasped around Solarades's arm, pulling the adversary back into their reality.

Gloria wasted not a heartbeat; her right fist became a nexus of raw energy, gathering the power of a hundred storms. With a cry that resonated with the force of her spirit, she released a magnificent beam, a lance of pure lightning that streaked across the sky with blinding brilliance.

Solarades met the attack head-on, his fall cushioned by an aura that ignited around him—a protective cocoon of green and brown light. He hit the earth with a muted thud, yet he rose, untouched by Gloria's fury, his arms lifted toward the heavens. Nature responded to his call, a beast awakened. Beneath Gloria's feet, the ground shuddered, upheaved, and chased her like a relentless predator. She ran, her instincts sharpened by a thousand days of battle, but the terrain itself seemed to hunger for her downfall.

She then dissolved into a brilliant streak of shocking blue electricity, zigzagging across the garden, a living bolt seeking shelter. She funnelled her essence into the greenhouse sanctuary. The murderous terrain halted its pursuit at the threshold, as if recognising some unspoken boundary. Inside, amidst the tranquil scent of earth and foliage, Gloria reconstituted into flesh and bone. Safety enveloped her like a warm embrace; under the glass panes above, her breathing steadied, her focus deepened. She was safe—for now.

"Stand down, Solarades!" On the other side, Rafaelzo's command cut through the chaos as he darted towards his foe, suspended mid-air with wings of light. He conjured a dagger of pure radiance, the embodiment of his resolve, and slashed at Solarades with a strike meant to end the charade. But the blade met wood, not flesh—Solarades had been a decoy, a wooden sculpture standing in silent mockery.

Rafaelzo's frustration was palpable as he surveyed the battlefield. Finding Solarades amidst the magic and mayhem would require all his cunning and focus. He knew time was against him, and the real Solarades was out there, a shadow among shadows. He also knew Gloria's impetuous nature often led her to act with her heart rather than her head. She was the storm, unpredictable and wild, but necessary in their struggle. He couldn't fault her passion, even as he yearned for a solution that didn't require such destruction.

Then, a subtle shift in the air, a mere whisper against his heightened senses, betrayed Solarades's presence. Spinning on his heel, he lashed out with his dagger, only to find empty space. His muscles tensed as he felt the firm grip of Solarades on his arm, the pressure of fingers like iron bands, yet lacking the intention to harm.

"Have you no desire to strike me down?" Rafaelzo asked, his voice tinged with confusion and an unexpected twinge of sympathy. For a moment, he glimpsed vulnerability within Solarades's silvery pupils. "Your mercy puzzles me."

"Mercy?" Solarades replied, almost contemplative. "Perhaps it's merely the recognition of a kindred spirit trapped in an endless cycle of conflict."

Rafaelzo seized the fleeting connection. "Then why do we fight? We could unite to implore the Son of Chaos for clemency, to halt this needless strife!"

"Naive. Do you think matters will be settled that easily?" Solarades scoffed. "You still think the Son of Chaos can be swayed after all the deception, all the corruption sowed by the Auras?"

"Is it so foolish to seek peace?" Rafaelzo reached for another weapon, channeling his diverse Elementro energies into the formation of a purple crystal sword, its glow casting eerie shadows around them. "Is war and violence the only way to give our people what they want?"

"Peace?" Solarades's laugh was bitter, cold. "There is no peace to be had with traitors. That is precisely why you are now drawing your weapon on me after uttering all those nonsensical words!"

In a fluid and seamless motion, Solarades summoned his own blade, a sword forged from the essence of living plants, dust, and the harmonious interplay of two forms of energy in perfect equilibrium. With a resounding crash, the crystal shattered against it, fracturing into a thousand glittering shards that reflected Rafaelzo's dismay.

As Rafaelzo braced himself for a fresh onslaught, Gloria's lightning form streaked across the battlefield. With agile grace, she darted between the duelling titans, using her speed to create openings and disrupt their clash. Her goal was to create an opportunity for her chief elder to unleash a devastating attack of greater magnitude.

"Let's end it today, shall we?" However, Solarades noticed her intention and a dreadful conclusion to the day's battle began to form in his mind. "With the death of this little Aura?"

"No way!" Rafaelzo felt a surge of unease, and he hastily abandoned the clash with Solarades, lunging towards Gloria instead. Above and below Gloria, reality itself appeared to rupture, forming two swirling vortexes—one emitting black light and the other radiating white. These manifestations were more than a mere spectacle of power—it was a snare, a Binary of Seal meant to entrap and neutralise.

In the pivotal moment, Rafaelzo poured his very essence into the Binary. The air burst into bright light with his efforts, a mirror to Solarades's own construct. The four clouds of energies collided with a thunderous roar, and at last, the Binaries neutralised each other, dissolving into sun and moon Elementro particles that glittered like stars being born and dying all at once.

Gloria's lightning form flickered and slowly receded, her human silhouette emerging from the diminishing glow. She returned to the ground, staggered, breathing heavily, the taste of ozone sharp on her tongue. She turned to see Rafaelzo. However, Solarades was nowhere to be found, and the mission had failed due to her own rabidness.

"I'm… terribly sorry," she panted while closing the distance to her chief elder, her normal confidence fractured by the near disaster. "I was… careless."

Rafaelzo dismissed her apology, the ghost of a smile touching his stern features. "You were facing one of the Trinity of Twelfianity, a powerful Aura whose wit is matched only by his strength. Even I am unprepared by his gambits."

She cast a shameful glance at him, her eyes continuing to search. "What should we do now?"

"Well, given the circumstances," he said thoughtfully, his eyes drifting to the lush greenhouse that had been under Solarades's fierce protection, "a change of schedule, for sure. We must seek an audience with the Son of Chaos in advance."

CHAPTER 25

HATRED TENDS TO CLING LONGER THAN LOVE

12 Aqual, W.D. 471
Teddix Castle, Teddix

Today was no ordinary day; it marked the birth of Queen Hurain, the shattered jewel of the once glorious Teddix Empire, and Paralloy Teddix in its sunrising era.

In the grand garden in front of Teddix Castle's west gate, Huricane, in his royal attire, usually resplendent in the court, was now marred by the dirt from the pots he carried, one by one, out from the inner sanctum of the castle. The delicate Icrings, nestled within earthenware, radiating an incipient lilac hue as they awaited the embrace of the Illuminator.

With each pot he delicately placed, it was a tribute to the Icrings, extraordinarily rare flowers that hailed from the frigid corners of Celestiloo; as their buds unfurled, they had a fleeting twenty-four hours to unveil their ultimate beauty before gracefully bowing out, leaving the stage of life forever; the only way to preserve their delicate existence was to store them in a realm of partial or complete darkness before they withered, decayed, and returned to the earth as soil and dust.

The castle guards knew the sacredness of this ritual, the sorrow that clung to their king like a shroud. The king's task was his alone—no hand but his would usher the Icrings into the light. They were more than mere flora; they embodied the fragility of life and the resilience of love.

"My King!" A voice broke the morning stillness. Huduson approached, his eyes reflecting a storm of concern. "I've been looking for you!"

Huricane paused, offering a nod of acknowledgment to his cousin. "The flowers require my care today, Huduson. It is a duty only I can fulfil."

"Of course," Huduson replied, his voice quivering. "But should you need me…"

The king rejected gently, "these blooms were my mother's favourite. She must feel my gratitude from the heavens above."

Huduson observed the Icrings. Memories of the queen's

kindness flooded his thoughts, and he saw her spirit reflected in Huricane's perseverance. Yet, he sensed an undercurrent of susceptibility—a longing for guidance once provided by the queen, and now sought in the echoes of her memory.

"Hmm... Anything, just say the word..." he offered again, unable to stifle his protective instincts. "I will be at your command."

Huricane's lips formed a wry smile, his hands bracing against a pot as he manoeuvred it into its designated spot. "I know, I know," he uttered, his voice tinged with a touch of annoyance yet also carrying unspoken appreciation. What Huduson mightn't have comprehended was that the king's mind wrestled with the duality of his role—the responsibilities of rulership conflicting with his personal desire for freedom.

"Hard at work, My King. It is a splendid morning, observing your lively energy." Wyach's arrival was heralded by the rhythmic clank of her high heels, a sound that had become as much a signature of her presence as the sharp intelligence in her eyes. The sapphire waves of her dress rippled with each step, reflecting the morning sun in a dazzling display of light and colour. She moved with an elegance that belied the urgency brewing within her.

"Hah, always," Huricane, who was meticulously arranging the final pots of Icrings, replied, his voice threaded with pride. "I need to. Everybody watches me, and they need me."

Yet Wyach's gaze lingered not on the king, but rather on the immaculate horizon where the Silensee Mountains jutted into the sky, their jagged profiles standing guard over Teddix. She watched as winged creatures soared through the thermals, their freedom a stark contrast to the world in which she was situated.

"Lady Hurain, may your soul continue to protect your son from any darkness that looms on the horizon," she whispered, offering a silent prayer. "The Creator... are you going to do the same for this kingdom?"

On the other hand, a nervous Huduson shifted uncomfortably. "My King, umm... Time presses against us, indeed. The Earthlings are awaiting our presence."

With a young and fresh mind that flourished, Huricane

turned, his voice booming across the garden. "Yes, yes! One pot remains, and then we shall depart!"

Kneeling beside the lone Icring, Huricane's hands hovered with reverence above the delicate bloom. He traced the contours of the pot, each line a memory of his mother's tender care. In the quiet of his heart, he reminisced about days filled with laughter, when shadows were merely playmates at dusk, before sorrow flooded his world like an insurmountable tide.

"Sea of Icrings..." he breathed, the words hanging in the air as a matter yet to be settled, and the day he had anticipated might have already dawned upon him. Waves of emotion crashed within him, love and loss entwined in an eternal war. For a moment, the king was simply a son, longing to turn back the clock, to bask once more in the warmth of a mother's hug.

25:2

12 Aqual, W.D. 471
T.P.S.E. Command Centre, Teddix

Following the Battle of Sun and Moon, there remained wounds in need of healing, but fortunately, the advanced technology provided by the Earthlings and the protective Wings of Moonlight mitigated the extent of destruction, keeping it under control and minimising the affected areas.

Amid the ongoing reconstruction, Huricane, flanked by Huduson and an entourage of personal guards, walked through the debris on their way to the command centre of the Earthlings. The building was as unremarkable as its purpose was crucial—a single-storey rectangular structure made of dull grey metal, with ten nondescript doors encircling it like sentries. Each door led to an elevator, descending into the earth to various clandestine chambers below.

Huricane's eyes took in the structure, recalling the agreement made years ago between his father and Lokiata Edward, the president of the Earth Alliance: a decision to burrow into the planet's crust rather than pierce its sky, an attempt to avoid attracting unwanted attention. It seemed almost quaint now, that belief in discretion. No matter whether they sought refuge underground or soared high in the sky, their enemies saw them regardless. The ending, inexorably, would be the same.

Before stepping in, Huricane cast a wistful glance back at Teddix Castle. The juxtaposition between the ancient stronghold of his lineage and the pragmatic bunker of T.P.S.E. wasn't lost on him. It was a collision of worlds—his birthright and his burden—as much as it was a fusion of old agreements and new realities.

Inside, Mark Carlo stood rigidly in the commander's tower, his gaze fixated on a screen that dwarfed his stature. Frustration simmered beneath his exterior as he awaited the arrival of the tardy royalty. His eyes swept over the scars marring the interior —damages from last week's battle, still raw and exposed—and his heart swelled with a bitter resentment towards Celestiloo.

But the screen soon recaptured his attention, displaying half the visage of Lokiata Edward, whose aura of power filled the base despite his digital confinement.

"I'll give them one more minute, Mark Carlo." The disembodied voice of Edward could be heard in the base, each word infused with impatience as if time itself bent to his will. "The Teddixians are wasting my time."

"Do I need to dispatch someone to ascertain the current condition of the king of this land?" Carlo inquired, his tone betraying none of the anxiety that fluttered like a trapped bird within his chest.

"No, it's not necessary at all." Edward's voice boomed. "Why is it that we are the ones who must wait, and not the other way around?"

Carlo clenched his jaw, turning away from the screen to scan the commander's tower once more. His mind raced with the potential fallout of this meeting. He knew that the president's confidence was a fortress, and he was but a soldier manning its walls. And yet, concealed within his loyalty, he harboured a grand scheme, a plot taking shape within the recesses of his mind. He was determined not to let the Teddixians ruin everything he had constructed in secret.

"Your minute is up." Edward's voice boomed again from the screen, a baritone of authority that resonated through the base. "I'll be disconnecting—"

"Wait, President Lokiata, please!," interjected Carlo, the words lodged in his throat as he caught sight of the door swinging open behind him. With the regal bearing of a true king, Huricane entered the commander's tower, his companions fanning out with military precision. Carlo's feet begrudgingly shuffled aside, creating a reluctant pathway for the young king.

"You're late," he muttered through gritted teeth, his gaze hardening into a glare as Huricane bypassed him without acknowledgment. "Grr, do the people in this kingdom not know the importance of punctuality?"

"Everyone seems to be quite occupied, President Lokiata, wouldn't you agree?" Huricane addressed Edward directly, his tone carrying a reverence reserved for those who held genuine power, showing no fear of standing in the shadow of the leader from another sovereign entity. "I am present now. I have been informed that you have a question for which you seek my answer. Please, enlighten me with the question."

Edward scrutinised Huricane through the screen, his eyebrows knitting together in disapproval. "Why isn't Huxtin here? I expected to negotiate with a king, not a child."

"I am the king of Paralloy Teddix," Huricane firmly stated, standing tall despite his lesser stature. "Furthermore, I am no longer a child. I have reached the age of sixteen, which deems me an adult."

A current sparked between them, electric and crackling. In the flickering light of their mutual hostility and dissatisfaction, their eyes locked—a silent battle raged across the void of cyberspace. Each man emanated a fierce intensity that seemed to warp the air around them, two sovereigns with a world to defend, a future to secure.

"Twenty-one is the age of majority in the Earth Alliance, anyway," Edward countered with bureaucratic finality before steering the conversation toward the heart of the matter. "Now, my question: where is Lokiata Zen? I demand an audience with my son."

Huricane had expected the imminent question and had rehearsed his response. He exhaled slowly, acutely conscious of the fragile lie that was about to leave his lips. "Your son, Lokiata Zen, has been deployed on a critical mission and is currently away from Paralloy Teddix."

The lie hovered in the air like smoke, its opacity a thin veil over the truth. Huricane understood the game at play, the intricate dance of deception. It was a performance where innocence masked intent, where every carefully chosen word acted as a step in a choreographed routine crafted to mislead.

"Is that so?" Edward's voice took on the sharp edge of skepticism, his stare penetrating the screen as if to dissect the falsehoods laid before him. "Where? Where did Huxtin send my son, and why my son of all people?"

Huricane's lips parted slightly, betraying no emotion as he responded with measured calm. "It's a classified mission,

President Lokiata. I'm afraid I'm not at liberty to disclose any specifics."

Irritated, Edward's fist slammed down, the resounding impact reverberating through the metallic walls, his frustration erupting into real and visible rage, threatening to lay waste to all around it. "If you are ignorant, then I demand Huxtin's immediate presence! Now!"

"My father is also on his own mission. He will not be joining us today."

The president's scowl deepened. Those same icy blue eyes that now challenged him were a mirror to Huxtin's, a bitter reminder of the man who had taken Lokiata Zen away. His nightmare had unfolded into reality. Regret flooded his being as he reflected upon the choices that had permitted his only son to embark on a perilous intergalactic mission. The burden of remorse grew heavier as he recognised the decisions influenced by the parliament members, who compelled him to demonstrate his resolve by appointing Lokiata Zen as a crucial member of T.P.S.E.

"Is your concern solely for your son?" Huricane's voice broke the tension. He leaned forward imperceptibly, the motion a silent assertion of power. "Because I have matters to address as well. May I?"

"Huh? You… How dare—"

"Reports have surfaced of groups of people known as the Cosmo Scavengers making landfall on Celestiloo. Two of their battleships have been found, no survivors. But what if more arrive? What then, President Lokiata? How did your government let this happen? And what recompense will we see if these intruders bring harm to our world?"

At this revelation, Carlo twitched nervously, his gaze darting away as he licked his lips—a cornered animal aware of prying eyes upon him. But Huricane's focus remained steadfast on the screen, his stare burrowing into Edward's conscience. Perceiving the subtle cues from his subordinate, Edward consciously chose to skate over them—his pawn would continue to play the dirty games that kept his own hands clean.

"I hold no knowledge of such events. This is the first I've

heard of it." His reply was curt, evasive.

In the silent aftermath, only the soft hum of machinery dared to speak. Huricane straightened, his posture regal despite his youth, knowing the game of political chess continued its relentless march forward. Each move was calculated, every gambit a step closer to unveiling hidden truths—or concealing them further. Carlo, meanwhile, struggled internally to maintain composure, his secrets clawing at the confines of his throat, desperate to spill forth. Yet, he must not falter; so much depended on the careful orchestration of lies and half-truths.

"For certain, this is your answer," Huricane responded after his mental calculations completed. His eyes scanned the base, taking in the uncomfortable shift of the guards, the nervous tic of Carlo's jaw, and finally landing again on the frustrated leader of the Earthlings. "Are you willing to take action on our behalf?"

"Assistance will be provided by Mark Carlo for any further investigation you deem necessary." Edward's tone was crisp, almost dismissive, as if he was washing his hands of the matter. "Mark Carlo, give me a report if something strange happens."

Carlo's heart lurched at the mention of his name, but his face betrayed nothing. Internally, he cursed—every second spent under scrutiny was a moment closer to his downfall. Huricane then tried to bring the meeting to a close. "Very well, if that is the stance of the Earth Alliance."

However, before anyone could utter another word, the unexpected whir of the door behind Huricane and Carlo added a new layer of complexity to the situation.

"Hey… Sorry, I didn't mean to come here… Just got turned around…"

It was Lokiata Kee who stumbled into view, his apologetic words tumbling from his lips before his eyes locked with his brother Edward. A collective inhale seemed to suck the oxygen from the base. Eyes widened at the sight of the scar that marred Kee's cheek—a mark of a shared history so tangible that it resonated like a struck bell. The glow of the screen cast stark shadows over Edward's features, rendering them frozen in an expression of sheer shock.

For a brief eternity, silence reigned, punctuated only by the soft electronic buzz of the equipment. Afterwards, with the abruptness of a cut transmission, Edward proclaimed, "This meeting is adjourned."

At the end, the screen flickered, leaving readings and charts in place of the president's stern countenance.

"Odd, isn't it?" Kee, attempting to dispel the sudden frost, gestured awkwardly towards the exit. "Just looking for the restroom, really." His hand cut through the air in a motion to leave, and then he was gone, a ghost swallowed back into the bowels of the command centre.

Huricane slowly took another breath, relief tempering the steel in his spine. He had braced for confrontation, for the inevitable clash of wills—but the reunion of the Lokiata brothers? This wasn't on his script, even though he had learned about Lokiata Kee's existence just a few hours prior. He cast another emotionless glance at Carlo, sensing the restlessness emanating from the T.P.S.E. deputy commander, hinting at unexplored depths and veiled agendas.

"Share with me what you know, Mark Carlo. If you dare, although I doubt your eagerness is anything more than pretence."

"King Huricane, if there is indeed anything that I know, any information that can be shared, rest assured that I will inform you without delay."

Without lingering, Huricane turned to leave, Huduson a silent shadow at his heel. Near the entrance of the commander's tower, Mu Mann stood, dressed in casual Earthling attire consisting of a white T-shirt, a navy blue short-sleeve jacket, sporty black pants and a pair of grey leather boots. She waved her hand in farewell to an unidentified figure, but Huricane couldn't help but suspect that he knew who it might be.

"Mu Mann," he called out, a grin tugging at the corner of his mouth, momentarily breaking through the tension that had ruined his mood during the heated argument. "I wasn't aware that the Earthlings' hospitality extended to allowing a suspended commander to wander these corridors freely."

Mann turned, her smile weary but genuine, though it quickly

sank into a sigh. "On Earth, I'd be behind bars for what I know," she confessed, her gaze drifting away. "But here, knowledge like mine is too valuable to lock away, even if it's a cage of a different sort."

He studied her, noting the slouch of her shoulders—a far cry from the commander whose spine was once as rigid as the steel beams of T.P.S.E.'s fleet. "I expected you to be shadowing my father on one of his covert escapades by now," he said lightly, trying to eliminate the gloom that clung to her.

She shook her head, her eyes dull like the matte grey of the metal walls. "That ancient Wood is preparing for departure, but I won't be joining him." She exhaled, a breath that seemed to carry the weight of Celestiloo itself. "For this mission, I am… extraneous. And perhaps, I need a moment—a real moment— to breathe."

His concern lit the dark pools of her eyes. "Is everything alright between you two?" His question was gentle, probing only as much as manners would allow.

"There's always something—good, bad, tangled in a web of complexity." Her voice was a whisper lost in the hum of the electric device nearby. "It's not simple, never has been."

Huricane sensed an echo of the same disquiet that often gnawed at his own heart. He realised that it was his turn to offer consolation, to pay back the countless times Mann had buoyed his spirits when the crown felt too heavy, the throne too large for his youthful frame. "If there's anything you need, simply let me know. I will ensure that my people take care of it. After all, you have already become one of us."

"Haha, am I pardoned for submitting my immigration application?" Mann then passed her well-worn notebook to Huricane, its cover bearing the marks of numerous hurried page-turns. Within those pages lay not only data and observations but fragments of dreams yet to be realised. "Added some new entries. Very interesting chapters."

Accepting the notebook with the familiarity of a long-standing acquaintance, Huricane's fingers gently tracing the edges before opening it to the marked pages, observing the new notes and drawings by Mann. "You are not mistaken. I will return it to you by the end of the week. More details will be added."

"Thank you, Huricane. I know you are very busy with those troubles… but you still make time for this little dream of mine."

"Of us. This is a welcome distraction. It's refreshing to immerse myself in something, well, pure, I must say."

"I just wondered what would people a thousand years from now feel after reading my clumsy drawings in it."

"A thousand years? I bet the world would be very different from now, and this notebook would be placed in some sort of temple as an object for worshipping. Your drawings could become some sort of divine oracle."

Huricane flipped through the pages again, noting the colourful bookmarks—more than he had ever seen before. A surge of delight welled up within him, imagining the secrets they guarded, waiting to be discovered.

"Time for me to head out," he announced after a moment, closing the notebook with care. His eyes met hers, seeking an affirmation that they were both on the same path, even if their footsteps now diverged. "See you soon, Mu Mann."

"See you soon." Mann watched him nod, the earnest set of his jaw speaking volumes of his determination to succeed, to lead, to rise above the chaos that had become their lives. "Keep it up, young king."

"Have a pleasant day," the king's chief of staff called out, the words coming only at that moment. He then turned and proceeded to follow in Huricane's footsteps, accompanied by the silent sentinels of the guard.

Mann's response was a smile, though it faltered the instant their backs were turned. Solitude pressed against her chest, a heavy cloak that threatened to smother the remaining embers of her spirit. They didn't know, couldn't know, the tumultuous maelstrom that raged within her heart, fuelled by the messages she received through the rare chance of cosmic communication today—whispers of fate and future that clawed at her resilience.

One message, in particular, held her fast in its grip, a dire harbinger perched upon a precipice, its talons dug deep into the edge. She desperately needed an update, any word to either quell the swelling tide of anxiety or confirm her darkest apprehensions.

12 Aqual, W.D. 471
Teddix Castle, Teddix

Meanwhile, Huxtin remained engrossed in contemplation at his rendezvous point.

"When the moment arrives and the restrictions are lifted, my hope is that you will tread the right path and forge your own destiny."

An incessant drumbeat was echoing through the blackness of Waxing Moon. Huxtin had always found peace in the quiet isolation, but now it seemed to be suffocating him. The shadows around him twisted and writhed unnaturally. His pupils, once a deep navy blue, had turned a fiery red, his eyes blinking rapidly in the dimness as though trying to dispel some unwelcome presence.

Desperate to regain control, he attempted to take slow, calming breaths, but each inhale felt like a vice tightening around his lungs. The more he struggled to relax, the stronger the feeling of dread grew, gnawing at his gut like a ravenous beast.

"Promise me. Protect our child no matter what."

Phrases burned into his consciousness, playing on repeat like a broken record. Each repetition was identical, drilling itself into his very being, shaping his instincts and actions. Images of Lunarcaria in her final moments and Hurain flickering through the dark purple fog kept tempting him.

Shutting his eyes tightly, he tried to block out the torment, only to hear other voices join the cacophony. Mu Mann, Lokiata Zen, Miria, Sheung Oren, Wyach, Latyu, Poet, Autaming, Lokiata Kee, and even his sons, Huricane and Huringo, his parents, Hurong and Huship, and several other important figures in his life—their words from days past clamouring for attention in his mind.

At last, he opened his eyes, willing himself to focus.

"Are you ready for your second fight?"

"I'm ready."

12 Aqual, W.D. 471
T.P.S.E. Secret Base, Teddix

At noon, Mu Mann experienced a sense of being adrift in a haze, her footsteps unsteady and her thoughts muddled. It was as though she had consumed too much alcohol, yet she hadn't touched a drop.

Entering the secret base of her former army, she felt an irresistible pull towards the Hokan, which stood in maintenance mode. The technician team worked diligently, ensuring the battleship's readiness for any future battles without the guidance of their team head. Their dedication reminded her of her own impulsive decision to support Huxtin in building this vessel, a choice that started with minimal aid but in the end became almost full-fledged support.

She didn't regret her decision, but couldn't help wondering what might have been. If she had turned Huxtin down back then, what would their lives look like now? She wandered aimlessly, but somewhere deep inside, she sensed that she was searching for an exit, a way out of the sadness eclipsing her heart.

As she made her way to a secluded corner, the muffled voices of a man and a woman arguing caught her attention, pulling her to a halt.

"Get away from me!"

"See? I'm still wearing the ring!"

"None of my damn business!"

"That's a totally stupid excuse! I know you're still in love with me! Just say it!"

"Stop it! Mark Carlo! Not everything has to revolve around you! I have my own life, and it doesn't need to be controlled by you... What I need is freedom!"

"Freedom? Do you really have the freedom you desire here, on this cursed planet?"

Mann, recognising the voices of her friend and her friend's old flame, found herself torn. She struggled with the decision of whether to intervene or respect their need for privacy in their personal affairs, all while the voices grew fainter, carrying with them heartbreaking emotion.

"Answer me, Oren… If you followed me, I could give you the true freedom you can't find here."

"Why don't you just give up…"

"Because I really care about you."

At that moment, something within Mann snapped. She couldn't stand idly by any longer. Emerging from the shadows, she confronted the arguing couple. Both Mark Carlo and Sheung Oren looked startled to see her there.

"Mark Carlo, stop being ridiculous!" Mann scolded, her voice trembling with anger. "You have no right to force Oren into pleasing you."

In a swift motion, Mann's fist connected with Carlo's jaw, channeling years of pent-up hatred and frustration. Carlo staggered back, his eyes blazing with fury. He raised his fist, ready to retaliate, but Oren halted him, gripping his arms firmly.

"What are you doing here?" Oren evaded Mann's equally burning eyes, seeking to conceal her embarrassment and disregarding the growing rift between them. "This is my personal matter… I don't need you to step in."

"Oren, you…" Those words struck Mann like a dagger through her heart, the crack in their sisterhood growing deeper and deeper. As she stood there, reeling from Oren's rebuke, she wondered if her choice to intervene had only served to sabotage everything they had built all along.

Nevertheless, if Oren decided to decline her assistance, Mann contemplated that it might be time to reassess her role as a friend, as an Earthling in an alien world, and as a human being destined to suffer from the complexities of existence.

"Very well," she said as she walked away from the scene. "I hope you become a favourite commander in the army, Mark Carlo. And Oren… I hope you can handle things just as you claim." Her words carried a touch of irony, but she meant them sincerely, encouraging Oren to consider offering an apology. However, in the end, no action was taken.

As Mann left the secluded corner, Oren issued a final

warning to her ex-husband. "Don't overthink this... I have no emotions left for you." Though she wasn't entirely certain if her words truly represented her heart.

With that, Oren too departed, leaving Carlo alone with his thoughts. In his mind, he took an oath: he would do whatever it took to achieve his desires and prove himself. Once that was accomplished, he would have the entire army, people on Earth, and perhaps even the entire universe gaze upon him.

12 Aqual, W.D. 471
T.P.S.E. Command Centre, Teddix

An hour later, Lokiata Kee, holding a can of beer, stumbled upon Mu Mann sitting under a tree near the command centre.

"Kid, if you need someone to listen, I'm right here," he offered.

Mann sat, Kee stood, and together they directed a penetrating stare at the majestic Teddix Castle in the distance. Finally, after minutes of silent struggle, Mann disclosed, "My younger sister… Mu Gwen… She is in heaven now."

Kee's initial shock gave way to understanding as he remembered that Mu Gwen had been raised alongside Mann in the same orphanage. The details of Mann's motivation for joining the army came flooding back to his mind: she had sought a better life, one in which she could provide for herself and secure the best medical care possible for her ailing sister.

"It's totally okay to be upset," he said softly, a slight breeze rustling the leaves overhead, casting dappled shadows on their faces. "You've been strong for so long. You can now show weakness and seek help from those who care about you."

His words pierced through her last defences, and her tears finally broke free like a dam bursting under immense pressure. As she sobbed, Kee listened with empathy, remembering his own past struggles when he was around her age. He saw in her a reflection of his younger self, battling to keep up appearances while contending with loss and grief.

"I thought that if… I was strong enough…" Mann choked out her confession between sobs, her voice raw with rare emotion. "If I fought hard enough… I could beat my fate. But now… I've failed!"

"Sometimes it feels as though our own echoes get lost, even when we shout into the depths of a valley, and all we receive is silence…" Kee's heart ached for her, and he couldn't help but feel a bitter pang of pity for both of them. "Love means battling against the world itself. You've come so far, and that alone is extraordinary."

Although Kee wanted to offer Mann further solace, he held a deep understanding that her narrative wouldn't conclude with a beautiful ending. The symphony of sorrow would persist, playing its haunting melodies throughout her life.

"This is the reality we find ourselves in, and we still have a long battle to fight," he concluded. "Just remember, one day, each of us must face our battle alone, regardless of how many friends we have had, or how many women and men we have fallen in love with. We are all alone in the damn end in this abhorrent universe."

25:6

12 Aqual, W.D. 471
Teddix

"You've lost, once again."

In the vast grassland situated to the south of the confines of Silverlight Overflow, Huxtin stood amidst a ring of twelve metallic longswords. The indigo hues of the blades shimmered under the gentle sunlight. His black cloak hid his trembling body, and his hold on the Revenging Shard was somewhat unsteady.

Before him floated an orb of indigo light. The beauty of the blossoms that peppered the landscape was lost on Huxtin; his focus remained solely on the task at hand: capturing Kousou, the Star Soul of Mateek. As he stared into the depths of the orb, the longswords quivered and shot toward it, disintegrating into pure Elementro particles along the way. The particles glinted like a million tiny stars, so potent that even human eyes could perceive them.

"I have been curious for a long time, the Son of Chaos," said a voice that was both arrogant and carefree, completely at odds with the atmosphere. It belonged to Mateek. "Why do you refuse to believe in your own destiny?"

"I believe in my destiny…" Replying with a steely expression on his face, Huxtin gathered his strength once more. "But I also believe in shaping my own path, not walking one predetermined by others."

A mocking laugh echoed around him, the sound grating against Huxtin's nerves like metal grinding against metal. "Oh, really? But here you are, defeated by me for the second time. Without power, how can you hope to shape anything, let alone change the world or the universe?"

In response, Huxtin's grip on the Revenging Shard tightened. However, he wasn't allowed to strike at Mateek in that moment, for doing so would mean forfeiting his right to seize control of the Star Soul.

"I will demonstrate my capabilities," he declared through

gritted teeth, his eagle eyes piercing into the ethereal floating orb, as he sought to uncover every hidden weakness of the Children of God, hoping to glean insights that would aid him in his yet-to-be-won victory. "I will find a way to transcend my past failures, and then I will take hold of my own destiny. Let's wait and see."

CHAPTER 26

THOSE WHO DEVIATE TOO FAR
FROM THE PATH DESTINED FOR THEM
CANNOT HOLD THE HOPE OF STARTING ANEW

9 Aqual, W.D. 471
From Silverlight Overflow to Teddix

A few days ago.

"Come and retrieve me aboard the Hokan!"

Tension filled the area as Huxtin sprinted through the corridors of Silverlight Overflow. The abundance of black metal tube structures behind him appeared to undulate like a swarm of killer bees, intent on delivering thousands, if not millions, of lethal blows.

"You should not repeat the mistakes I once made!" Mateek's voice was a harsh reminder of the choices confronting Huxtin. "Accept the offer from the Umbras, or face sabotage by the Auras!"

"Impossible!" Huxtin shouted defiantly. "I'll capture you! I swear!"

He navigated the labyrinthine passages, eventually returning to the damaged corridor left in the wake of the Hokan's destruction. Without hesitation, he leaped through the gaping hole that Magic Mirror of Mateek had failed to mend. And just as he did, the flow of metal tubes followed suit, culminating in the unveiling of Kousou, the Star Soul of Mateek.

Shattering the metal tubes into pure Elementro particles, Kousou floated away from Silverlight Overflow, the illusion of Mateek's upper body emerging from the luminous orb. Brandishing a colossal longsword that gleamed with indigo light, he assumed the visage of a mighty warrior, reminiscent of Flammando, albeit in an altered war suit and demeanour. Unaware of Huxtin's presence, he glanced around only to find the Hokan circling overhead, its trajectory aimed directly at him, batteries primed for attack.

Thinking quickly, Mateek manipulated the Elementro particles around him, forming a large floating metal shield which intercepted the incoming laser beams from the Earthling battleship. Despite the barrage of energy, the Hokan showed no signs of stopping. With its impulse blade activated, it clashed against Mateek's shield, generating a scream that haunted all the creatures in the sky.

Mateek couldn't help but feel impressed by the sheer power of the battleship as he observed the surface of his shield gradually reverting back into Elementro particles. He acknowledged that it was his own doing, unintentionally embedding traces of his knowledge into every Earthling. Now, his own technological creations presented an obstacle, disturbing his peaceful slumber.

The moment the energy of the Hokan's impulse blade ran out, Mateek wasted no time in transforming his nearly shattered shield into a massive hammer, poised to strike down the battleship from above. Inside the Hokan, Sheung Oren's brow furrowed in focused concentration as she firmly grasped the controls. At the same time, she shot a warning glance at Huxtin, who appeared to be gearing up to depart from the battleship once more.

"Huxtin! What's our strategy now?" she called out, her voice brimming with urgency. "Our target is unstoppable!"

He responded without hesitation, "It's about time. Launch the magic shield immediately."

Oren nodded, her fingers flying to a red trigger above her head. With a decisive pull, a small cube-shaped gadget, tinted in red and blue, was detached from the Hokan, floating just above it. As Mateek's hammer came crashing down, the cube burst open, releasing a cascade of silvery beads that rapidly expanded to form an incomplete sphere around the battleship. It appeared half-silvery, half-transparent, resembling a beautiful amalgamation of metal and crystal. The surface shimmered, reflecting the colours of the surrounding environment, casting a magical glow that made it seem almost alive.

With that, Mateek's hammer came to an abrupt stop in mid-strike, and he ceased his attack. His initial admiration for the Earthlings quickly transformed into irritation. "Earthlings! How dare you!" he exclaimed. "No one should dare to blaspheme my Magic Mirrors!"

Taking advantage of Mateek's momentary loss of balance, Huxtin issued a new command to Oren. "He won't strike us now. Unleash full force and bring him down. Pour the liquefied Thunderites on him while keeping up the bombardment."

As she complied, the Hokan retracted the magic shield, compressing it into a newly formed orb. Concurrently, two metal boxes, affixed to the wings of the battleship, were launched towards the Children of God. Mid-flight, the boxes shed their outer surfaces, revealing their contents—a torrent of shocking yellow liquified Thunderites poured down around him, while laser beams continued to pelt his position.

The torrent of Thunderites had no effect on the illusion of Mateek's half-body; instead, they swirled and seeped into the Star Soul itself, which began to pulse with unstable intensity. In that moment, it became evident that even the mighty Mateek couldn't withstand the combined assault of Earthling technology and the raw power of electricity.

With the indigo light of Kousou flickering and dimming, the once imposing illusion shattered, each Elementro particle returning to the orb. The weakened Star Soul commenced its descent towards the ground below. Huxtin, standing on the right front wing of the Hokan, clutched Litorio's Star Soul, Hekireki, in his hand, with electric sparks dancing around the orb. Uncertain if there was any internal conflict within him, he disregarded the dizzying distance between himself and Mateek and leaped from the battleship.

While Huxtin plummeted, Mateek's attention was drawn to the presence of his brother. "You, Litorio. I can sense that your intentions are far from noble," he muttered, his voice tinged with suspicion.

"Oh, brother." Litorio's voice emerged from the depths of the lightning-imbued Star Soul. "You must suffer a bit more. The Son of Chaos is in control right now."

Ignoring their verbal exchange, Huxtin knew that mere free-falling wouldn't bridge the distance; he needed to take action. He tapped into his air Elementro power, and an orange aura enveloped his body, propelling him vigorously ahead. Nonetheless, the resistance of the air was still immense, buffeting against him like an unforgiving avalanche.

Moments before Mateek would have succumbed to

unconsciousness, the sky above turned dark and grey. A cyclone of lightning Elementro particles converged within the cloud, culminating in a massive bolt that struck the Star Soul with a force sufficient to strip it of colour. Lightning arced outwards in a horizontal circle, discharging its energy until it gradually dissipated. Kousou, now unresponsive, continued to plummet.

"He's all yours now, the Son of Chaos," Litorio urged, just as the colour of Hekireki vanished, disappearing from Huxtin's grasp.

"Just a little more…" Huxtin thought, pushing himself to the limit as he redoubled his efforts to maintain his air Elementro power in the face of the punishing air resistance. Every muscle in his body screamed in protest as he summoned Windalia's Star Soul, Kyuusou, into his left hand instead. Meanwhile, his right hand stretched out, desperately reaching for Kousou. However, the falling distance between him and the now transparent orb seemed to close agonisingly slowly.

"Tsk!"

Just as Huxtin's fingers almost grazed Kousou, its core blazed to life again with indigo radiance. Mateek's consciousness returned in an instant, and he skilfully manoeuvred away from Huxtin's reach. Huxtin's eyes widened in a mix of shock and disappointment, realising that he had failed the trial.

"You've come so close," Mateek barked, the mighty half-body illusion reemerging to seize Huxtin by his neck, preventing him from channeling his Elementro energy and causing Kyuusou to vanish. "But maybe you should try harder next time."

The armoured warrior guided their descent to the grassy ground below, releasing his grip on Huxtin's neck as his own feet touched the earth. Huxtin gasped for breath, his muscles taut and quivering from exhaustion. He had entered the trial with the belief that he could succeed in a single attempt, but now it was clear that he had severely underestimated the magnitude of the challenge.

Finally, Mateek's illusion disappeared, leaving behind only his echoing voice in the air. "It is not so simple to earn my recognition and wield my power, the Son of Chaos. I would appreciate it if you understood when it is time to surrender."

12 Aqual, W.D. 471
Teddix

In the present moment, Mateek continued to sow doubt in Huxtin's faith. "Why can't you just relieve yourself from this endless struggle?" the Children of God demanded.

Battling to regain his footing and energy, Huxtin countered, "Then why did you depart from your duty to bring peace and maintain order? What were you thinking? Perhaps you can enlighten me with the reasons behind it, and then you may reassess and judge my determination afterward."

Mateek's expression flickered with hidden pain. "I made a mistake," he admitted. "A mistake that has cost me dearly... Why haven't you considered why we became Star Souls? Why we're forced to watch the universe unfold without tangible existence? I've already paid my price for that."

"Because," Huxtin replied, his voice firm with conviction, "you gave up when your faith faltered."

"No! I gave up because there was no hope!"

In fact, Huxtin did have a clearer picture of the Children of God, which granted him a deeper understanding of the motives and minds of those beings who had once also had blood flowing inside their bodies. While he couldn't condone their choices, he could empathise with the pain that drove them to such desperate measures.

Despite the exhaustion tugging at his limbs, he managed to stand tall, his eyes locked with the Children of God's. "I will not heed your words," he declared. "If you seek to persuade me to surrender, do so at your own discretion. However, I will only follow the guidance of my heart.

Mateek observed Huxtin intently for a moment, his tone carrying a solemn weight. "If you genuinely hold that belief," he stated, "then bring me back to my Starfall Tomb for your third and final trial. Keep in mind the trial objective and be well prepared."

With those words, the indigo radiance within the Star Soul

gradually diminished, leaving behind a silent, motionless orb that gently descended onto the grassy ground. Huxtin let out a frustrated sigh, feeling the weight of Mateek's demands pressing heavily on his body and heart. Inwardly, he grumbled about the troublesome nature of these trials and the fact that he had no idea where Mateek's Starfall Tomb even was. Still, he knew better that dwelling on it in the present moment would serve no purpose.

As he bent down to retrieve the silent Star Soul, carefully tucking it away in an outer pocket of his combat outfit and concealing it beneath his black cloak, he became aware of two unfamiliar beings nearby. Straightening up, he turned to find Rafaelzo and Gloria waiting, their presence resembling two soft lights in the air.

Rafaelzo brought his hands together dramatically, but his admiration was sincere. "What a magnificent fight," he praised wholeheartedly.

"What's the matter?" Huxtin stared warily at the Auras. "Typically, my visitors have been nothing but enemies."

"Easy, the Son of Chaos. Allow me to introduce ourselves," Rafaelzo stated in a pleasant and professional manner. "I am Rafaelzo, and this is Gloria."

"I know you, the chief elder of the Auras. No worry. I have not taken the lives of any of your kind... at least not yet."

"Whoa, okay, splendid. It seems you are already acquainted with the reason for our visit. That saves us from having to explain."

"It's not a good time for a conversation," Huxtin declared, raising the Revenging Shard and pointing its tip towards the Auras. "A fight? I would say yes."

Rafaelzo couldn't be sure of Huxtin's remaining reserves of Elementro energies or what conditions would allow him to harness the power of Six Xenxes—or even Chaos. Weighing his options, he decided not to push his luck. "I agree we should talk later," he conceded, "but would you at least allow us to accompany you for now? I bet you the whereabouts of my fellows?"

Despite the intimidating demeanour displayed in front of

him, Rafaelzo managed to maintain a calm disposition. On the other hand, Gloria appeared visibly anxious, her chest heaving as if she were suppressing a flurry of questions on the tip of her tongue.

"As you wish," Huxtin replied curtly at the end, striding towards the direction of Teddix Castle without another word.

While her silvery eyes widened in frustration as she stared at Huxtin's retreating back, Gloria was troubled by the cloud of negative energy emanating from the Son of Chaos. Unable to hold herself back any longer, she surged forward. "There's a question I need to ask, and I must have the answer beforehand!

Rafaelzo reached out to restrain her, but he quickly realised that stopping the determined Aura was fruitless.

"I'm looking for Miria, my sister. She had a mission on Celestiloo," Gloria continued, knowing full well that Huxtin might already be aware of the true purpose of her sister's mission and the potential danger it entailed. Her voice trembled with desperation, even though the power and order of Huxtin intimidated her to some extent. "I... I need to know if she's safe."

Huxtin stopped in his tracks but didn't turn around, his silence only serving to fan the flames of Gloria's agitation. With fists clenched tightly at her sides, she held her breath, waiting for a response that never came

"Gloria, if we want answers, we have no choice but to follow him," Rafaelzo concluded, his tone resigned. "He isn't willing to speak for now, I can tell. Let's stick to the plan."

Gloria's nerves jumped erratically, her anxiety flowing through her like an endless surge of electricity. "I have a terrible feeling about this," she confessed.

"Me too."

"If anything happened to Miria, I... I will get even with him for that."

12 Aqual, W.D. 471
Teddix Castle, Teddix

At the same time but in a different location, in a corridor on the first floor of Teddix Castle, a cloaked figure clad in complete darkness stood motionless. The brim of the hood concealed the face, blending seamlessly with the cloak. Although there were Teddixian soldiers marching past, they were completely unaware of the presence of the cloaked figure, save for a subtle distortion in the air. Lacking the necessary perceptiveness, they remained oblivious to this intriguing phenomenon.

In the mind of the cloaked figure, there were several voices —venomous whispers originating from the four individuals who had orchestrated and manipulated their actions along this path.

"The Pioneer, you are exactly what we desired."

"The task ahead will be... challenging, but... but... I think he is the perfect choice!"

"We shall make the Auras our slaves!"

"Will our revenge finally succeed this time? Are we destined to rule the universe once again?"

These voices slithered through the thoughts like poisonous serpents, cursing their puppets and forcing them into a servitude they once refused. With no opportunity for retreat, the cloaked figure had willingly volunteered for this perilous undertaking, driven by an insatiable desire to to attain something of greater significance.

Meanwhile, on the second floor, Wyach walked down a separate corridor, her high heels clicking against the stone floor. She carried a stack of scrolls in both hands, providing reports for her king. As she moved, she sensed an odd atmosphere. Her instincts heightened, and she deliberately dropped the scrolls, feigning clumsiness as she knelt to retrieve them. Then, she tilted her glasses and rose, pretending not to notice the growing energies behind her. Internally, though, she was on high alert. The water vapour in the air carried a strange taste of wood and soil, which only amplified her suspicions

The energies behind her continued to grow stronger, and when she tapped lightly on the door to her king's suite, the distance between her and the source of the energies remained constant.

"My King," she called out, her voice steady despite the unease gnawing at the edges of her composure. "I have come with the reports you requested."

"Come in, Wyach," Huricane replied, his voice muffled by the thick wooden door. "It's unlocked."

Wyach pushed the door open and entered the cluttered room. Papers were strewn about on a large desk where Huricane sat, surrounded by open books flipped to random pages.

"Here are the reports from the military, the royal family, and the minutes from the previous meeting," Wyach said respectfully, carefully placing the scrolls on the desk without disturbing his work.

"Thank you, Wyach," Huricane said, not looking up from his papers. "Your attention to detail is commendable, as always."

"Not at all. Your hard work and dedication are truly inspiring," Wyach replied modestly, while her eyes fell upon a stack of papers partially covering a set of wooden cards, remnants from Huricane's last confrontation with his brother. She cautiously reached for the pile, pulling it aside to reveal the card she sought. With deft fingers, she slid the card across the desk, ensuring it captured her king's attention.

As Huricane's eyes locked onto the card, his body tensed, the hair on his arms standing on end, and goosebumps prickling his skin. His dilated pupils traced each familiar stroke of the words etched upon it—words that transformed into a torrential river of blood and tears before his scorching gaze, obscuring everything else from view. Dazzling fragments circled wildly in his mind. He knew that the "Easter Egg" he had dreaded for a week had finally arrived, leaving him with no means of escape.

The message had been delivered. Wyach watched as Huricane's expression shifted from curiosity to alarm.

"Listen, Wyach. Whenever an opportunity arises, dash out with your utmost speed," Huricane instructed in a hushed and cautious tone. "Alert the guards, sound the alarm."

"But, My King, this time I must protect you from him—"

"No, you mustn't. Instead, protect the people of my kingdom."

Understanding that she couldn't change Huricane's mind and that there was no time for further debate, Wyach nodded gravely, mentally and physically preparing herself for the worst to come. She comprehended the importance of placing trust in Huricane at this critical moment, even though every fibre within her being warned her to stay by his side and protect him. Reluctantly turning away from her king, she caught a glimpse of the Azure Dragon glinting in his grip. The magnificent weapon infused her with a sense of courage, just as it did for Huricane.

No sooner had Wyach taken her first step toward the door than it burst open with a deafening crash. The entrance revealed the cloaked figure, wielding an intangible sword that emitted daffodil-coloured glimmers. It urged Huricane to rush forward, his blades clashing with the intruder whom he instantly recognised as his older brother, Huringo.

"Run! Now!"

Torn between her duty and her desire to stand beside her king, Wyach hesitated for a brief moment before sprinting from the room. Huringo's gaze tracked her departure, contempt flickering in his eyes, before he redirected his full attention to his brother.

"Oh, little brother, aspiring to be a merciful king and willing to be sacrificed?" he taunted, applying greater pressure with his sword against his younger brother. "You've made a grave error by sending the powerhouse away!"

"Are you certain I can't handle you on my own?" Huricane sneered resolutely. "You will pay for the sins you've committed, causing such devastation in my kingdom!"

"Your kingdom? What a joke!"

The air thickened with unspoken thoughts as the siblings stood face-to-face, their pasts intertwined like the roots of an ancient tree. Huricane couldn't help but recall the years they spent together, both good and bad, each memory stinging like salt in an open wound.

As their swords clashed once more, Huricane found himself pushed off balance, compelled to take a few steps back. The strength of his sibling proved to be a formidable challenge. Under the hood, the face contorted with a cruel and deranged expression, causing a hollow ache within Huricane as he witnessed the extent of Huringo's descent. However, amid the changes, those navy blue eyes remained unaltered—brilliant jewels that outshone all other lights in the universe.

"It has been a long time," Huringo snarled, his gaze fixated on the very jewels he believed Huricane unworthy of possessing.

"Far too long," Huricane responded, his voice strained with suppressed emotion. "But this time… I won't let you win!"

The brothers circled one another, each assessing the other's weaknesses and strengths, their minds calculating strategies and anticipating their opponent's moves. With a roar, Huringo launched again into action, slashing his sword, the Blazing Sun, through the air with breathtaking velocity. A beam of raw energy erupted from the blade, hurtling towards Huricane with lethal intent. Huricane barely managed to avoid the attack, gritting his teeth as the desk and glass windows behind him were consumed by the furious onslaught. Papers crumbled into ash, leaving a deep black scar that marred the old wooden desk, an heirloom with a long history tied to their bloodline. The shattered remnants of the glass windows lay in chaotic disarray on the floor, resembling sharp and jagged crystals.

"Weak… I had expected that Latyu would have imparted at least a few tricks to you," Huringo jeered, purposely invoking the name of his former mentor to underline his own superiority. "It seems his death isn't worth it at all!"

"Is this truly what you have become?" Huricane spat, the

familiar anger bubbling up within him, fuelled further by the grief for the fallen marshal. "I'm ashamed to say these words, but... you were my role model... I looked up to you! I never thought I could be stronger than you, but after all you've done, I swore to surpass you one day. For Teddix, for our mother, and for myself!"

"Fool... and I'm curious. How do you plan to achieve that, little brother?"

With an air of cruelty akin to that of a blood-drinking animal, Huringo unleashed his newly acquired power, manipulating the light and shadows in the room and causing the wooden structures to tremble with his sinisterness. The display was both mesmerising and terrifying, temporarily leaving Huricane breathless in its wake.

"If only you had wielded your power for good..." Huricane's eyes scanned the Elementro uprising, and in that moment, a specific memory struck deep within his mind. "Mother would not have died... and our family would not be broken!"

"Blaming me for her death?" Huringo roared, his arrogance and fury seething like molten lava beneath his words, the memory of that fateful day etched vividly in his mind as well. "You share that responsibility with me! If it weren't for you!"

With a feral growl, Huringo charged forward, causing the Azure Dragon to slip from Huricane's grasp and clatter onto the floor. Huricane narrowly evaded the deadly slash, but before he could regain his footing, his brother teleported, appearing right before him in an instant.

Cornered and weaponless, Huricane glared at his deranged sibling. "How dare you claim her death wasn't your fault, Huringo!" In his eyes, it was clear that Huringo had become a madman, consumed by dark emotions and twisted desires.

Ignoring the accusation, Huringo brought his sword down upon Huricane, but his younger brother reacted quickly, raising his right hand to release a shield that promptly shattered the blade into flying Elementro particles. Huringo's surprise was short-lived, his fury quickly returning as he witnessed the extent of Huricane's Elementro power.

"You are unworthy... of wielding such power!" Huringo

reshaped the Elementro particles into a complete sword. With a fluid motion, the sword transformed into a torrent of radiant energies, sparkling with daffodil hues, crashing against Huricane's shield. "Your shield won't save you! I will burn it down!"

The force Huringo unleashed wasn't merely a manifestation of Elementro power; it was enhanced by a deep-seated hatred and jealousy, born from the darkest recesses of his heart. The once transparent shield began to shrink, its surface becoming opaque and peeling away. In the moment of utmost urgency, Huricane found his voice and let out a resounding shout, infused with willpower. "Do not dare to underestimate me, Huringo!"

He took a deep breath, feeling something click into place within him. He finally understood why he had dwelled on the memories of his past, because they were the ingredients to cultivate his inner power.

"I am the son of Huxtin, just as you are!"

In that instant, a strange phenomenon occurred: everything seemed to slow down in front of Huringo's eyes. He watched in disbelief as Huricane methodically stepped away from his melting shield, calmly evading the torrent of energy it had been holding back. With deliberate movements, his younger brother approached the fallen Azure Dragon, picked it up, and continued walking. He could do nothing but observe the chaotic scene unfolding before him in slow motion, his mind racing to comprehend the turn of events.

As time resumed its normal flow, the shield once surrounding Huricane destroyed, causing the torrent of energies to collide with the wall. The impact dislodged several stones, releasing a faint scent of a familiar metal into the air. Huringo swiftly turned around, only to discover that Huricane had vanished from his sight. A shiver ran down his spine as he reached a chilling realisation: it wasn't time itself that had slowed down, but every cell within his own body.

As if to mock his failed attempt, the blaring sound of the alarm reverberated throughout Teddix Castle, signalling danger within Teddix City. He stood alone in his brother's suite, consumed by emotions that were easily perceivable. The room that should have rightfully been his, had fate dealt him a different hand, served as a bitter reminder of what he desired but couldn't attain.

"Run, my little brother!" he bellowed into the room subjected to violence, certain that Huricane would hear his declaration. "But know that running is meaningless before me, for I am far more powerful than you!"

Having uttered those words, Huringo crumpled to the floor, his knees hitting the ground with a dull thud. Negative thoughts swirled within his mind, tearing at his confidence and sanity. He had once believed himself to be the sole unique being in the presence of his father, but witnessing Huricane's ability to manipulate not only mind but also illusion Elementro—and perhaps even more— shattered his arrogance and left him gasping for air.

26:4

12 Aqual, W.D. 471
Teddix City, Teddix

One confrontation ended, another began. The mournful wail of the alarm pierced the peaceful afternoon, plunging the castle and the city into a state of chaos for the second time within two weeks. Hordes of Teddixian soldiers darted like panicked ants through the courtyards and castle corridors. Meanwhile, reinforcements stood prepared, ready to flood the city streets at a moment's notice.

In the midst of the crisis, Wyach stood in a shadowed alley, her focus solely on the unexpected intruder before her—Solarades. His form flickered between visibility and invisibility, as though reality itself wavered in uncertainty of his existence. Wyach felt disoriented, much like encountering a mirage in close proximity

Two ethereal circles of energies were encasing her: one black halo hovering above her head, and another, white, beneath her feet. They pulsed in rhythm with her heartbeat, tapping into the very core of her being. She knew better than to move, lest they unleash their full power upon her. All she could do was watch as Solarades demonstrated his phenomenal mastery of Elementro power, all the while subjecting her to his taunts.

"With every stream diverging into countless directions, do you still possess the ability to foresee the future, Wyach?" Solarades questioned, his voice echoing eerily in the air. "Do you truly believe that the Son of Chaos will be the saviour, but not the destroyer of all?"

Wyach's watery eyes burned with conviction as she stared down her adversary. "I will always believe in Huxtin. I have no doubt."

"Interesting," Solarades mused. "I thought your rank would have made you more… adaptable."

"I don't need you to tell me what I should do," Wyach fired back. "I can choose what to believe for myself."

"I remember when we first crossed paths, you were

tormented by doubt, uncertain of the purpose of your existence in this chaotic universe... and now, look at you."

"No, it is you who should be looked at... still planning to topple the balance of the universe. That is precisely why I made the correct choice to align myself with Huxtin, not you!"

Internally, Wyach searched for an opening, a weakness in Solarades's seemingly impenetrable power. She longed to take action, to break free from the energy bindings that held her captive. But every time she tried, the circles pulsed with a warning, and ultimately she knew it would be foolish to test their limits. On the other hand, Solarades was acutely aware of Wyach's capabilities, and he was cautious not to make any missteps that could jeopardise his grand scheme.

"Topple?" he argued, his form briefly solidifying as if to emphasise his words. "I have said it countless times. I am not trying to destroy the balance. I simply cannot bear the stagnation that plagues this universe. It is like a pool of still water, desperate for a ripple."

Wyach understood there was truth in what he said, but she couldn't accept his methods. "You don't have to resort to this... Plunging the universe into darkness does not equate to progress!"

"Aah, but I do. Everything now hinges on the actions of the Son of Chaos and the so-called The Pioneer. They alone can accelerate the evolution of this universe."

"This is a delusive rambling of a fool!"

"Wyach, Wyach... Why can't we just turn fantasises into tangible reality?"

On impulse, Wyach wanted to stop Solarades from wreaking further havoc, but she was powerless under the constant threat of the two light circles. As if sensing her resolve, Solarades acted without warning, causing the black and white circles to begin rotating in opposite directions. Their motion was hypnotic, almost entrancing, and Wyach felt her strength waning.

"Solarades!" she cried out, but it was too late. The circles converged at their midpoint, swallowing her whole. In a blinding flash of light, she was silenced, disappearing as she was transported into a sealed dimension where she would be shielded from witnessing the upcoming destruction.

Solarades's body flickered once again, akin to the shimmer of a high-tech protective cloak, as he surveyed the chaos that awaited the kingdom. Amidst the unheard screams of soldiers and civilians and the yet-to-be-perceived scent of smoke and blood, he harboured a sense of compassion for the inevitable losses—both necessary and unnecessary—that would be brought forth by the chosen ones destined to usher in the downfall of Celestiloo.

"Huringo, The Pioneer... Let us bear witness to the full extent of your capabilities, befitting of your title," he muttered to himself, expecting the anarchy to come. "Now, unleash the transformation we so desperately seek."

12 Aqual, W.D. 471
T.P.S.E. Command Centre, Teddix

The news of the alarm ringing in Teddix Castle and Teddix City hadn't yet reached the heart of T.P.S.E. Instead, Earthling soldiers and technicians could be seen hurriedly packing up equipment and making preparations for an unannounced departure. The once prosperous collaboration between the Teddixians and Earthlings had deteriorated into a tense standoff, with the Earthling faction eager to sever ties and minimise further losses as soon as possible.

Mark Carlo, who had finally achieved the coveted position he had long desired, had made the unilateral decision to evacuate all the Earthlings from Paralloy Teddix, supported by the president of the Earth Alliance. The Teddixians were left in the dark, unaware that their erstwhile allies were breaching their agreement and leaving them to fend for themselves.

Meanwhile, deep within the underground facilities of the Earthling military, Lokiata Kee was on a search for Mu Mann. She had mentioned the necessity of retrieving some personal belongings from her dormitory, and he felt an urgent need to inform her of the Earthlings' clandestine plans to abandon the Teddixians. As he transitioned from one section to another, his senses caught the soft sound of a woman's voice murmuring in the distance.

"Kid? Mu Mann? You there?"

Suddenly, a figure emerged from the shadows—an Earthling woman, relatively young, clad in a white one-piece dress, barefoot, with disheveled hair falling to her neck. Her eyes blazed with an unfocused rage as she clutched a knife in both hands. Kee's heart raced, his instincts telling him to be cautious, but he pushed forward, trying to project bravery.

"Excuse me, do you... know where Mu Mann's dormitory is?" he asked hesitantly, but before he could blink, the woman lunged at him, her knife slicing through the air. He dodged, stumbling back and raising his hands defensively by his ears as a sign of peace. Cold sweat trickled down his spine, his breaths coming in short gasps. This was too close for comfort, and he couldn't help but feel a deep sense of unease at the woman's unpredictable behaviour.

"Get away from me!" the woman screamed, her voice trembling as she brandished the knife. Her eyes darted around, wide with paranoia and fear.

"Wait! I'm just looking for my friend," Kee replied hastily, trying to calm the situation. Despite his best efforts, his smile was feeble, unable to mask the rapid thumping of his heart. Having experienced various instances where weapons were directed at him in the past, he knew that familiarity didn't grant immunity to fear. Even though the woman before him didn't appear to pose a significant threat, his apprehension remained.

"You'd better not be telling lies." Her hands shook, but she didn't lower the knife. "Or you will be going to hell with me!"

"Why... Umm... Why are you walking around with a knife?" He kept his smile on his face. "Is there anything or anyone that needs to be guarded against?"

"You have a laser gun with you," she stuttered, eyeing the weapon at his waist. "So, what are you carrying that for?"

His gaze shifted to the laser gun holstered on his right side. "Self-defence," he admitted. "And I'm sorry if I startled you."

"Same here," she said quickly, her voice barely above a whisper. "You're right... I'm just trying to protect myself."

Kee observed the woman carefully, perceiving the pain buried beneath her anger and fear. Something terrible must have happened to her, and a pang of sympathy welled up within him.

"Listen," he said gently, lowering his hands. "I'm really just trying to find Mu Mann. She's my friend. My name is Lokiata Kee."

The woman's grip on the knife faltered, and her eyes widened in recognition. "Lokiata Kee?" she echoed, her voice shaking slightly. She might have heard the name somewhere before, but its origin eluded her. Her mind, muddled with confusion, struggled to connect the scattered fragments of her memories, leaving her in a state of bewilderment.

"May I ask your name?" Kee ventured, hoping to help her

feel more at ease.

And after a moment of hesitation, she lowered the knife and whispered, "Kayley Mien."

Kee's suspicions were confirmed, but he chose not to mention the story he had heard about her recent troubles. Instead, he said, "It's nice to meet you, Miss Kayley. I promise I don't mean you any harm. Can you tell me who you are trying to protect yourself from?"

Mien simply replied, "The soul reaper."

"The soul reaper?" Kee knew the reference, but couldn't resist asking for more information, if only to hear her version. "Who or what is this soul reaper?"

As if an earthquake had ceased on the surface, Mien's demeanour shifted to a disarming calmness. She seemed to be mustering every ounce of strength left within her to recount her harrowing memories. Her hands tightened around the knife, her knuckles turning white. "The soul reaper was once a man— someone like us. But he was... possessed, transformed into something monstrous... a murderer."

Kee could see the potent blend of love and hatred promiscuously drawn on Mien's face, a mask that bore the imprint of a life that was never meant to be hers. He believed he understood all too well the nature of the demons that she was wrestling with. Nonetheless, he has underestimated the possibility of aftershocks from an earthquake that might reignite any dismissed vigilance.

"I know how it feels to be haunted, but..." he confessed quietly, wishing to reach out and touch her hand. However, he hesitated, afraid of forging an intimate connection with someone else. "We can't let fear dictate our lives."

"It won't work..."

"Huh? What?"

"It won't work..."

Kee wasn't entirely taken aback by Mien's response. "I know, I know... Things won't be easy—"

But Mien's abrupt shift in mood did surprise him. "No! You don't understand! He's still here!" she shouted, tears streaming down her helpless eyes. "Inside this underground building—

136

lurking, calculating, an unseen horror... waiting for the perfect moment in the shadows to strike again!"

CHAPTER 27

ONCE THE SOUL IS BROKEN,
IT POSSESSES AN INHERENT CAPACITY
TO MEND AND RESTORE ITSELF AUTOMATICALLY

12 Aqual, W.D. 471
T.P.S.E. Command Centre, Teddix

"Alarm?" Mark Carlo, the newly and officially appointed commander of T.P.S.E., inquired of the soldier standing beside him. "Where is it?"

"It's coming from Teddix Castle and Teddix City," the soldier reported. "Something serious seems to have occurred concerning the Teddixians."

"See? I've made the right decision. We must evacuate this cursed kingdom in advance before we get into any trouble."

Outside the underground facility, Carlo was leading his subordinates in the final stages of the evacuation procedures. He no longer bothered himself with the affairs of the Teddixians and treated the inquiry as a routine matter. With all the major equipment, resources, and chemicals being transported to the designated parking areas of the two transport docks in the Kuna Plains, the end of the Earthlings' time in Paralloy Teddix was undoubtedly destined to be written in the history books of both Celestiloo and the Earth Alliance.

There were voices opposing the evacuation, though Carlo remained indifferent to his subordinates' murmurs and disregarded their gestures. Motivated by greed, their dissent amounted to nothing more than cheap tricks in his eyes. He revelled in the intoxicating pleasure that coursed through his veins, fuelling his thirst for power. The command centre of T.P.S.E. would soon be empty, but it only further cemented his position, leaving him completely satisfied.

Just as Carlo believed all obstacles were cleared, Mu Mann, the former commander, made her appearance with a dark green backpack on her back.

"What the hell is going on…" she muttered, clearly confused. Then her gaze fell upon the person she needed to question. "Mark Carlo!"

Carlo ignored her, arrogantly commanding his subordinates and purposefully walking away from her. However, this only served to further ignite Mann's irritation. Forcefully grabbing the collar of a nearby soldier, she clenched her fist and raised her voice, cursing, "What the hell are all of you doing?"

"Com-commander Mu... No... Umm... We're..." the soldier stammered, glancing at Carlo, seeking guidance.

Unable to tolerate Mann causing a scene, Carlo finally intervened, saying, "Hey! Release him! We're evacuating Paralloy Teddix. If you want to join us, there's still a place for you, but I doubt you'd want to take it."

Stunned, Mann pushed the innocent soldier aside and confronted Carlo directly. "Why are you doing this? Who gave you the authority?" Her loud voice was filled with the aura of a leader, enough to make everyone question who should be in charge in that moment.

"You have no right to know the specifics of the operation," Carlo emphasised, his face contorted with the ugliness of corrupted power. "I am the commander now, Mu Mann, and who are you? A woman without any title. I believe you would rather align yourself with the Teddixians than with us, am I right?"

"Everyone! Stop!"

Ironically, no one dared to defy Mann's stern command, except for Carlo, who rolled up his sleeves, intent on displaying the absolute power he believed he was privileged to possess.

"You should be the one to stop! To stop messing around! Are you willing to let our comrades go and sacrifice in vain?" He quickened his pace, closing in on Mann. "All for a man named Huxtin?"

As a result of his words, a punch came hurtling towards his face, but he managed to catch the incoming fist this time. Sporting a victorious smile, he had become too absorbed in his own little world of power to notice another punch heading towards his right.

"You bastard!" Mann cursed, her breath heavy. If she lost control, she would undoubtedly unleash more merciless punches on him.

"Damn... you!" Carlo shouted, his hand pressed against his right cheek, trying to alleviate the pain, both physical and inflicted upon his wounded pride. "You pathetic little woman!"

The commander's assault left his subordinates speechless, with some even revealing hidden smiles, clearly relishing the moment. In truth, Mann understood that she had no authority to interfere with matters involving T.P.S.E. anymore. The attack was merely a farewell to her past.

Regardless, their dispute had to be put aside as a colossal column of light, glittering with shades of brown, green, black, and white, shot up into the sky. It collided with the transparent dome encompassing the area of Teddix Castle and Teddix City, creating a spectacle that captivated everyone's attention.

"The castle... That light..." Mann's concern grew with each passing second as the light column grew brighter, leaving only a harsh and intense radiance. "Is that... Elementro?"

12 Aqual, W.D. 471
Teddix Castle, Teddix

From the garden and courtyard before the west gate of Teddix Castle, the assembled crowd witnessed a breathtaking entanglement of colours as the protective dome above them began to corrode. Streaks of blue, purple, golden, and silvery hues reappeared across its surface. The originally invisible barrier now bore the furious mark of the assaulting light column, which had drilled through a small hole in the weakening defence.

After an intense fifteen seconds, the light column vanished suddenly, leaving behind a gaping wound in the dome that failed to return to its transparent state. Huricane, his energy nearly depleted from halting the assailant—who, unsurprisingly, turned out to be Huringo—collapsed, unconscious, among the Teddixian soldiers. The soldiers, hesitant to approach their fallen king or confront the wrathful mad prince, stood back in apprehension.

"Who dares to stand in my way?" Huringo bellowed arrogantly, his eyes sweeping over the terrified expressions. Some were unaware of the true identity of the young man before them, but they could sense the danger emanating from him. They knew that even stepping an inch closer to their intended target could lead them to their demise. Others, however, recognised him as the long-lost prince and instinctively avoided his disdainful stare, unwilling to meet his scornful gaze.

"Of course, none of you would dare challenge me!" Huringo continued, his voice dripping with contempt. "I should be the one seated on the throne all of you worship, not that weakling lying there on the ground! This kingdom has failed me, every single person in it has failed me, and I will ensure that each of you pays the price!"

"King Huricane is not weak!"

A challenge arose, and Huringo scanned the crowd, searching

for the challenger. His eyes finally landed on Huduson, whose face, though pale, radiated bravery. Huduson pushed past the motionless soldiers, stepping forward to stand before Huricane. Despite his inner fear, he refused to back down against his other cousin, Huringo, who appeared genuinely surprised by this unexpected show of courage.

"Really, the timid and nervous Huduson? Anyone but you..." Huringo sneered, his eyes narrowing dangerously. "Why defend someone who has taken everything from me? He deserves to have nothing!"

"No! You... you can't say that about your own brother!" Huduson gulped, his voice quivering but resolute, trying to convey his thoughts while facing a seasoned warrior who could easily end his life. "And... he's my king... my cousin! I must defend him!"

Huringo's laughter rang out cruelly. "Defend? You truly believe you can do that?"

"Yes... even if it costs me my life!"

"Bah, you are such a joke..."

Huduson was well aware that Huringo could sense his inner fear, but he steadfastly refused to let that deter him; he had to try. However, little did he know that his words were akin to poking a sleeping dragon of craziness, inadvertently igniting the flames of jealousy.

"The two of you share quite a strong bond," Huringo remarked, his hand raised as he gathered the dangerous Elementro energies once more. "And you remind me of how unwelcome I was in this family."

"You just said that... We're a family, Huringo," Huduson trembled. "We... shouldn't be fighting like this. I've seen how we suffered over these years, and I... I can't bear it any longer!"

"Have you said everything you wanted to say?" Annoyed, Huringo asked coldly of his cousin. "If you have, it's time to meet your doom."

Huduson smelled a dreadful burnt odour of the implied countdown, causing his heart to race even faster, yet he refused to abandon Huricane. Without warning, Huringo channeled his Elementro energies into the Blazing Sun, preparing to strike down his cousin. The courtyard held its breath, soldiers watching in horror, unable to intervene. But then, Solarades materialised, his left hand outstretched to halt Huringo's advance, and his sudden appearance shocked everyone, leaving them paralysed in an additional layer of fear.

"Enough," Solarades demanded. "We are not meant to create a massacre here. Fate will lead them to the end of their road, not us."

Huringo reluctantly held his anger, but his grip on the Blazing Sun tightened. "What does it matter if everything ends in death and destruction?"

Knowing it was futile to argue, Solarades chose not to respond to the question. Instead, he issued a warning. "The Constraint will return soon, and perhaps even the Son of Chaos and the person in charge of the Auras. We must be ready for what's to come. You need to focus on your task."

As the words sank in, Huringo's rage subsided, and he acknowledged the truth in Solarades's message. With begrudging acceptance, he closed his eyes, his chest heaving with the struggle for control. When he opened them again, three pairs of wings shimmered in the light, unfurling from his back. Their green and brown hues embodied the power of nature, while black and white dust swirled around the wing edges, which were sharp as wharncliffe blades, representing the energies of the Illuminator and the Engulfer.

Raising the Blazing Sun high above his head, Huringo channeled the massive Elementro energies skyward. The same colours glowed around Solarades's outline, connecting him to Huringo in an unspoken pact. The resulting surge of power sent out waves of energies that washed over Huduson and all others in the courtyard. They shielded their heads, hands pressed over their eyes to block out the blinding radiance.

The tug of war between the light column and the dome's defences resumed, but it was clear which side would prevail. The hole in the barrier grew larger, and the defeated Elementro dissipated into the air like melting colourful flakes. With nearly half of the protective dome destroyed, the light column finally vanished, leaving only a faint afterglow as the remaining section of the barrier returned to complete transparency. Huringo's wings faded along with the Blazing Sun, and he stood there, panting heavily.

From his pair of silvery eyes, Solarades studied Huringo's expression, sensing an unspoken request. Yet, he also understood that there was no such thing as "enough" for this young man driven by an insatiable thirst for unlimited power.

"We've done enough," he stressed. "The Throne of Immortality is now left unprotected. It's time to place our next pawns on the chessboard."

"Fine…" Huringo conceded, knowing he had no leverage over Solarades. He turned away from Huricane, Huduson, and the battlefield that had consumed his obsession. "Let's go then."

Shutting his eyes tight, Solarades focused on the energies within him, preparing to teleport them away from this scene of destruction. Within a matter of seconds, a large Binary of Teleportation formed beneath them, whisking them away in an instant. The Teddixian soldiers, some still shielding themselves from the remnants, hesitantly lowered their hands and looked around, uncertain of what to do next.

Huduson, who had been a witness to the devastation, could only stare at the spot where the intruders had disappeared, shaking, but he never once forgot his loyalty to his king. After a few moments of mental restoration, he hurried to Huricane's side, gently cradling the fallen ruler's head in his hands. "My King!" he called out urgently. "Please! Answer me!"

No response came from Huricane, who lay immobile and silent. It was only then that some of the Teddixian soldiers dared to approach, inching closer to assess the situation. As the king was carefully escorted back to his suite, Huduson lifted his head towards the sky, scanning for any trace of Huxtin or Wyach, fervently praying for their imminent arrival.

12 Aqual, W.D. 471
T.P.S.E. Command Centre, Teddix

Not knowing the emergency situation outside the Earthling facilities, Lokiata Kee and Kayley Mien sat side by side, their backs pressed against the cold metal wall beneath the bold red letters that read "Section UCDC-106." The darkness of the adjacent section loomed at their side like a physical presence, urging them to leave this place behind. However, there were still stories left to be told.

Kee glanced over at Mien, her eyes still hollow but with a faint shine of hope. "The Earthling soldiers are leaving Paralloy Teddix. You should go with them," he said softly, breaking the silence that had settled between them for a while. "That way, the soul reaper won't be able to harm you."

Mien stared blankly at the opposite wall, her mind drifting elsewhere, but she did feel a glimmer of healing starting to mend the broken pieces within her. Taking a deep breath, she mustered the courage to find her voice and speak. "You mentioned you were betrayed," she said, turning to look at the scar on Kee's chin. "What really happened?"

"It was a mess... a disaster," Kee replied, his tone hesitant. "Hey... You don't actually need to force yourself to talk to me. We can just leave whenever you're ready—"

"What if I want to know?"

Kee shifted uncomfortably on the cold, hard floor beneath them, his own ghosts hovering in the shadows of his thoughts. He had been trying to avoid making the atmosphere even more awkward, but he now realised that Mien's reluctance to leave stemmed from something deeper than mere fear. As he gazed into Mien's innocent eyes once more, he came to the conclusion that by sharing his story, he might be able to help her find her own path forward and give her a reason to to stay alive.

"Tell me how you managed to survive after being betrayed by your beloved," she insisted. "Tell me what May Dori did to you. Tell me everything."

"Alright," he said quietly, taking a deep breath as he prepared to delve into the depths of his past. "You asked me how I survived... You know, I have thought about ending my own life before, but..."

His voice trailed off as the first chapter of his story emerged in his mind—a wonderful tale that brought a bittersweet smile to his lips. The sweet taste of love and the fresh scent of happiness lingered as he recounted the days of his beautiful youth.

"But what?"

"Ultimately, I realised that aside from dying from natural causes, disease, unavoidable incidents... there's no meaning in death if it's not for protecting the ones we love and care for. That's... what kept me going."

As Kee spoke, Mien stared down at the knife in her hands. Why was she holding onto it? Was it really for self-defence? Or, was it a symbol of something darker in her mind?

"Well... Let me start my story from the beginning then," Kee continued. "I was born into a prestigious and influential family, as you know, the Lokiata family, one of the most powerful and wealthy families in the Earth Alliance, with almost unparalleled military strength and financial resources, capable of controlling half of the planet."

Kee's words flowed like a river, painting vivid images of love, loss, and survival, a time when he was still the pride and joy of the Lokiata family, before betrayal shattered his world.

"Being raised in this family was far from easy. I wasn't the eldest son. I'm the third in line, with two elder brothers and two younger sisters, so I was spared the responsibility of leading the family's development, which was fortunate because I never had a taste for power struggles, let alone violence. While I was exempt from carrying out unsavoury tasks for my father and still reap the benefits of being part of the family, I realised that sharing my wealth with those less fortunate and engaging in charity would bring more fulfilment and purpose to my life.

My family didn't stop this idea; in fact, they believed it would enhance their reputation. So, I thought, why not? Over the years, I built several schools and orphanages in almost every district of the Earth Alliance. I opened a hospital in Matankasch, where I met May Dori. She was an intern nurse, around the same age as me. I was instantly captivated by her, and it seemed she was attracted to me as well. May Dori was beautiful, with charming eyes, expressive eyebrows, full lips, a pointed nose, a cute curling braid... Our paths intertwined, igniting an unstoppable flame of love. We quickly became lovers, and I... never expected such a change in my life—"

NTG527-UC6-D7
Image 0, Rictor Island

"Love blinded me, and my eyes could only see May Dori. I left my charitable acts behind, just to spend my days and nights with her. It's just sad that I couldn't openly reveal our relationship. My family would not approve of me falling in love with a nurse, as they expected me to be involved with someone from another high-ranking family on Earth, someone with money, power, and connections. But she said, she didn't mind being in the shadows. She said, she just needed to know that I loved her, and that would be enough for her.

It was at this same time that my family urgently summoned me back to my home in Image 0. My eldest brother had passed away suddenly from a severe, undisclosed illness. He was being groomed by my parents to become the pillar of the Lokiata family. With his passing, the situation changed, leaving my second brother and me to compete for a position, a chance to represent the family in a new era.

I didn't want it, but my father chose me because of my high profile and positive reputation. I turned him down. I refused my family's request. After all, I returned on the same day only to be confronted with the lifeless body of my eldest brother, the one who had shown me the most care and affection. In the face of such a heartbreaking loss, how could I possibly find the inclination or mood to engage in matters about money and politics?

I tried calling May Dori to share my sorrow and explain that I might be unable to return to Matankasch for an extended period. I needed her. I needed her support, her hug, her kiss. But she didn't pick up the phone. I called again, again, again, and again. What had happened to her? Did she no longer wish to hear my voice? Were there hidden secrets I was unaware of? I was depressed, lost, and I found myself forced to make a crucial decision.

In the end, I accepted the most audacious offer I had ever

had. I didn't know. I was actually sending myself to a devil's lair. I was doomed to lose a significant part of myself."

27:5

NTG527-LC11-D11
The Kernel, Rictor Island

"My family forged my future to head towards brightness, but my soul was submerged in the undercurrents. The Lokiata family had successfully seized control of Earth, and I was about to become the president of the Earth Alliance. I must admit, it made me quite pleased, and it was truly a supreme honour. While power had never been my personal aspiration, when it was bestowed upon me, there was an undeniable magnetic pull that compelled me to embrace it.

On the eve of my inauguration, I found myself consumed with busyness at the presidential palace, thinking that when I woke up the following morning, life would be as I imagined— trapped in a cage, unable to fly freely, forced to act against my own wishes in order to uphold the reputation of my family name. It was then, quite coincidentally, that I received an anonymous call, and to my surprise, it was May Dori on the other end. My heart instantly spiralled into chaos, and I questioned her sudden disappearance. Yet, I realised that instead of focusing on her whereabouts, what I truly needed to express were 'I love you,' 'I miss you,' 'I can't live without you.'

May Dori said she wished to explain something to me in person. So, I quickly arranged a private meeting at the palace. As soon as I laid eyes on her, she couldn't contain her emotions. She was pregnant, and I went speechless. I held her in my arms, experiencing the strange sensation of recovering what was once lost, while our shared moments played out like scenes from a drama film in my mind. She then whispered in my ear, and at first, I was overjoyed. Every fibre of my being yearned for her words to be drenched in love and apologies. But as I listened, something felt increasingly wrong, and before it reached the end, I became frozen, unable to think. All I could manage was to ask why and what exactly had happened.

As it turned out, I had been betrayed.

The government accused me of utilising my collaboration

with the hospital I had funded as a cover for manufacturing biochemical weapons. The trial took place behind closed doors, with assurances that no press or organisations would uncover any information. There existed an abundance of evidence against me, including sealed confidential documents, weapon samples, testimonies from alleged witnesses within the hospital, and even a recorded conversation. The source of these fabricated pieces became glaringly obvious—May Dori, a professional spy hired by Lokiata Edward. What a treacherous duo.

I couldn't solely blame myself for not being more cautious, for failing to exercise discernment, for being so deeply immersed in love that I almost disregarded anything unrelated to it. I did not regret the time we spent together. I cherished it, as every moment with love was an invaluable treasure. But, entwined with love, there was also hatred, and that hatred began to exert terrible effects on me."

NTG527-UC12-D1
Utopian Prison, Rictor Island

"I couldn't sleep, enduring the entirety of the night until my body couldn't take it anymore, collapsing as day broke. In a daze, I saw the prison gates wide open, and several unfamiliar figures came in and whisked me away. I didn't concern myself with what would happen next, allowing them to handle it as they pleased. All I wanted was to close my eyes and find respite in a long, uninterrupted sleep.

Never could I have imagined that it would be the Cosmo Scavengers, the group described by the outside world as the epitome of villainy and evilness, who would come to my rescue from the prison. By the way, we actually called ourselves 'Gathiv.' My rescuers enlightened me about the truth behind everything—it was all part of a scheme to seize the presidential position. People around me had been bribed, and even my eldest brother had fallen into a trap and died unjustly, while I, too trusting in someone's words, ruined my own life.

Lokiata Edward took my place as the president of the Earth Alliance, while Gathiv took the risk to save me. It all made sense —May Dori was originally a member of the group, and there were also informants within the government, operating under the guise of injustice, seeking to combat the true scoundrels responsible for perpetuating injustice in the world. Stripping me of everything would be a symbol of triumph for my brother, but for Gathiv? I was precisely a trophy of victory as well.

It wasn't necessary for me to know every detail of the betrayal, just as it wasn't crucial to uncover who had contacted my rescuers to plan and execute my prison break. There was only one question that held the power to determine my fate, and it demanded an answer. I needed to meet May Dori for one last time."

NTG527-UC12-D2
The Kernel, Rictor Island

"The universe, with its intricate web of unpredictable relationships, was something I had always hated. If only I had not been chosen to take the spotlight within my family and assume the position of president. If only May Dori had been an ordinary person without ties to thieves or espionage. If only Lokiata Edward had been born a humble and contented man. What would have become of the palace then? Perhaps a wondrous and fulfilling home for some. However, it ended up turning into a cage for the three of us—a cage of hunger for power, a cage of a puppet's life, and a cage of memories that I failed to bury.

On the following night, I infiltrated the palace. Neither May Dori nor my brother seemed surprised, as if they had foreseen my eventual return to confront them. I asked May Dori that question, but she dared not answer with words. I pressed on, only for my brother to silently draw a dagger. If it weren't for May Dori pulling me close just in time, that dagger may have found its place embedded in my skull instead of leaving a scar on my chin.

I understood it finally. That was May Dori's answer—her tears, her sorrow, her pity.

She pleaded with my brother to spare me, but nothing could ever be so simple. Lokiata Edward, renowned for his ignorance and coldness, and I, Lokiata Kee, sentimental and prone to meddling in all sorts of matters, were destined to be nemeses. I couldn't afford to look back. I feared that I would soften, that I wouldn't be able to sever the ties.

And then, I heard the thunderous sound of gunfire outside, followed by the ship's cannons shattering the walls behind me. My Gathiv brothers and sisters awaited me. I made my choice. I leaped through the opening, saying goodbye to the Earth Alliance forever.

The chapter between May Dori and me had reached its

conclusion. She had her new life, and I had my resolute cultivation. The flames of love burned some precious memories, turning them into unattainable ashes. I swore, from that day forward, I would never forgive May Dori, and I would never allow myself to fall in love with anyone else, absolutely not. I hated her. I hated her for deceiving me. I hated her for destroying everything I had, changing me into something else for the remainder of my days. Hatred became my greatest driving force for survival. If I had chosen love over hatred, I might have no power to face my goddess of death after that forlorn night.

I hated her, because I understood that, if I had to move on, if I had to avoid my own destruction, I had to let go—let go of all my love for her, for my dearest May Dori."

12 Aqual, W.D. 471
Teddix Castle, Teddix

The eternal battle between love and hatred was a narrative that transcended boundaries, resonating within the empty command centre of the Earthlings and the royal chambers of the Teddixians. Both places were filled with a murky air of negativity as the forces of love and hatred clashed.

In the king's suite, once a symbol of power and authority, now stood heavily guarded like a fragile fortress. The faces of the guards were taut, their eyes scanning for any sign of danger. But deep down, they all knew that it was merely a facade, an illusion of security. Huduson paced anxiously, his thoughts racing like a wild storm. He glanced at Huricane, who lay asleep on his bed, recovering from the recent fights that had left him drained. Despite the impossibility of Huringo being inside the room, he couldn't shake the nagging fear that the mad prince was still hiding somewhere within the castle.

Outside the suite, Wyach stood guard with lines of Teddixian soldiers. The weight of the past weeks' troubles bore down on her—the war with the golden army, the emergence of Silverlight Overflow, Huringo's return with Solarades, and the incident in the Earthling realm as recounted by Huxtin. All these events seemed to be interconnected somehow, pointing towards a dark scheme plotted by the Umbras, and she could only hope that she would be able to protect those dear to her.

Lost in her thoughts, Wyach was startled as Huxtin appeared, a dark visage emerging from even darker shadows, his demeanour eerily calm. The sight of Huxtin sent a wave of nervous tension through the ranks of guards, each man and woman stiffening under his piercing gaze. He approached Wyach, who immediately bowed her head in shame and sorrow. "I'm terribly sorry, Lord Huxtin," she whispered. "I failed to protect your son."

Huxtin's expression remained unchanged as he replied, "It's

not your fault. Your opponent was Huringo."

Wyach hesitated before continuing. "But... it wasn't just Huringo. There was someone else."

"Who?" His voice lowered even further. "Solarades?"

Nodding, she confirmed his suspicion. "You guessed it right... Huringo was under Solarades's protection all along."

Huxtin clenched his jaw in response. He knew that the time for decisions was upon them—decisions that would affect the fate of their entire kingdom. "From this moment on," he murmured, barely audible even to Wyach, "execute 'Evening Star'."

Shock rippled across Wyach's face, but within seconds, she realised that it might be the only viable solution in these dire circumstances. "I understand," she whispered back with her steady gaze. "I'll make the arrangements immediately."

"I'll leave it to you," Huxtin replied, his voice returning to its normal volume. "Now, tell me how my son is faring."

"He's recovering and asleep now. It seems like the first time he's used so much Elementro power in such a short period."

"Then he'll be fine."

"Would you like to go inside and check on him yourself?"

"No, that won't be necessary."

Wyach bit her lip, knowing full well that Huxtin was just afraid to show his true emotions. If he didn't care for his son, he wouldn't have come to this part of the castle in the first place. For all the years she had served by his side, she held an unwavering belief that he would do everything in his power to protect his family. Yet, she also knew better than to try and persuade him otherwise.

Before Huxtin turned to leave, Wyach spoke up once more. "Lord Huxtin, please pardon me for my uselessness."

Huxtin paused and looked at her, his expression softening just a fraction. "If you're truly sorry, then protect him at all costs. It may be that only you can do it, as he'll be the target of both sides of power."

Wyach nodded again, feeling a deep sense of gratitude toward the former king who had once given her a purpose in life. "That will be my only task before my duty must be fulfilled.

I promise."

"Very well. Wyach… Thank you."

12 Aqual, W.D. 471
Shell Valley

Soon after, near the Alva River, Rafaelzo and Gloria hid among the trees, observing Huxtin as he crossed the river towards the beach area of the Shell Valley. The night was quiet, with only the gentle lapping of water against the shore and the rustling leaves above them as their soundtrack.

"Is he heading for the Temple of Moon Shadow?" Gloria whispered, her curiosity piqued.

Rafaelzo shook his head. "There's no point in him going there now. The Binary written with the power of Wings of Moonlight has been depleted. We'd have to wait for an incarnation if any Aura wants to replenish the energies."

"Then we should get closer to him, so we don't lose track of where he's going."

"No, we just wait. He knows we're tracking him, and he doesn't want to be followed. Let's stay here for a while longer; there may be something interesting ahead."

The two of them remained hidden, their eyes never straying from Huxtin's path until he was about to enter the wooden house by the beach. The door creaked as Huxtin pushed it open, his tall silhouette framed by the starry night sky. The familiar scent of aged wood and damp earth filled his nostrils, bringing back memories of past encounters within those walls.

Inside the room, Remezo and Jeremia sat on the bench, maintaining a close watch over the golden sphere cell caging the Fallen. The cell's surface reflected the flickering light emanating from several floating crystal-like shards, but they weren't substances created by crystal Elementro; instead, they were a combination of light and illusion Elementro channeled by Remezo from the Auras clan of the Major Spirit.

"Hey, big guy," Jeremia greeted Huxtin with a crooked smile, standing up from the bench at the table. "We kept our promise and waited here. Did you see our chief elder?"

In response, Huxtin said nothing. He strode past the Auras,

his only focus on the floating cell, the object of his current obsession, a key piece in the trial in which he was currently involved. As he reached the cell, he extended both hands. With a single touch, he nullified the effect of the Elementro particles that created it, shattering it into fragments in no time before their very eyes. The white feathers inside fluttered free, but their desperate escape was thwarted by Huxtin's powerful, intangible grasp.

"Impossible..." Remezo breathed, shocked by what he saw. He had crafted the cell to be unbreakable by mere touch, but Huxtin's power surpassed even his wildest expectations. "The Son of Chaos... what are you really?"

Jeremia also stared wide-eyed at Huxtin, his earlier bravado replaced by hidden fear. He exchanged a glance with Remezo, the unspoken question hanging between them: what would happen next? Through sheer force of will, Huxtin caused the white feathers to coalesce, and Poet involuntarily reformed into her human shape. As she solidified, Huxtin's hand shot forward, grabbing her by the neck and pulling her towards him.

The violence threatened Remezo, while his eyes darted from Huxtin's arms to his fingers, noting the faint glowing red circles of light that surrounded them. He recalled the reports of the Rings of Chaos, the manifestation of unimaginable power wielded by the Son of Chaos himself. He then shared another uneasy look with Jeremia, who shrugged helplessly, signalling that they shouldn't intervene.

On the brink of mental collapse, Huxtin's consciousness teetered on the edge, with only a fragile thread of sanity keeping his thoughts intact. He yearned to uncover the answer to a burning question, yet a darker aspect of his being craved something far more sinister.

"Poet," he demanded, his voice colder than the depths of the darkest sea where the most monstrous creatures dwelled. "If you wish to survive, it would be in your best interest to answer my question right now."

CHAPTER 28

DRIVEN BY THEIR MISSION, THEY DEFY NORMS,
EMBRACING REBELLION TO SUCCEED

12 Aqual, W.D. 471
Shell Valley

Writhing in pain, Poet's moans echoed off the wooden walls of the beach house. Her smoky makeup was now a mess of tears and desperation. Huxtin's eyes, which had turned from blue to red, posed a real threat to her soul, which had resided in this universe for far too long.

"Please..." Poet rasped through clenched teeth, "release me... and eliminate those Auras in the house... for the sake of the universe."

But Huxtin merely stared at her, his face impassive. "Where is Mateek's Starfall Tomb?" he asked, his tone particularly detached.

Poet blinked back fresh tears, her mind racing. "Why do you... need to know?" she weakly countered, desperate for any reprieve from her tormentor.

"I just need to, and you shouldn't question why."

"I don't know..." Poet emphasised her ignorance, but Huxtin wouldn't relent, convinced that she had found him in the Starfall Tomb of Sealina—surely, she must have knowledge of the others.

The atmosphere in the room grew increasingly suffocating. Jeremia and Remezo both tried their best to stay calm, but the uneasiness made their nerves restless.

Faced with no other option, Poet lied again, "I know nothing! I have no idea... what you are talking about!"

Huxtin then issued an ultimatum. "If you refuse to reveal what you know, I will force you to do so."

"No, you won't—"

"Three." Huxtin's voice turned from ice to steel, each syllable chilling the air around him. "I'll keep counting."

At first, Poet didn't believe Huxtin would kill her for just a small piece of information—but when he uttered "two" with the same conviction, panic set in. Her fear escalated, and it became clear that her previous tactics wouldn't save her now.

"One."

And for a fleeting moment, Poet's heart seemed to stop entirely. "Huxtin! You made a promise... My sister... You remember?"

Upon hearing the same excuse he had heard countless times before, Huxtin refrained from taking immediate action against Poet. Relief surged through Poet as if the entrance to her tomb had closed before she could step inside. She believed she had made the right decision by remaining silent about the location, resorting to a deceitful tactic she had always despised—but she was gravely mistaken. In the next instant, her body splintered into white feathers, her screams silenced as she underwent her final transformation. This would be her ultimate metamorphosis, for she had been killed by Huxtin.

As the feathers dissolved into pure Elementro particles, Poet's soul remained, hidden from sight but visible to Huxtin's red gaze. A network of golden soul shards spread out before him, their brilliance fading with each passing moment. With methodical precision, he delved into her library of memories, discarding inconsequential fragments as he sought the vital information he so desperately needed.

At last, he found it: the location of Mateek's Starfall Tomb. He saw Poet there, aiding the Auras and the Children of God in constructing their initial resting places before becoming a Fallen. His search also revealed something he hadn't expected— the recollection of his promise to her sister that he wouldn't harm or kill her, but it was all too late for remorse. He had chosen the worst possible path. There was no turning back, and there would be no forgiveness for him.

Until the very last flicker of Poet's golden soul shard faded away, Huxtin was left alone in a cold darkness in his vision. Far beyond mere shadows, this darkness was a living, breathing entity that seemed to seep into his very core. He started to feel an uneasy sensation, like a ghastly presence traversing through his mind. Soon after, two hauntingly beautiful eyes with dark purple pupils materialised before him. They fed on the mysterious energy flowing from him, thriving off the essence known as Chaos.

Thirteen long seconds ticked by, each one fraught with breathless tension. Believing it was a time when action was necessary, Remezo finally glanced up from the bench, disregarding the potential disadvantageous consequences. He cautiously approached Huxtin, but was suddenly struck by an unseen force, instantly causing him to crumple to the ground in agony. Jeremia, eager to check on his companion, was met with a stern order to stay put.

"Stay there! Don't come close... Something's seriously wrong!"

Remaining in his position, Jeremia observed as the six glowing red loops encircling Huxtin's hand and fingers expanded infinitely before vanishing into nothingness. From their vantage point overlooking the whacky wooden house, Rafaelzo and Gloria also witnessed the perplexing red loops coursing through the walls, seemingly intertwining with every physical substance in its vicinity.

"This is not a good sign," Rafaelzo said, his face turning serious in an instant. "We must put a stop to it."

As the mysterious dark purple eyes continued to draw power from Huxtin, the darkness surrounding him thickened like a viscous liquid. He struggled to maintain control over his own thoughts as he watched a small black dot expand within the various layers of darkness, morphing into the shape of a creature. Eventually, the creature took over the pair of eyes, becoming a tangible presence and bringing them back to the realm of reality. The creature possessed six featherless pairs of pointed wings, its body resembling that of an adult male human, dripping with the same thick black substance.

"Welcome, My King," the creature rasped through an incomplete mouth. "I am here to serve you in this universe. It is time for us to join the grand army awaiting our command."

Huxtin, his eyes returning to their normal navy blue hue, displayed shock and confusion, rooted to the spot. A memory flashed before him—a vision of himself lying in a sea of blood. He tried to shake off the disturbing image, but it clung to him like a stubborn leech.

"What the hell are you?" he questioned. "What do you...

166

want from me?"

Without waiting for a response, the creature lunged forward and grabbed Huxtin, its pointed wings fanning out as they took to the sky. Startled, Jeremia hurried over to his companion after witnessing a chaos. "Are you alright? What just happened to you?" he asked, kneeling beside Remezo.

"I bet I'm fine…" Remezo forced a smile. "You should stay here, though; I don't think we can handle whatever's happening with the Son of Chaos."

"Of course, I'll stay, to protect you." Jeremia offered a playful grin.

"Wow," Remezo replied dramatically, "thanks. I knew it."

While the creature tried to carry Huxtin deeper into the Shell Valley, Huxtin managed to break free and fell to the ground, landing on his feet after creating an air cushion to soften the impact. The creature reacted swiftly, only to be slashed in half by a wind blade. However, it was only a momentary triumph.

"I don't believe you are capable of killing me at this moment," the creature sneered, his black substance fusing and stitching back together to reform his body. "My body remains connected to Chaos, and as you are aware, you cannot destroy what is a part of yourself."

The creature then melted like molten black lava, reshaping himself into a blanket in a matter of seconds. Huxtin futilely attempted to push the blanket off, but he found himself immobilised, bound by the black substance that clung to his combat attire like a second skin, repulsed by the blanket's viscosity and elasticity.

"My apologies, My King." The creature formed his head by extending a portion from the blanket. "But I must bring you to see the queen."

As he spoke, he released a dark purple mist into the air through the black substance, causing Huxtin's consciousness to fade rapidly. Just before succumbing to a deep slumber, Huxtin's attention was caught by a glimmer of light in the distance, growing brighter. It cut through the darkness like a beacon, warming him and pushing back the coldness of the dark purple mist. It appeared to be the precise strength he required to mount a counteroffensive and reclaim control of the situation once more.

"Huxtin!"

It was Mu Mann's voice that carried on the wind. Huxtin saw Mann perching upon the large palm of Tunpatter, the guardian beast of the Shell Valley. The beast's pastel and light grey fur stood out against the black sky, and the cross symbol on his chest was the spotlight star of the night, casting a unique radiance over the scene.

"Help him, Tunpatter!" Mann ordered, leaping to the ground.

"Roger that! Hahaha!" Tunpatter responded with his distinctive laughter. "No intruders are allowed in the Shell Valley!"

Scorching energy pulsated through his veins as Tunpatter charged towards the creature with his massive hand reaching out. The creature squirmed, but was unable to escape the iron grip of the ancient beast.

"Your intrusion into the Shell Valley has sentenced you to death!" With a sudden flick of his wrist, Tunpatter pulled the blanket off Huxtin, but the black substance contorted and expanded, transforming into an even larger blanket that sought to ensnare the beast. The same dark purple mist enveloped Tunpatter, but it had no effect on his mind at all.

"Illusion-based attack? Do you know what I am made of? Huh?" Letting out a mighty howl, Tunpatter displayed a similar set of abilities, reshaping his body into a small, nimble cat-like form without a tail, maintaining the same pastel fur and markings that adorned his original appearance. His claws lengthened slightly, and his horns extended beyond his body, flowing like silvery ribbons. In this new form, he darted around, the ribbons undulating against gravity, enticing the creature into a perilous game of cat and mouse.

"Too slow, animal," the creature taunted. "Is that all you've got?"

"You want more?" Tunpatter countered, leaping gracefully through the air as the blanket attempted to engulf him. "Let me show you more!"

The creature closed in, trying to compress himself to a size

168

that could wrap his little target. But Tunpatter escaped, his true form restored, and unleashed a devastating golden shockwave by striking with both palms, obliterating the creature into nothing more than wisps of mist within seconds. The malevolent voice was silenced, but the soothing laughter continued. The negativity dissipated, and life within the valley temporarily returned to harmony.

"How dare you cause trouble in my homeland!" Tunpatter roared, turning his attention to Mann, who was tending to Huxtin, leaving him somewhat disappointed, because he had just performed a remarkable and heroic feat.

"Hey, Wood," Mann said softly, kneeling beside Huxtin.

"Hey, the Great Detective," Huxtin weakly replied. "Why are you here?"

"Umm… I was just passing by."

"Oh, really?"

"So, how about you?"

Huxtin could barely remember losing control of his emotions and doing something terrible. He wanted to tell Mann the truth but couldn't find the words. His gaze then moved away from hers as Rafaelzo and Gloria arrived on the scene. An uncomfortable silence settled, a weight that burdened them all.

"Well, it seems we don't need to interfere in the situation, as it has been settled," Rafaelzo spoke first, his deep voice echoing through the serene landscape. "I am glad that everyone's okay."

Mann's eyes darted anxiously between the two newcomers, whom she recognised as the Auras. She attempted to maintain a sense of calm, carefully observing their approach. However, the events that had transpired left her questioning whether these Auras were truly allies or potential enemies. Although the other two Auras she had met on the Isle of Sealina were kind to her, she was still tainted by the uncertainties of the past.

To her surprise, the Auras exchanged respectful nods with Tunpatter, who stood tall and proud beside Huxtin.

"It is a pleasure to meet you in person, the Judge of Life and Death," Rafaelzo said, his tone full of reverence, and Gloria echoed the sentiment.

Tunpatter chuckled, a deep rumble that seemed to shake the

ground beneath their feet. "I didn't know I was so popular among the Auras, hahaha!"

"Wow... You..." Mann mumbled, her brow furrowed in confusion as she struggled to process the idea of Tunpatter being worshipped by the Auras. It felt surreal, almost absurd.

"The lady there, you must understand that the Judge of Life and Death is a guardian as ancient as Celestiloo itself," Rafaelzo clarified. "A few days older than me, perhaps?"

Mann's jaw dropped, and she turned her questioning and uneasy gaze toward the two strangers. "Who are you?"

"Earthling." Gloria raised her head, a hint of disapproval in her expression. "You should show more respect to our chief elder"

"So, you are the one mentioned by Remezo and Jeremia," Mann muttered as she finally realised the Aura before her was the true leader of the Auras, and yet he greeted Tunpatter with such respect. "You came to Celestiloo for Huxtin."

"Yes, I did," Rafaelzo confirmed, his attention now focused on Huxtin, whose mind was a labyrinth of thoughts, their depths impenetrable and incomprehensible to anyone else. "We must have a conversation, the Son of Chaos, about everything."

Back at the wooden house by the beach, the group gathered for a serious meeting. Remezo, thankfully recovered from his internal injuries, stood beside Gloria and Jeremia. Their leader, Rafaelzo, sat with a confident expression, while Huxtin and Mu Mann took their seats opposite him.

With practiced ease, Mann lit some new candles on the long table. Rafaelzo expressed his gratitude, while Tunpatter, now in his small form, leaped onto the table and settled in front of Mann, purring contentedly as she stroked his fur. Eventually, he drifted off to sleep, finding peace among all the tense faces.

"I hope the candlelight will suffice for all of us," Mann said, trying to lighten the mood. "I thought the Auras could use Elementro to create some light, though?"

Rafaelzo chuckled, glancing at Remezo. "One of us is quite skilled at it, but I didn't want him to expend his energy right now. As for Gloria, the light she generates would be too intense for this confined space." He grinned, but Gloria looked serious, silently urging him to stay focused on their primary objective.

"What about you?" Mann turned her attention back to Rafaelzo after looking at Gloria, unable to contain her curiosity. "Do you also harness sun Elementro?"

Rafaelzo's surprise briefly flickered across his face before he studied Huxtin's indifferent expression. "The Son of Chaos must have taught you many concepts about Elementro, hasn't he?"

Embarrassment flushed Mann's cheeks. "I do have some knowledge, but it's rather complex." She paused and then turned to Huxtin. "You must have many questions for the Auras, right?"

Huxtin stared back, his face shifting to one of resigned acceptance. "Alright," he muttered without turning his gaze toward the Auras, his voice low and gravelly. "Tell me, the chief elder of the Auras, what do you actually know about me?"

Rafaelzo assumed a composed posture, sitting upright in his seat. He interlocked his fingers and rested his elbows on the table, projecting an air of attentiveness.

"The Son of Chaos... No, I would prefer to address you as Huxtin out of respect. To be blunt, I know you're dangerous. You possess powers from both our kind and our adversaries, as well as the unique ability known as Chaos—a force so potent that it has attracted attention from all corners of the universe. I bet some of our people have already conveyed this to you. You are a being difficult to contain, and our options for coexistence with you are limited: either persuade you to join us or force you to comply. Otherwise..."

Mann's irritation suddenly flared up, cutting off Rafaelzo. "So, you do have a plan to confine him and eliminate potential threats, such as his..."

Huxtin gave a gentle look to Mann who couldn't finish her sentence, appreciating her boldness in asking the question he himself couldn't bring to the surface. He crossed his arms, his fingers firmly pinching his own skin, as if to confirm that his soul still resided within his flesh and blood.

"There is a plan, but it wasn't my idea," Rafaelzo continued, his demeanour becoming even more serious than before. "I did, however, cast my vote in favour of it. As the leader of the Auras, I bear the responsibility of making tough decisions to ensure the safety of my people. I believe you understand this, Huxtin, since you are a ruler yourself."

Huxtin relaxed his arms, but then he clenched his fists under the table, fighting the urge to lash out. He knew Rafaelzo was speaking the truth, but admitting it was a bitter pill to swallow. Meanwhile, Mann fell silent, her emotions simmering as she made a conscious effort to quell her temper. She recognised that, as a former army commander, if placed in a similar situation, she might have made the same choice.

"One wrong move can trigger a chain of disastrous consequences. The universe is not forgiving to beings like you and me." Rafaelzo closed his eyes, reflecting on the chaotic past and the potentially even more chaotic future. When he opened his eyes again, his gaze was steady. "If you could learn to control your emotions, things might become more manageable."

"Are you here to teach me how to control my emotions?" Huxtin countered.

"I'm afraid that falls outside my area of expertise."

"In that case, what is the purpose of your presence here?"

"I am here to apologise for the mistrust my people have shown you, and I believe that if we can set aside our disagreements and work together, we can overcome the challenges that lie ahead."

This wasn't the answer Huxtin had expected, leading him to realise that there were still Auras who were open to negotiation and had some flexibility in their terms. Noticing that Huxtin's mouth remained tightly shut, Mann took it upon herself to speak up on his behalf. "Next question, then... What exactly happened at Teddix Castle earlier? And what are we getting ourselves into now?"

Rafaelzo sighed, the lines on his face deepening as he recounted the events, his silvery eyes fixating on the navy blue gems. "Once there was a force protecting the entire planet of Celestiloo, but it has been reduced to covering only the area around the Throne of Immortality—or Teddix Castle, as the common people here call it. That was our first problem."

He paused, giving the information a moment to sink in before continuing. "Then, someone managed to blast a hole through the protective dome, adding another layer to the issue. Solarades, an immensely powerful Aura, and Huxtin's elder son... are the culprits. We have to take them down as soon as possible. If not, we will face even greater trouble."

Mann connected the dots between the rogue Aura and the ancient tales of two Children of God, Litorio and Mateek, joining forces with the Umbras to bring destruction upon the planet. "How could an Aura commit such acts? What could Solar... that individual, and Huringo possibly desire?"

"I am uncertain of the exact answer, but our best course of action is to locate them and confront them directly. I have been tracking their movements. They are currently situated in a fixed spot within a closed dimension and have yet to emerge. If they move again, I will be able to ascertain their new location. I believe I know where Solarades may be heading."

Huxtin, who had been brooding silently, suddenly expressed suspicion. "How do you know all of this?"

"I'm gifted with power, though I never asked for it. Sometimes it just troubles me, but it's what made me the person to lead the Auras—responsible for countless lives of our kind. I must adapt and utilise this power to our advantage," Rafaelzo explained, emphasising his point. "I believe that we share similar experiences, and you understand the depth of my emotions regarding all this suffering."

"No, you don't," Huxtin responded in the coldest and most distant tone. "And neither do I. If you expect me to act according to your needs, that's fine, but let's not go any further than that."

Rafaelzo smiled, relieved to have reached a conclusion after the lengthy meeting. "Fantastic. Do we have an agreement? Will you join us in this fight?"

"Join you? No," Huxtin replied firmly. "I will take care of my son, and you will handle Solarades. We are not allies, but our enemies are one and the same."

"Very well," Rafaelzo said, inclining his head. "It's a deal."

A temporary alliance had formed; however, burdened by her

sister Miria's disappearance, Gloria could no longer suppress her need for answers. She gazed at Mann earnestly, grateful for her earlier interruption as it had emboldened her. Rafaelzo sensed her intention, contemplating whether to stop her, but his careful thoughts were still not as quick as her impulsiveness.

"Wait! You still haven't told me what happened to my sister!" Gloria's voice started off loud and rushed, but she quickly composed herself, speaking more slowly to Huxtin. "She's been around, right?"

Rafaelzo admonished gently, cautioning her, "Not now, Gloria. This is not the appropriate time."

"I apologise, Chief Elder Rafaelzo," Gloria murmured softly, avoiding direct eye contact with her senior. "But this is something I cannot ignore. It has been ages since I last saw Miria."

There were more pieces of shocking news for Mann, who nearly lost her mind trying to digest so much information all at once. She had thought Miria and Gloria bore a resemblance, but she hadn't realised they were real sisters until now. She probably understood why Huxtin wanted to evade the question, but to her surprise yet again, he was willing to provide a statement.

"Zagatan, an Umbra, hired a Fallen named Poet to capture Miria." Huxtin's hands were now gripping the edge of the table, his fingers caressing the wood grain as he envisioned a connection between himself and the natural world. He hoped that this seemingly lifeless piece of wood could come alive, restraining him whenever he went berserk. "I sent the Constraint of Flammando to rescue her, but they never returned."

"Poet?" Gloria questioned sharply. "The same Fallen you just killed?"

"How come you haven't sought forgiveness after doing something so terribly wrong?"

Huxtin shut his eyes, while Mann stared at him in disbelief, her sudden movement startling Tunpatter from peaceful slumber. She didn't know whether to criticise or worry about

Huxtin, but based on previous experience, she decided it was better to pretend not to care about this matter for now.

Sensing Huxtin's reluctance, Rafaelzo spoke up in response to Gloria on Huxtin's behalf. "Yes, the same one. I knew her, and I know what she became in the end. What a shame. She was once a very strong warrior among us."

But Gloria hadn't given up on pressing Huxtin. "What do you mean by 'never return'?"

Huxtin's mind raced back to the incident at the command centre of T.P.S.E a few days ago. Nevertheless, he remained steadfast in his approach. He knew he was being evasive, but his focus was on preventing any unwanted details from slipping through his lips, including the fact that he had attempted to kill Miria before.

"It simply means I have no information about their current whereabouts."

"Then why did the Umbras want Miria alive?" Gloria murmured, more as a question to herself than to anyone else in the room. She looked at Rafaelzo for guidance, but he merely exchanged a knowing glance with Huxtin, indicating that he too had deduced something about Miria's fate.

As the flames of the candles on the long table flickered, on the verge of extinguishing, Mann swiftly lit some fresh matches to revive the dwindling light. Huxtin seized the moment to direct a question to Rafaelzo. "What have I done? What did I do to Poet? What exactly is… Chaos?"

"Oh, it's interesting that you had the chance to ask me this question before but ended up choosing a less significant one. Why the sudden curiosity about the fundamentals of Chaos?"

"I'm sorry, Huxtin," Rafaelzo responded, crossing his arms. "I don't know much about Chaos, nor do the Auras. It's a power beyond our comprehension. All I know about Chaos comes from the report of… Lunarcaria."

The name Lunarcaria felt like another encroaching fog that threatened to choke Huxtin, not the illusive dark purple, but something scared in nature. The pressure mounted on him as he recalled how greatly he had failed the only Aura he had ever trusted with his heart.

It was at this moment that Tunpatter, who had been walking on the wooden table, decided to speak up. "I do have some information about Chaos," he admitted, his bestial voice contrasting with his current appearance. "Not everything, but a piece of the puzzle."

All eyes turned towards the Judge of Life and Death, but the chief elder of the Auras was particularly interested in the mystery surrounding the user of Chaos.

"Please, enlighten us with the truth about Chaos," he inquired. "Even a glimpse of understanding would be invaluable."

Tunpatter ceased his restless pacing around the table with an elegant flick of his ribbons, his whiskers, only appearing in his cat-like form, twitching as he began to speak, "Among Auras and Umbras alike, Chaos is considered a myth, but what if it existed long before the creation of our universe? I cannot say whether Chaos predates even the existence of The Creator, but the Children of God once mentioned that Chaos might draw its power from a dimension beyond our knowledge.

You see, the twelve of them together compose the entirety of our known universe, and yet Chaos has never resonated with them. This suggests that The Creator did not forge this special power, and perhaps it belongs to another realm, or another universe entirely."

The concept of another universe was alien to everyone in the room, and the shock of it showed on Huxtin's normally stoic face. Rafaelzo's brow furrowed, deep in thought, and even Mann's adventurous spirit seemed momentarily quelled by this revelation. It wasn't until Tunpatter's laughter, a sound both comforting and jarring, burst forth that everyone's focus returned to his explanation.

"Although my title is the Judge of Life and Death, I cannot create or destroy life with just a single command." He paused for effect, his gaze meeting each person in turn. "My power draws from the illusion Elementro of Imortalli, granting me the

176

ability to sense the activities of every cell in every living being. This means I can discern when a life will be born or when it will end. But the power of Chaos... that is something totally different. It can create and destroy life in an instant. The only being capable of such wonders might be The Creator. Even the Children of God took time and effort to turn Celestiloo into a flourishing planet."

Then he locked eyes with Rafaelzo, who asked with grave seriousness, "With the Rings of Chaos... Did Huxtin create an Umbra from Poet's 'Bad Deeds'?"

"Involuntarily, yes," Tunpatter replied solemnly.

"And 'Bad Deeds' within the soul of a Fallen was always the strongest... You, the Son of Chaos, have nearly caused a calamity that you might not even be able to handle. Luckily, that Umbra was destroyed before reaching full form."

"And that's why both the Auras and the Umbras fear the wielder of Chaos..." Mann interjected as she observed Huxtin, whose soul appeared to be lost in some distant place. "It's also why both sides covet the power within Huxtin..."

"Exactly, hahaha!" Tunpatter exclaimed, returning to Mann's side and playfully nudging her as if asking for more pets. Mann relented, her fingers sinking into his soft fur, the sensation providing her a brief moment of comfort. His laughter, his spirit, and his latent steadiness all reminded her of Autaming, and amidst all the troubles, it allowed her to find solace in the grace of the world.

In that very moment, Huxtin's mind was plagued by haunting images of the woman he had unintentionally killed—a life taken against his will for the second time, although the first victim miraculously survived in the end. His hands, which had once been wielded proudly as instruments of justice and restoration, now felt like shackles binding him to commit heinous acts.

"Do you wish to venture once more to the sea of blood? To the astronomical clock? I know you hold a fondness for

that place. If it is your desire... If you dream of it... Just make your wish known."

"Perhaps it is time we conclude this meeting," Rafaelzo finally proposed, signalling the end of their extended conversation. "We shall be well-prepared for the upcoming battles."

"I have a trial to attend," Huxtin stated. "You all must wait for me until the end of tomorrow."

"Oh, yes, of course," Rafaelzo agreed, nodding his head in understanding. "We won't interfere with your challenge with Mateek. But I must urge you to return as soon as you're able, for our enemies could resurface at any given moment."

"So be it," Huxtin responded tersely, still avoiding eye contact with Rafaelzo and everyone else in the room, except perhaps for Mann.

Aware that trust had yet to be fully established, Rafaelzo realised that he would need to demonstrate his commitment through actions rather than mere words. Meanwhile, Gloria's mind was consumed by fear and suspicion as she tried to make sense of her sister's fate. Did Huxtin or even Rafaelzo know something they weren't disclosing? Her nerves were like live wires, dangerously close to sparking into a burst of explosive electricity.

Unable to contain herself any longer, she stormed out of the wooden house, leaving everyone behind in her wake. Jeremia called after her, but Rafaelzo stopped him with a raised hand. "Let her be alone," he advised. "She needs space to process her emotions."

From the corner of his eye, Huxtin watched the scene unfold, realising the potential devastation that could occur if Gloria were to uncover the truth about Miria and the impending crisis. The electricity coursing through her veins possessed the potential to ignite a war, and the gravity of that power wasn't lost on any of the Auras present.

"The Umbras? The Auras? Whom do you wish to lead? Whom do you aspire to become? If you are drawn to the

allure of the third path, what will it entail? Where do you believe you will discover the extraordinary? Will it be—"

"Chaos."

"Huxtin, do you still have something to say?" Mann sensed something amiss in Huxtin's demeanour and decided to divert his attention with a random question.

"No. All good."

"Okay… Let's return to Teddix first."

Mann's question had served its purpose, drawing Huxtin away from his introspection. Even if his answer was potentially false, it was the most desirable response she could hope for in that moment.

12 Aqual, W.D. 471
Teddix Castle, Teddix

Eighteen vibrant red candles cast chaotic reflections across the suite of the Teddixian king, illuminating the scattered and broken objects within. Huricane awoke from what felt like a long sleep, his mind clouded with the remnants of a forgotten nightmare. In the company of only Huduson and Wyach, their faces displaying exhaustion and worry, he remained oblivious to the heavily guarded door of his bedroom.

Surveying the room, Huricane lamented the disastrous scene before him. Important documents and scrolls lay burned, their significance lost forever. Pages from various books were torn and detached, but thankfully, Mu Mann's notebook remained unscathed. He reached out, delicately flipping through its pages, his fingers tracing over the writings and drawings, unintentionally creating one crease after another. It was a bittersweet reminder that their fragile alliance with the Earthlings had officially come to an end.

Setting the notebook aside, Huricane began to pace the room, his eyes catching sight of the charred cards given to him by Huringo, now strewn across the floor. The words on them were barely legible, their purpose fulfilled in tormenting him, at least in his interpretation of the situation.

"This is the end."

Returning to his seat, he leaned heavily against the back of the chair, allowing his body to relax. The accumulated work pressure magically vanished, no longer burdening him with complex calculations or meticulously crafted dialogues for his subjects. He now resembled a leader in ruins, stripped of luxurious adornments and devoid of grandeur. The once mighty king of Paralloy Teddix had fallen into a realm of emptiness.

"You know, just a few hours ago, I still had great expectations placed upon me. I believed I could govern the kingdom properly, prove to my father that I possessed the ability to carry on the prosperous era he established... I thought I could..." His voice trailed off, and he let out a hollow, cold laugh. "Everything has become a dream, an illusion."

"My King, it's not your fault," Wyach stressed. "I also bear the responsibility—"

"No, Wyach, no. I know it's not my fault. I did everything I could, gave my all without giving up for even a single second! But still..." Tears streaked down Huricane's face as he spoke, his words filled with hopelessness, with those navy blue eyes reflecting his deepest sorrow. "The kingdom will perish under my watch..."

Feeling a genuine ache in his heart, Huduson attempted to ignite the king's determination. "We cannot give up at this time, My King! We all believe that you can do it. You can lead us through this difficult time. You will... We need you... All of us..."

However, as he witnessed the king's defeated and despondent appearance, his usual encouragement seemed futile, and he felt increasingly powerless. Despite the fact that the red candles hadn't yet burned down even halfway, the suite was pervaded by an unusual dimness.

"I'm truly exhausted, Huduson." Huricane wiped away his tears, though the stains remained evident. "Why can't I give up? This kingdom cannot be saved. I cannot be saved. I was just fortunate enough to have the chance to sit on a throne that was never mine to begin with. The Stars of Teddix... and those inspiring stories... I should have never dared to dream of being the protagonist in any of them. Well... I am still a part of those stories, but everyone will remember that there exists a weakling who couldn't protect what he held dear."

"How could that be, My King?" Huduson exclaimed, refusing to let go. "With you and Lord Huxtin, and with your formidable abilities, Paralloy Teddix will—"

"It is precisely because of our power that Paralloy Teddix is destined for ruin."

The king's proclamation about the future of the kingdom left his chief of staff speechless. Huricane's self-abandonment was especially disheartening. Despite having been forced to abandon his lively and cheerful nature for years, the extent of his current decadence was simply pathological.

What true secrets were hidden within the Elementro power that Huxtin and Huricane possessed? Huduson couldn't decipher how having such extraordinary power could have the opposite effect on the very land it was meant to safeguard. During the civil wars, Huxtin's presence, akin to that of a divine being descending from the heavens, had turned the tide and propelled the crumbling empire to its zenith. It had unified the continent and deterred neighbouring rulers from expanding their influence. So, why would Elementro now bring about the downfall of Paralloy Teddix?

Huduson then glanced at Wyach, who stood to his left at the back. He wasn't entirely sure why she remained particularly silent tonight.

"My King... No, Huricane, my dear cousin." With one final attempt, he abandoned the formalities and addressed the king in a way he had never imagined before. "Are you truly willing to let Paralloy Teddix be trampled upon by those who despise us? Are you satisfied with the idea that our land will be ravaged, our people slaughtered, our resources plundered, and our pride as the brightest stars on Celestiloo reduced to a mere paragraph in a forgotten corner of the history book that nobody will remember or even care about?"

His tongue, chest, neck, and arteries quivered with a terrifying surge. For the first time, he realised that he couldn't simply stand there like a robotic entity, regurgitating beautiful phrases or dramatic adjectives. He no longer feared how his words might affect the king's emotions or how the king would perceive him, but regrettably, the king remained unmoved.

"Th-this... This is wrong, Huricane! This is all wrong!"

With the king isolating himself in his pitiful state and Wyach silently sighing on the side, Huduson hastily rushed out of the room without uttering a farewell. The more he yearned to break free from the confines of their predetermined master-servant relationship, the more he hated his own helplessness within this royal family. He had exerted his utmost effort, but it seemed insignificant in shaping the future of Paralloy Teddix.

"My King, I believe it is necessary for me to accompany you to the emergency meeting early tomorrow," Wyach finally stated, adjusting her slipping glasses while intentionally concealing her troubled expression. "During the meeting, we shall discuss the subsequent steps for initiating 'Evening Star'."

"Uh-huh, leave me be for now," the king simply replied.

The sound of Wyach's high heels echoed on the stone floor, gradually fading away. An hour passed, and even with all the candles extinguished, the king remained seated, fixated on the same spot. His mind was occupied by no one and nothing, awaiting the brutal conclusion of his own story.

CHAPTER 29

THEY WILL MAKE EVERY LIVING BEING RECOGNISE YOU,
SUPPORT YOU, AND ADMIRE YOU

12 Aqual, W.D. 471
Somewhere in Timeloss

"Are we prepared? Can we leave right now? Are there any other obstacles?"

"Yes, we are fully prepared! Of course, we are!"

"Just wait a little longer, and the time will come."

"And then we will… we will… conquer Celestiloo… once again…"

The endless expanse of broken, colourful crystal shards that stretched as far as the eye could see was a magnificent yet horrifying scene, especially under the oppressive, gloomy sky, making it impossible to discern whether it was day or night. Standing amidst this desolation was a long-haired woman, her blood red skin adorned with purple markings and draped in black cloth. She walked close to a pulsating energy source emanating from a floating black orb surrounded by shades of purple, resembling an eclipsed sun with its corona.

"Enough of your 'mind-blowing' games," the woman snapped, glaring at the orb as if it were a living entity.

"What? You don't like me being this way? Why didn't you say so earlier?"

"Clam down. There's no need to be emotional."

"But she… hurt us… badly."

"I can't stand it! Annoying woman!"

The pulsations of the orb ceased, and four beings emerged from it, unfolding like ink black blankets before transforming into identical hound-like creatures. As they took shape, the substance of the orb depleted and disintegrated. The four creatures then merged together, their forms intertwining like the threads of a quilt. The result was a single, enormous hound, four times larger than the originals, with rough black skin and four long tails, each tipped with a large cross that emitted vibrant purple light.

"Does this satisfy you, Conew?" The hound, Ganavanda, spoke in a normal male voice, defying its monstrous appearance.

"Such a bothersome shapeshifter," the woman, Conew, grumbled.

"Come on! You know I am more than just a shapeshifter," Ganavanda corrected her, the purple light at the crosses of his tails intensifying. "If you want me to make you forget how constantly bothersome I can be, or if you wish to believe that you are passionately in love with me, I can fulfil that for you, right here, right now."

"Suit yourself. I don't have time for this," Conew replied, rolling her eyes and dismissing his offer. "The queen is summoning us. We should make our way there."

"Which queen are you referring to?" Ganavanda inquired mischievously. "The true queen or merely the shell that contains her?"

Conew narrowed her eyes, shooting him a warning glare. "The queen is doing everything she can to stabilise the shell. Don't doubt her abilities, and don't overestimate your own."

"Ahh, but I'm not doubting," Ganavanda replied smoothly, maintaining his enigmatic grin. "I've simply observed them conversing with each other, arguing over who's right and wrong, who should control the shell... just like beings with split personalities."

"Isn't that just like you?" Conew countered, gesturing at his massive form. She stepped closer to him, undeterred by the possibility of his beastly mouth widening further, with his sharp teeth threatening to puncture her already bloodied, red skin. "Always talking to yourself, indulging in your... four distinct personalities. Or should I be counting five? I never even know which of you is the real one... I suggest you keep quiet and behave yourself."

"One of us is very disciplined in behaviour, but it's hard to say for the others."

"I advise you—"

"Oh, wait! They're arguing who is the more disciplined one, and even I don't know—"

"Ganavanda! Do you understand?" All Conew could smell from Ganavanda's mouth was a sinister and bloodthirsty scent, but she had no fear of it. "I bet you don't want me to keep repeating myself. You know the consequences, don't you?"

Ganavanda's smile grew wider. "Yes, I witnessed what happened to that unfortunate Umbra last time," he replied, displaying equal fearlessness. "Let's not keep our queen waiting then."

Conew couldn't help but reciprocate with a smile, albeit a reluctant one. She truly had no regard for creatures like Ganavanda, who seemed nothing more than pets to their masters—at least, that was her initial perception. But when she allowed herself to envision escaping this infernal place for something greater, a purpose more suited to her wicked nature, she felt a surge of joy. It was this desire that fuelled her determination to survive.

Unknown
Unknown

While the Umbras were weaving their sinister scheme, Huringo stood at the edge of an eerily still garden, reminiscent of the one in the Shell Valley owned by Solarades, in a realm where time and space melded together. He focused his attention on the lifeless stream, searching for any sign of movement—a fish, ripples, even a reflection of himself—yet found nothing. The air surrounding him was heavy and stagnant, devoid of any scent or freshness from the woods, grass, or flowers, contrasting sharply with where he had once resided.

Clenching his fists, he reflected on his past actions. He harboured no regrets, but he loathed his own inadequacy. Despite borrowing power from Solarades, it hadn't been enough to defeat his brother. He no longer aspired to the throne or to rule as the ultimate authority; there was only one thing he genuinely yearned for. And now, he found himself grappling with how far he still needed to go to fulfil that desire.

"Damn it," he muttered, frustration seeping through his words. "Huricane... Father..."

He made his way back to the greenhouse, where Solarades sat at ease, savouring a cup of tea. The older man's countenance showcased the traces of age, pain, and countless tribulations, but those marks might simply be tricky cover-ups. Huringo had never asked about the real motive behind Solarades's betrayal against the Auras, yet they had come such a long way together that it seemed inappropriate or useless to question their accomplice.

"I have to get out of here," Huringo demanded. "We're just wasting our time."

Solarades was well aware of the impatience that characterised the young man he had saved twice. He intentionally finished the cup of tea, studied Huringo for a moment before replying. "If you're ready, you can go anytime."

"I know what you're implying. I'm not qualified... I haven't done enough to strengthen myself," Huringo confessed. "But I've already reached my limit."

"Then kill me and take it, my power," Solarades suggested nonchalantly, as if discussing the weather. "It would be all yours. It's just a matter of time."

Huringo shook his head vehemently. "You know I can't do that. You… saved me. I still need you to fight by my side. The Auras are pursuing us, and we are outnumbered."

Setting his cup down, Solarades sighed, "Look at you. The Huringo I knew would stop at nothing to obtain the power he required, no matter how insurmountable the task."

"I want you to understand that I am someone who honours my oath. I won't hurt you to obtain your power."

"But what about your father? Aren't you causing pain and suffering to him by pursuing your own desires all this time?"

"That's different!" The young man momentarily lost his temper, but he quickly regained control, recognising that Solarades might have uncovered his one and only vulnerability —the most delicate part of his heart. "Hurting my father is the only way to achieve the ending we both desire."

"It's the ending only you desire, young man. Speaking of power, may I ask you a question? What is the strongest power in your mind?" Solarades continued, "Oh, wait, I do have an answer for you. Many will say love or hatred. While I admit that love brings forth both destructive and constructive outcomes, and hatred makes one hesitant, confused, fearful, unfortunately, both of them hinder the progression of the universe. To me, it is to be devoid of emotions: not to love, not to hate. Only then can I make the most accurate judgments, avoid committing foolish mistakes, never miss any details in the big picture."

After digesting Solarades's long speech, one burning question stung Huringo's rarely weakened heart. "How can I possibly let go of love and hatred when they have been the driving forces of my entire life?

Solarades smiled, and the cup on the tea table burst into mere bubbles. "You're still young, Huringo. You have yet to experience life without those burdens."

"If I have the chance to live long enough to experience that life you talked about."

"We will find out very soon."

The bubbles then reassembled, restoring the cup to its original form. Solarades took the cup, had a sip of his new imaginative tea. The illusion baffled Huringo, for it wasn't a power display of Elementro; it was more like he was in a dream sequence belonging to someone else. In dreams, all kinds of illogical stuff might happen.

"If we proceed with our plan, the Auras will have their eye on us." He raised his head to the ceiling of the greenhouse, scanning the surroundings, taking in the pots and plants. He didn't feel comfortable about everything in the area that lacked substance in reality. "Sometimes I just wonder how many hours I still have to live under the sky, by the ocean, and surrounded by the freshness of the air."

"They already have, the Auras," Solarades calmly stated, ignoring Huringo's murmuring about life and death. "The moment of change will come very soon."

12 Aqual, W.D. 471
Somewhere in Timeloss

Before their departure from Timeloss, the Umbras gathered at the behest of their queen, who would soon lead them to the land of fate. Conew and Ganavanda stood among the waves of Umbras, each one with a unique and grotesque appearance. Some were missing eyes, noses, ears, or mouths, while others resembled fearsome beasts. A few had a semblance of humanity, albeit with unnatural skin tones and purple glints in their eyes. Despite their differences, they all shared a common negative energy and a singular purpose—to wreak havoc and destruction across the cosmos.

In this assembly, the elites occupied the best spot to worship their queen, who sat on a throne crafted from crystal shards that extended from the very ground beneath them. The throne was reached by more than twenty steps, which were guarded by six representatives from the six distinctive tribes. Although there was no clear hierarchy among the Umbras, those with the greatest powers naturally rose to prominence—a system not unlike that of the Auras or ordinary beings.

Conew and Ganavanda, being among the ranks of the elites, both bowed their heads in respect, acknowledging the queen's authority. The other Umbras followed suit, silently pledging their allegiance to their enigmatic ruler.

"Rise," commanded the queen, and not a single Umbra dared to defy her order.

"Long live My Queen!" the queen's army roared in unison, their twisted faces contorted with glee. Only then did some of them dare to observe their queen's porcelain features, shadowed by a white hood that revealed only the curve of a slight smile. Her silvery hair was neatly tucked within, and her white dress with black underlying shades shimmered as she crossed her legs and arms upon the crystal throne.

"My loyal dukes and priests." The queen's voice was exceptionally soft, a melody that belied the darkness. "The time has come for us to claim what is rightfully ours. The shield of Wings of Moonlight is at its weakest, and we must seize this opportunity to harvest the riches from The Pioneer."

Conew opened her mouth to speak, but Ganavanda cut her off with a wicked grin, baring his spiky teeth. "Let me serve you and lead the way, My Queen. I know the shortcut to Paralloy so tragically opened by our dearest Zagatan, who will never join us in our triumph."

Irritated, Conew's squinted at Ganavanda, her anger barely contained. She understood that showing too much on her face could be lethal in the presence of the queen, but the sting of having her thunder stolen was difficult to ignore.

"Very well," the queen continued, her eyes sweeping over the gathered Umbras. "I require each of you to swear your allegiance to me, to fight for me, die for me, and strive to reclaim the glory days of the Umbras!"

"Long live My Queen!"

As the echoes of their loyalty faded, the queen held her subjects in thrall with her bewitching presence. Storms of ambition, lust for power, and perhaps even darker secrets raged within her eyes. However, amidst this sea of monstrosity, she seemed oddly out of place in her contrasting white attire.

"Let it be known," she declared, her voice rising to a crescendo. "We shall not rest until the universe is ours to command! Know that you are all my capable soldiers, together, this will be…"

Tension filled the air as the queen trailed off, her eyes shut tight, her voice faltering as if something deep within her was struggling to break free. Conew and Ganavanda both worried about the unforeseen changes that might occur if the queen's inner struggle disrupted their plans. However, they held slightly different concerns. Conew feared the queen's position would be shaken, while Ganavanda questioned if it was the right time for the Umbras to take action.

The assembled Umbras waited with bated breath, their anticipation growing heavier by the second. After what felt like an eternity, the queen stood tall, her eyes shining with renewed vigour. "We will depart when we are all ready," she declared, her voice now ringing with the authority that had been momentarily lost.

"My Queen! Victory! The Umbras! Conquer!"

"If any of you harbour doubts." Her dark purple eyes glanced over Conew and Ganavanda, as if she had seen through their capriciousness. "There will be only one outcome—death—either by being killed by your enemies or by your master—me."

CHAPTER 30

SACRIFICE IS THE GREATEST EXPRESSION OF LOVE

13 Aqual, W.D. 471
Teddix Castle, Teddix

Left exposed to the sunlight for two consecutive mornings, every pot of Icrings in the garden wilted, their petals turning into dust that flew away aimlessly. Their remaining parts resembled corpses after a tragic war, dumped on the battlefield. This sight served as a reflection of the current state of the castle and the kingdom itself. After enduring countless wars that the Teddixians had once cherished, they found themselves in a brief period of peace. However, now they were plagued by unpredictability, unsure of where fate would lead them next.

Teddix City was unusually quiet today, as if time itself had come to a standstill. Farmers wept before their abandoned fields, traders closed their shops that might never reopen, and children clutched their toys as anxious parents hurriedly led them along. Following the 'Evening Star' protocol, everyone in Teddix Castle, Teddix City, and the soldiers from the barracks on the Kuna Plains began their reluctant exodus towards the cities of Kilidaci. None knew if they would ever return to the land they once called home, and doubts lingered about finding a sense of belonging under the shelter of another.

As he stood behind the large glass window on the castle's third floor, Huricane placed his hands on the cold surface, absorbing the sight of his people leaving behind everything they held dear. He could still hear the powerful chant echoing in his mind:

"The Stars of Teddix never set!

Despite numerous warnings, the king stubbornly insisted on staying in the castle. Even the troublesome nobles in the royal assembly offered their rare but unwavering support to the king, declaring that they would await his arrival, ready to restore the kingdom's glory under his rule. Nevertheless, Paralloy Teddix had lost the backing of the aliens, and the one person who had always shown the greatest support for the king was absent.

With these thoughts stirring in his mind, tears finally spilled down Huricane's cheeks. He was drowning in a sea of loneliness. He couldn't bring himself to turn and face the six flags of the Stars of Teddix that hung behind him, for the symbolism of the flags would only crush him. He feared that just one look could cause an instant kill.

As he continued to wallow in his dejection, he heard the familiar sound of high heels clicking. Wyach, who had been by his father's side and now stood by his, approached. Huricane's soul, deep in the abyss, momentarily found a brief moment of calm in the rhythmic tapping, pulling him away from his woe. When the clicking stopped, however, the darkness within him swelled once more.

"My King, everyone has evacuated," Wyach stated, her weary eyes fixed on the solitary figure before her. "A total of 5058 Teddixians are migrating to the three cities in Kilidaci, and Teddowa City is prepared to receive households in case Kilidaci becomes saturated."

"Uh-huh," Huricane responded, not turning to face her. He could see her blurred reflection in the glass, but his shame and fear kept his gaze trained on the city beyond.

"Are you wishing to remain—"

"I won't leave, Wyach."

"I'm not asking you to leave," Wyach stressed, her tone both firm and gentle. "I know you won't abandon the castle. I simply wanted to know if you'd like to stay here or go back to your suite. Lady Huala and Lord Zaewa will take care of the arrangements in Kilidaci while you are absent. You don't have to worry too much about the procedures. I believe they can handle it with great care. And please know that I'll be here with you, ready to protect you no matter what happens."

Huricane didn't intend to respond, feeling the ache in his heart, his nose tingling with a sour sensation as he watched and assumed that the last of the soldiers guide the people of Teddix City away from their homes, towards the distant refuge. He couldn't help it—the tears began to flow again. There was no need for Wyach to stop the outpouring, for she understood that the young king needed this release as a lesson in growth. She still had faith in him, believing that he would mend the broken pieces and rise again from this dark place, despite the bleak circumstances they faced.

After a while, the king wiped his tears and asked, his voice trembling, "Where's... my father?"

"Lord Huxtin is on a mission. He left the castle late last night, but I assume he will return tonight."

"And what about Huduson?"

"I haven't seen Huduson around. Perhaps he accompanied the royal family and left the castle with them. I imagine Lady Huala wants her son by her side, after all."

"I've failed them both, haven't I?" Huricane whispered, his self-doubt like a tumour in his brain, attacking his confidence. "I couldn't keep my promise to be a good king for Paralloy Teddix. I said something terrible to Huduson yesterday, and he disapproved of me... I'm such a loser..."

"Huduson spoke the truth—about your struggles, yes—but he never doubted you. He believed you were a great king. He looked up to you. And I share that belief. I wouldn't lie about it because I know how difficult it is to sit on this throne, in this kingdom whose fate is often uncertain and faces endless challenges. Only someone like you or Lord Huxtin has the strength to overcome them." Wyach paused, taking a deep breath and recalling a memory from the past, then asked, "Do you know why your father chose you over Huringo to be the king of us?"

The king shook his head slightly. "It was either Huringo or me," he admitted, still gazing out the window, secretly observing Wyach's expression. "Wasn't it because Huringo did something terrible to the Silensers, causing him to lose his qualification as the firstborn?"

"It wasn't because your father lacked faith in your brother that he chose an alternative candidate he had never previously considered. You were never a secondary option in your father's eyes. You were always his first choice. It was something you said when you were a child."

"What did I say? I don't really remember."

"Your father asked both of you if you ever wanted to be the king of a new kingdom when all the cities in Paralloy would be unified one day. Your brother said yes, but only because he wanted to prove to your father that he was capable of ruling and expanding the kingdom for the glory of the royal bloodline. He sought praise for his achievements, from Lord Huxtin. But you said something different," Wyach reminisced, her voice growing softer as she recalled the innocence and purity of the children of Huxtin in days gone by. "You told your father that you weren't sure if you wanted to be king. But if you were, it would be to protect everyone in this kingdom because you loved them."

The body of the boy who lived in this castle for sixteen years tensed as the memory flooded back—the two little boys standing before their father, in the same spot where he stood now, their answers reflecting their true desires. He remembered his father's rare smile, warm and proud, but that intimacy felt distant after all these traumatising years.

"My King," Wyach continued, "you were chosen for your love and devotion. The royal family's opinion of Huringo was simply a tradition that your father couldn't ignore. Lord Huxtin loved both of you, but you are the only one he—"

"Stop it! Don't say it any more... I can't bear it... I just can't take it!" As more tears streamed down his face, Huricane's voice became barely more than a choked whisper. Not a single word could empower him with the courage he had momentarily lost; instead, each word only intensified his pain. When he imagined the destruction and suffering that would befall the kingdom due to his failure, the crack in his heart widened even further.

In the quiet moments that followed, with only the sound of wailing filling the air, Wyach pondered the chain of events that had led them to this point. If Huringo hadn't acted foolishly, if Huxtin hadn't succumbed to the darkness within him, if Huricane had been nurtured as the true successor to the throne from the beginning, perhaps the fate of them and the kingdom would be different. She tried to find someone or something to blame, but the truth eluded her—a complex web of actions and reactions that defied easy understanding.

13 Aqual, W.D. 471
T.P.S.E. Command Centre, Teddix

With each light within the commander's tower flickering back to life, Lokiata Kee witnessed a scene vastly transformed from when he first arrived. All vital equipment had been salvaged, leaving behind only non-essential and immovable items. Fortunately, the Earthlings hadn't managed to sever every source of electricity, allowing Kee to carry out his crucial mission.

"This should work," he remarked, surveying one of the intact devices with a monitor. He turned to Kayley Mien, who appeared more spirited than before. "I believe we can still establish a connection to the system through this device?"

Mien came by slowly and took a seat in front of the device, her fingers still somewhat stiff and lacking confidence, but she gradually regained the familiarity with operating the equipment. Her fingers then freely navigated the keyboard as data scrolled across the black screen in green text. Suddenly, a line of red text halted her progress.

"Access denied," she calmly informed Kee, glancing back at him. "The password has been altered."

Surprisingly, Kee remained calm compared to Mien. He instructed her to move aside, and after entering a series of codes bypassing the system's security measures, he let out a breath. After a brief moment of loading, the red text vanished, granting Mien the clearance to proceed with her tasks.

"You... know how to do this?" Mien asked, taken aback by Kee's proficiency.

"You have no idea how extensively I contributed to the development of the military." Kee placed a hand on the monitor frame as he quietly spoke to himself, "I never thought I would have the chance to use these coding sets again... And this system... Lokiata Edward didn't abandon Protocol 1W... Well, I suppose it's just his way, isn't it?"

Mien continued entering various data on the keyboard,

aiming to gain remote control of a system located outside the command centre. It was only today that she learned about the extermination protocol, a truth revealed by Kee, and she finally realised that the explosion that occurred years ago in Bagoland wasn't solely the result of an assault by a mysterious power on Celestiloo, but also the arrogance and ignorance of her own kind's higher power.

"I'm sorry. You could have left with the rest of your fellows," Kee sighed, observing Mien's focused expression with a sunken heart. "I know it may be overwhelming for you, to manipulate the life and death of someone else, especially after our conversation yesterday, but... Ahh, why am I doing this?"

"I don't really care anymore." Mien's response stunned Kee. "And it turns out, it's not such a bad thing to be a partner in crime with a Cosmo Scavenger like you."

"Gathiv, if you are one of us," Kee responded, a faint smile gracing his lips. However, as thoughts of their game-changing actions occupied his mind, a sudden chill coursed down his spine. "I really hope we're doing the right thing."

As they conversed, the device's screen displayed three names from left to right: Hanmuk, Noira, and Yeesin, respectively. Above the first two names, there were two filled red squares, while above the third name, there was no word or symbol.

"I'm in," Mien announced, turning to Kee. "The doors of the transport docks have been locked by a hidden program, as suspected." She then looked away, fully conscious of the identity responsible for the manipulated scenario.

"Alright... Thank you, Mien." Kee slipped an earpiece onto his right ear. "I will take it from here."

"Are you sure... we shouldn't unlock the doors for them right away?" Mien seemed skeptical, though she still placed her trust in the decisions from the man she had newly acquainted with.

And Kee remained resolute in his certainty. "No, not yet. We must wait. We are exploring several possibilities, and fate will soon reveal what we need to do next."

13 Aqual, W.D. 471
Kuna Plains

"Access denied!"

For the thirteenth time of trying, the Earthlings still had no way to open the doors to their transport docks. Mark Carlo, along with his entire team of T.P.S.E, stood on the Kuna Plains, eagerly waiting to board and move all their equipment, resources, and secrets back onto the carriers that had brought them to Celestiloo in the first place.

These specially designed models, built exclusively for T.P.S.E., had triumphed over the vastness of the universe, surpassing the Earthlings' previous belief that such intergalactic journeys were insurmountable. Carlo vividly recalled his initial unease upon setting foot on this alien planet, apprehensive that man-eating beasts, poisonous flora, or otherworldly creatures would emerge from every corner. Eventually, he discovered that there were humans who bore a striking resemblance to the Earthlings, as if they were kindred brothers and sisters. One had received an education in advanced technology, while the other dwelled in seclusion, intimately connected with nature.

He thought the Earthlings and the Teddixians would be able to coexist peacefully. He had truly dreamt about it, but over time, the truth was gradually unveiled—Earthlings simply couldn't live peacefully on Celestiloo.

"Access denied!"

"For the damn fourteenth time!" Carlo let his frustration loose. "We can't waste any more time on this trivial matter! One more time, and we'll have to blow the doors open!"

Sheung Oren, standing nearby with a cold gaze, couldn't help but mock her impetuous superior and former lover. "Mark Carlo, what's wrong with you?" she questioned. "You know the material those doors are made of, right? How do you plan to blow them open?"

"Then what do you suggest we do?" Carlo stopped, sensing that he had overreacted a bit, reminding himself that he couldn't speak to Oren in such a manner. "We need to leave as soon as possible. It's not safe for us to stay here any longer. This kingdom is an inferno."

"You are such a coward," Oren insulted Carlo once again.

Unable to bear the accusations this time, Carlo snapped, "This isn't cowardice, Oren!"

"If that's the case, then why did you run away?"

"We will die if we don't leave Paralloy Teddix! Don't fight for those people. Fight for us! Fight for anything else, go to somewhere we were meant to be! You saw what happened to the castle yesterday. That place was cursed... That place will be doomed! And we Earthlings were not meant to be the burial goods of the Teddixians! And that's why you're standing here, right in front of me, isn't it? You do want to leave with me, don't you? Tell me, Oren!"

Carlo's thoughts were a jumble of work and personal matters, unable to focus. He hadn't figured out the next step, but he couldn't stop pondering his ex-wife's willingness. Noticing her teary eyes, he felt that perhaps there was still a chance to rekindle the dying flames between them.

"Oren, you know what I want," he pleaded, gripping both of her hands, and this time, there was no resistance, giving him a final glimmer of hope.

"What do you want?"

"Come with me... We can start over, and I won't let go. I promise!"

However, Carlo had misinterpreted the complex intention behind Oren's question, and in his eagerness, he failed to provide the correct answer that might have had a slim chance of changing her mind.

"Stop dwelling on it," Oren stated, her voice as cold as the first snow of winter, and speaking of the season, reminding her of the very first date she had with Carlo, when their warmth was capable of withstanding frigidity. She didn't shake off Carlo's hands, but her words were clear. "I won't go with you. Just... give up, Carlo, give up on me."

His hopeful plea fell upon deaf ears as her expression shifted. At last, he released her hands voluntarily. He immediately dampened his once fervent passion, though he still refused to admit an official end to their relationship. He never understood how to cater to her needs, and now he was even more at a loss. Both of them were simply exhausted from the ongoing battle of love and hatred.

"Tell me you love me, Oren," Carlo pleaded, longing to hear the truth before everything turned even more bitter. Still, Oren stayed silent, unable to utter a word. The urgent calls of the other soldiers compelled Carlo to divert his attention and attend to the pressing matters at hand. Reluctantly, he acknowledged that he had no option but to go back to his duties.

"I still have time to hear you answer," he said before he turned away. "Please, make the right choice."

13 Aqual, W.D. 471
Nugloo Mounting, Teddix

Although Huxtin had initially refused to let Mu Mann accompany him to the final confrontation against Mateek, the nature of the task required him to bring someone who could assist in retrieving a treasure from Mateek's Starfall Tomb. Huxtin had originally intended to bring Lokiata Kee, but Mann insisted that she was the best candidate, leaving him with no choice but to allow her to come along.

Rejuvenated from her sorrows, Mann radiated an exceptional spirit. Having liberated herself from previous obligations in T.P.S.E., she had also severed ties with her own people. It was her clear decision to continue her adventure on Celestiloo and assist Huxtin in his goal: to collect all twelve Star Souls and seal the existence of the Umbras, if that was still Huxtin's main objective.

On their journey to their destination, they found themselves at the base of a large, isolated grassy hill known as Nugloo Mounting. This hill, situated at the southern end of the vast grassland on the south side of Teddix, remained shrouded in mystery. Even Huxtin had overlooked it and had never ventured to its summit. Despite previous attempts by Earthlings to search for resources in the area, nothing of value had been found. However, it was precisely the location that Huxtin had discovered through the memories trapped within Poet's soul, which he obtained by taking her life. Recalling the events of yesterday night, Huxtin still felt a slight unease, causing his grip on the Revenging Shard to tighten while his other hand trembled.

As Huxtin's earpiece beeped in the gentle breeze, he glanced at Mann before answering, his face a mask of focus. "Is everything set?"

Unintentionally overhearing the conversation, Mann assumed that Huxtin was talking to Sheung Oren, as usual. She didn't want to waste her energy on navigating their strained relationship and pondered whether Oren would accompany the rest of the army or choose to stay in Paralloy Teddix. If Oren chose to stay, she assumed that the primary reason might be the man standing before her.

"Alright. Stick to the plan."

"So, what about Sheung Oren's situation?"

"It's not her."

"Huh? Then who were you talking to?"

"Lokiata Kee."

"Uncle Kee? Why?" Mann demanded, her instincts itching with unease. "What's going on?"

"I offered him an important job," Huxtin replied, avoiding her eyes. "You don't need to know the details."

Mann frowned, disappointment creeping in, but an instinctive impulse urged her to remain silent and refrain from speaking up. "I'm not interested," she lied. "I just know it's another secret of yours."

As they continued their climb, Huxtin suddenly halted, his back rigid as he stared into the distance. Without turning around, he spoke, his voice heavy with a thousand of worries, "I need to talk about... what I did to Poet."

"Listen," Mann interjected quickly, her heart racing, "we've already discussed this. You were out of control, and I won't hold it against you."

Huxtin's shoulders tensed. "But what if I wasn't out of control? What if I truly wanted to hurt her, to kill her, and I was just... following my heart?"

"Shut up," Mann whispered to him, her vision focusing on the familiar black cloak and the gleaming silver-white sword, once possessed by his son. What she saw was a valiant and righteous warrior, one who consistently endeavoured to vanquish darkness with scared illumination, rather than a monster revelling in slaughter and mindless destruction.

"Thank you... for believing in me," Huxtin murmured, before resuming his stride.

"Again and again," Mann sighed, yet overjoyed by the comment replaying in her mind. "Are you tired of saying that?"

As they climbed higher, the wind grew colder. Reaching the

summit of the hill, which stood 200 meters above the ground, they were greeted by a relatively circular peak adorned with a lush carpet of vibrant green grass. Positioning himself in the central area of the mountaintop, Huxtin extended his left hand and channeled his Elementro energy. The silvery light on the ground in front of them traced dotted lines that spiralled outward, and as the last of the glowing tendrils connected, the grass and soil within the circle disintegrated into pure Elementro particles, instantly revealing a gaping hole about five meters in diameter.

Mu Mann approached the edge cautiously, peering down into the abyss below. "Another bottomless pit," she grumbled. "Who the hell designed all these terrible facilities, and how is anyone supposed to get down there?"

"Exactly," Huxtin replied. "The builders never intended for these places to be accessed by others."

Mann bit her lip, embarrassed by her outburst. "Umm, okay. I guess you have a point." She looked closely at Huxtin, curiosity piqued. "But how were you able to open this entrance so easily?"

"It's just a simple lock, designed using mind Elementro particles," he explained. "It's similar to the door that opened for you last night. I mean, that door leading to the Temple of Moon Shadow."

"Wait, what door?" Her heart fluttered at the mention of the temple, her eyes darting between him and the abyss. "Oh, you mean that door from before? It wasn't yesterday."

His eyes narrowed slightly. "But you were in the deeper part of the Shell Valley last night."

Pretending ignorance, she quickly replied, "I don't know what you're talking about. Besides, I was there because I was looking for you, believe it or not. I just happened to run into Tunpatter on the way. Nothing special about that."

Confused, he stared at her for a moment, his wooden expression betraying nothing, and a cool breeze stirred the grass around them. Finally, he said in a frivolous tone, "Never mind."

He chose not to reveal his secret: that he had used Elementro power to link the door in question to Mann's soul, ensuring it would automatically open for her whenever she was near the Temple of Moon Shadow. He knew she had entered the temple, and he knew why she had done it. But he didn't want her to admit it just yet because those words he wanted her to read would be even more meaningful later, when the time was right.

Soon, they were inside the cylindrical pit, surrounded by walls adorned with occasional peculiar and cryptic glyphs and inscriptions. These strokes and symbols were unlike anything from Celestiloo, Earth, or any known Auras or Umbras, nor did they resemble any variations of the sacred marking. Mu Mann quickly noticed that the surrounding wall was made of metal, which had a distinct smell she wasn't quite familiar with, but had some prior knowledge of.

Thanks to cleverly structured anti-gravity layers inside the area, they could descend slowly without the need for any additional tools or forces. Under their feet, a deep shadow loomed, and although Huxtin assured Mann that it was absolutely safe, it didn't prevent her from imagining the possibility of an accidental free fall. For a split second, her body and mind felt as if they were separated in time.

"Tell me more about Teddix Castle," she said, making an effort to divert her attention from constantly looking down at the lone path ahead of them. She retrieved a small glass bottle from her tool pocket, attached to her waist. The bottle was filled with a metallic substance of intertwining shades of purple and silver, its concentration exceptionally high. It appeared as both a solid and a liquid at the same time. This tiny bottle contained a mystical compound capable of transforming into countless magical forms—Magic Mirror of Mateek.

"I understand that it's the most significant legacy of the Teddix Empire, and I'm aware that it serves as the heart of Celestiloo. Correct me if I'm mistaken, but I've heard about it from, well, Miria," she continued, her voice brimming with her usual curiosity. "You nearly killed yourself to protect it from Silverlight Overflow. Remember? What would happen if it were to truly collapse and crumble? What would be the consequences?"

As far as she understood, Teddix Castle had been hailed as a fortress crafted by celestial beings, and it mightn't be merely a legend. She recalled the earlier conversation they had before arriving at Nugloo Mounting, during which Huxtin mentioned that behind its exquisite craftsmanship lay a dark history closely related to the Children of God. The castle was actually aligned with the positions of the twelve Starfall Tombs, which served as the original dwelling places of the resting souls.

"Teddix Castle is no ordinary stone and rock structure," Huxtin further explained. "Its outward appearance is merely a disguise, concealing the hidden metal within."

"Magic Mirror—the metal that even we Earthlings cannot detect..." Mann grasped the truth, looking at the mysterious blend of Elementro in her hand, realising its world-altering potential. "How fascinating it is..."

"You have to understand that Teddix Castle was actually constructed by Mateek. It was built in conjunction with Silverlight Overflow. While that gigantic battleship served as the vessel to transport the Auras to their new habitat, the castle, often referred to as the Throne of Immortality, stood as a symbol for heroes, kings, or any group of individuals who chose to remain on Celestiloo and take the oath to protect the planet, regardless of the circumstances.

No, there wouldn't be any actual consequences even if the castle was destroyed, and even if Silverlight Overflow did crash into it, there wouldn't be any magical devastation inflicted upon the planet. But both the castle and the battleship could never regain their original structures, instead transforming into something else that nobody can predict... except maybe Mateek himself."

Mann concluded based on her knowledge and belief, "So, you wanted to protect the legacy. You wanted the people in Teddix, or even the entire Celestiloo, to remain hopeful about their future?"

With a gentle tone, Huxtin replied, "Protecting only the castle would be meaningless if the king wasn't inside of it."

"The Stars of Teddix..."

"I told you. I made an extremely terrible decision, and you wouldn't approve of it."

Huxtin's words carried deep meaning, but Mann was able to fully decipher the intricate complexities of his thoughts. As they drew closer to the bottom, a chilly breeze grew sharper. The cold air trapped in the pit seemed to carry the accumulated resentment of thousands of years. Despite her fears, Mann trusted that Huxtin would protect her in times of danger, and this assurance brought her a sense of serenity, as well as love.

"Wood, you don't have to apologise for it," she said, attempting to comfort him. "I am here to help——"

But he interrupted her, "After learning about what I have done, after knowing about my selfish actions, which I myself cannot fully justify, you still believe that there is goodness within me?"

"If I were in your position, I believe I would have done the same." Her warmth was momentarily overshadowed by unhappy memories that surged forth, causing a sharp pang in her heart. "You've made significant sacrifices to protect someone you love, someone you care about, and I can truly relate to that sentiment."

He didn't respond to her assurance, and as they finally set foot on the ground, a large Binary of Teleportation just stood right before them, ever-present and unchanging.

"We're here. Mateek's Starfall Tomb. I won't let it slip away from me this time."

13 Aqual, W.D. 471
Starfall Tomb of Mateek, Teddix

After being teleported to a spacious, pure white room with an almost cubic shape, resembling the original Waxing Moon but on a much larger scale, Huxtin and Mu Mann found themselves face to face with the illusion of Mateek's upper body emerging from his Star Soul. Mateek had been waiting patiently for a considerable amount of time for the Son of Chaos and his companion to arrive.

"The first trial: to knock me out while we were in mid-air and catch me as we fell—you failed. The second trial: to evade my swords and remain untouched for three minutes—you failed," Mateek stated, scanning Mann with a hint of surprise. He hadn't anticipated that Huxtin would bring not an extraordinary warrior, but rather an apparently ordinary woman to participate in the final trial. "Now, your representative will unlock and retrieve the artefact from the treasure box behind me, while you must ensure her safety... from me. Alternatively, you can defeat me and claim the treasure. Different routes, same target. The choice is yours. No power from any Star Souls shall prevail this time."

"Well, okay, here he is... Mateek, the true form of that Star Soul..." Mann acknowledged, encountering the wielder of metal Elementro for the first time. She took in her surroundings, noticing the distinct purplish crystal treasure box positioned behind the levitating Kousou, clearly out of sync with the overall ambiance. "And that box is my target. I got it."

While Huxtin and Mateek tightened their grips on their swords, their eyes brimmed with an indomitable spirit. The tomb of the Children of God interestingly morphed into a battlefield, but this was no ordinary clash between a man and a god-like being; Huxtin transcended mere humanity, while Mateek was nothing more than a captive soul trapped within a crystal coffin.

"You will acknowledge your defeat and return to your empty

vessel, Mateek," Huxtin's voice resonated with aggression as he declared, and with a swift motion, he cast aside his cloak, revealing his ultimate combat armour, the Starry Fortress, crafted from a rare azure metal called Lost Stars, found in the underwater space of the Reflection of the Stars.

The armour, shining with a mesmerising blend of metallic black and light blue hues, bore a golden dodecagram symbol on its breastplate. Having been worn in numerous pivotal battles during the Parallian Civil War, it stood as the epitome of refinement and durability among the Teddixian military. Huxtin was shielded by two dodecagrams now—one providing physical defence and the other symbolising the eternal love encapsulated within the pendant of his necklace.

"Hmph… You expect me to do nothing within my Star Soul while you delude yourself into escaping a shell that has always trapped you. Is that fair?" In response, Mateek's eyes narrowed into a thin, ominous line, and his voice took on an eerie tone. The gap in his helmet radiated a malevolent energy, as if it could unleash deadly rays, instilling fear in all who beheld it

"I have made my decision, and there shall be no further argument," Huxtin asserted firmly, assuming a resolute stance. "You will not stand in my way."

"Very well, but I don't appreciate your answer." Mateek raised his gleaming indigo longsword above his head. "If you can pierce through my illusion and cleave it in two, you shall emerge victorious!"

"Mann, it's time!"

And Mann braced herself, ready to spring into action. "I'm ready. Let's go!"

The battle commenced, with Huxtin and Mann moving in near synchronicity, displaying a relentless pursuit akin to that of a pair of predatory beasts. One focused on defence, while the other aimed for the coveted treasure, but she had to match his pace and aggression, even if she lacked his physical strength. She had to persevere.

Charging forward together towards the left, they passed by Mateek. Huxtin swiftly pivoted to intercept Mateek's sword strike. Although the Children of God and his weapon appeared formidable in size, the illusion of a Star Soul was merely a convergence of Elementro particles, and thus, leaving the strength between the adversaries evenly matched.

"You bring along a defenceless human woman for your trial." Mateek looked back at Mann who had already reached the crystal treasure box, exerting even greater power onto his longsword. "You will regret it… when she dies before your eyes!"

Hearing this, Huxtin's irritation flared. He skilfully slid his sword aside, generating sparks from the friction and causing Mateek to momentarily lose balance. Seizing the opportunity, he aimed for Mateek's heart, but a colossal left hand loomed, ready to sweep him away, making him no choice but to step back.

"I'm not going to repeat your failure!" he exclaimed, and he charged forward again, striking Mateek's longsword and shattering it into a cloud of particles

"You'll see!" Mateek roared. "What a fool you are!"

The shattered blade had been Mateek's true intention all along. The cloud of Elementro particles instantly divided into two equal portions, reforming into two weapons that matched the original in size and volume. One weapon remained in the illusion's grasp, while the other hurtled towards Mann. The speed was astonishing, causing a flicker of fear to briefly cross Huxtin's typically composed face.

On the other side, with no apparent lock mechanism on the treasure box, Mann pondered how to unlock it. She rummaged through her tool pocket, retrieving a screwdriver, large nails, and a small hammer. As she caught glimpses of the ongoing battle through the crystal's reflective surface, she was aware of the imminent danger. Her eyes darted around, beads of sweat trickling down her forehead and back. However, she warned herself not to panic, knowing that she held the solution in her hands. She then bravely turned around, removed the stopper from the glass bottle, and simply poured the solid-liquid compound into the air.

Magic Mirror of Mateek, a fusion of metal and crystal, contained Elementro particles that retained the memory of their position within a structure. If the overall structure was destroyed, these particles, in the form of silvery beads, could immediately restore the original form and shape. The Earthlings' final scientific research in Paralloy Teddix had resulted in a breakthrough—a prototype that harnessed the creation of the Children of God in a novel manner: a retractable metal shield, which had also been utilised in the recent battle between the Hokan and Mateek a few days earlier.

As the spilled compound dispersed, it rapidly solidified, transforming into an umbrella-shaped shield firmly rooted in the ground. While the experimental product possessed a relatively fragile structure, it proved sufficient to halt the onslaught of Mateek, who had pledged not to harm his own creation. The longsword came to an abrupt stop before the shield, its forward momentum halted, and it flew back into the grasp of its owner.

Humanity had begun to unlock powers that were once thought to be the realm of mythical figures. This was merely the dawn of a new era.

"Human... I granted you the potential to develop your knowledge of my expertise, but you should never wield it as a threat against me! Do you think I won't dare to shatter it?" Mateek erupted in anger, his Magic Mirror both a source of pride and an indelible stain on his life.

"Will you?" Huxtin seized upon the weakness of Mateek, advancing with forcefulness. "Will you break the promise you made with Kristalanna?"

Enraged, Mateek swung both longswords with full force, each strike imbued with infuriation. Huxtin successfully blocked every attack, prompting Mateek to escalate the ferocity. He divided each longsword into four, and then those four into eight, as all eight replicas charged uncontrollably towards their target. Their movements were disorderly and erratic, reflecting the turbulent state of their wielder's mind, making the situation exceedingly challenging for Huxtin in this battle.

Soon, the number of longswords multiplied from eight to sixteen under the control of the Children of God. However agile Huxtin was, he could barely evade the indiscriminately launched blades, narrowly avoiding them coming mere inches from his head. It was then that Huxtin decided to abandon blocking and instead utilised his opponent's weapons as stepping stones. With precision and skill, he hopped and steppcd on the longswords one by one, ascending to the highest point. Extending both hands, he held the Revenging Shard at its very tip, assuming a posture akin to a parachutist descending, prepared to land a perfect strike on Mateek's helmet.

Simultaneously, his attention was drawn to Mann, who was struggling to unlock the treasure box. This momentary distraction caused his strike to deviate from its intended target, missing the helmet but sliding the sword from the left cheekbone to the throat. As the sword shattered Mateek's clavicle and penetrated his chest cavity, its trajectory was deflected by a massive hand, suspending Huxtin mid-air.

"Tsk!" With his hands still tightly gripping the sword hilt, Huxtin raised his head to glare at the crumbling armour of the giant. "I don't think it counted, right?"

Mateek yanked the sword out from beneath his sternum. "Try harder!" he exclaimed, flinging away the Revenging Shard and Huxtin, causing the royal armour to collide with the ceiling, creating a thunderous noise. Unbeknownst to him, it was only the armour boots that made contact with the ceiling.

"I'm trying!" Huxtin pushed back with force, his face now slightly distorted, revealing the underlying beastly nature hidden within his human form. The sword impaled Mateek's heart, driving both the floating Kousou and the illusion emerging from it against the wall, right next to Mann and the treasure box.

"It's you, the Son of Chaos!" Mateek shouted, thrusting Huxtin back towards the centre of the room. Around them, thirty-two longswords now revolved as if they were the central axis of the universe. "By refusing to accept your fate, by rejecting the choice between 'Good Deeds' and 'Bad Deeds,' you have plunged the universe into a state of true and absolute nightmare. You bring forth the most dreadful punishment upon all life!"

Huxtin extracted his sword and landed gracefully on the ground, observing that the fractures on the illusion had once again sealed shut. Then, his gaze shifted to Mann, who was using a sharp file, searching for the weakest point on the treasure box. She had forsaken her ordinary life for him, and he desired nothing more than to see her embrace a happier future alongside someone better than himself. Thinking of this, he heard the sound of his heart breaking, stupidly wondering why he still felt the pain of it even though he had already made up his mind.

Redirecting his focus to the Children of God, he declared, "I won't reiterate the words I've spoken in the past. Simply surrender and become my captive!"

As their steely eyes locked, a surge of desire welled up within Mateek's heart, urging him to defeat Huxtin and intensifying the energy of Elementro he channeled. When had he last willingly expended such a massive amount of Elementro energy? It came back to him—in a duel with Flammando, he had triumphed in the fight, but he had also destroyed the woman he loved with his own hands. The crystals exploded, the purple jewel turned to smoke, and crystal-clear tears splashed onto the sea of fire, igniting an unforgettable purple afterglow.

Buried deep within his heart for over a hundred thousand days, could he truly abandon the promises of his past? Could he disregard the genuine reasons for why he had fought so hard to earn the love and trust of Kristalanna?

"It worked!"

Finally, the method had proven successful as Mann cracked open the treasure box, fulfilling the task entrusted to her by Huxtin. However, it wasn't time to celebrate just yet. Glancing behind her, she noticed that while her shield remained intact, a stray metallic longsword had impaled a newly constructed transparent wall before the tangible shield, rotating and gradually slowing down until it crashed to the ground with a resounding thud. The transparent wall then fractured, degrading to resemble a milky eggshell before disintegrating into sparkling dust.

"You, the Son of Chaos.... truly willing to sacrifice yourself to save her..." Mateek's thoughts temporarily slowed, leaving him in a state of blankness for a few moments. He couldn't believe that Huxtin, with thirty-two longswords pointed perilously close to his head, had extended his trembling left hand, his face growing rigid and pale, only to place his one and only shield in front of the human woman. At the same time, he felt a deep sense of shame for himself—he did have a plan to break his promise.

He scrutinised the human woman, whom he had initially thought would be nothing more than a victim in this battle. Unsure of her exact emotions at that very moment—whether she was frightened, fearless, or experiencing a myriad of other feelings—he couldn't help but be impressed by this remarkable pair of individuals.

Unaware that the trial had concluded, Mann proceeded to retrieve a sword from the treasure box, an exact duplicate of the one Huxtin was holding, featuring a turbine-like device above the hilt and twelve gems that shimmered with dazzling, magical light. They were crafted as a pair, and when wielded together, they were said to have the ability to slice through water, cleave the air, shake the earth, and ignite flames into the sky.

After a few more moments of silence, all the indigo longswords returned to Mateek's grasp, merging into a single entity, while Mann presented the ultimate award to Huxtin. In the end, Mateek's disposition softened due to Huxtin's actions.

"We need not continue this fight. I have won the duel," he declared, closing his eyes. Unconsciously, memories of everything he had shared with Kristalanna flooded his mind. "However, you have passed the trial. I shall entrust the other half of the Key of Create and Destroy to you. Your fate now rests in your own hands. May you not come to regret it."

The conclusion of the trial brought about an unexpected twist when the Children of God returned to the floating indigo orb, but the mission had finally been accomplished.

"Mann, were you scared?" Huxtin asked softly, now holding two identical swords in his hands.

"You promised I would be safe, so… Okay, I admit, I was a little bit scared," Mann replied, though her greater fear lay in the possibility of losing Huxtin in any form, rather than her own safety. "We now have another Star Soul, and it's time to confront your son and whoever that other person is."

"Yes, the time has come," Huxtin spoke as he quickly turned and started walking away, "but you will not be coming with me. There's no turning back now."

Mann's instinct urged her to reach out and grab Huxtin's hand, but it was too late. They were now only a short distance apart, yet she could only touch a transparent wall—golden when seen from the outside. She also saw two Star Souls circling Huxtin—one silvery, the other golden—and finally realised she was trapped within the same kind of cell that had once imprisoned Poet.

"Huxtin! We agreed to find the remaining Star Souls together, to seal the Umbras together, didn't we? We said we would do it together!" she screamed in terror, her voice echoing and tearing at her throat as she desperately tried to compel Huxtin to return for her. "Damn you! Huxtin! No... this can't be happening... You're not going... You're not... Huxtin!"

In fact, Huxtin was unable to hear anything from the outside. Lost in her own madness, she risked injuring herself as she repeatedly slammed her body against the cell wall. But the wall was constructed from the strongest material—the will and the perseverance of a living being. No matter how much pain her fists endured, she couldn't break through this fortress designed specifically for her.

Huxtin was leaving her. It seemed that everything had been nothing more than a beautiful dream, but she didn't want to wake up from it. She then recalled the times when she had dreamt of Huxtin enveloped in a mysterious dark purple fog. Sometimes, it was a poetic and picturesque sight, while other times, it appeared incomprehensible, like a riddle. Peering through the fog, and radiance, she often found herself trapped in interconnected mazes without any exit or entrance, watching innumerable stars in the sky with a big scar slip away, beautiful yet unattainable.

Before departing from the tomb from the permanent Binary of Teleportation, Huxtin commanded his newly acquired servant, "Mateek, protect her for me with all means."

The Children of God wouldn't argue, for he was now bound

by the orders of the Son of Chaos. With the pair of the Key of Create and Destroy in his possession, no Star Soul could hinder Huxtin from achieving his goal any longer, and Mann was no exception.

CHAPTER 31

LOVE IS THE GREATEST EXPRESSION OF SELFISHNESS

13 Aqual, W.D. 471
Shell Valley

The wooden house creaked and groaned amidst the Shell Valley's whispering winds, while the Auras huddled around the table, the remnants of numerous burnt-out candles scattered about. Shards of light created by Remezo now illuminated the room, as he had already recovered from the incident the previous night. After witnessing Huxtin's power firsthand, they collectively decided that, though not unanimously agreed upon, the best approach to dealing with the Son of Chaos was through communication rather than physical confrontation.

Their senior, Rafaelzo, found his thoughts drifting to his history with Solarades. The once admired warrior, part of the revered Trinity of Twelfianity, had been a force to be reckoned with, harnessing his unique Elementro power like no other among their ranks. Despite Rafaelzo's higher social standing, Solarades, Novaubri, and Lunarcaria were considered the strongest Auras in the past.

Sadly, the Trinity of Twelfianity had since fractured; one dead, another betraying the Auras, and the last exerting pressure on their people's development.

Solarades then observed Gloria, who appeared preoccupied as she sat across from him. "Can you still continue with our mission, Gloria?" he asked. "If you can't, just let me know."

Gloria's eyes darkened like thunderstorm clouds about to unleash their fury, barely containing her desperation. "I'm in this until the end."

Rafaelzo comprehended that revealing the truth about Miria would only cause Gloria more anguish, and he firmly believed that it wasn't the appropriate time to broach the subject concerning her sister. He had deduced what had happened to Miria, and it was a nightmare not only for the Auras but for everyone on Celestiloo. If they couldn't resolve the impending challenges in time, the fate of all would be like the melted wax pooling at the base of those lifeless candles before them.

"Excellent then," Rafaelzo pretended, forcing a weary smile, though he secretly wished for Gloria to quit the mission for the greater good. He couldn't afford to let any conflict tear them apart, especially when they were so close to either victory or defeat.

Beside him, Jeremia questioned, "Why haven't the enemies made their appearance yet? We've been waiting for what feels like an eternity."

"What would your eternity be like? I thought you had lived long enough to disregard the notion of eternity," Remezo admonished him from across the table. "Just be patient. Grumbling won't make them appear any faster."

"Ahh, so what will?" Jeremia retorted with a smirk.

Closing his eyes, Remezo took a deep breath. "If there's a way to sew your mouth shut," he muttered.

"Remezo, Jeremia." Their chief elder's firm tone cut through their bickering, silencing them like a knife. "We are the Auras, not the Umbras. We must maintain peace and unity among ourselves."

Upon hearing that statement, Gloria briefly squinted at Rafaelzo. It was as if her gaze conveyed the truth she clung to regarding the Auras. They weren't actually beings who believed in peace and unity. They had abandoned every human on Celestiloo and Earth, and they aggressively hunted down the Fallens. Both species were originally their families, friends, as well as lovers.

"I just hope we can reunite with Anari and Sarukan very soon. We have been on Celestiloo for quite some time now, yet they are still out of our reach," Rafaelzo continued, redirecting their focus. "By the way, Remezo, when you encountered the Son of Chaos on the Isle of Sealina, you mentioned a human man accompanying him, carrying an artefact resembling a book. Can you provide a more detailed description?"

Remezo nodded, recalling the scene vividly. "The book's cover appeared to be made of a reflective material, like a mirror. Other than that, there was nothing particularly noteworthy about it, but it emitted a strange energy which I couldn't determine whether it was related to Elementro or not."

"A book kept by Sealina..." Rafaelzo murmured. "The Testament of Life and Death.... But why would the Son of Chaos want it?"

He tried to understand the connection between Huxtin and the artefact by replaying in his mind the conversation with Tunpatter, who had suggested the possibility of another realm or even another universe, along with the unknown secrets within Chaos. The Testament of Life and Death, he realised, wasn't crafted by the Auras or the Children of God. Its presence on Celestiloo was nothing more than a myth, akin to the existence of The Creator in the universe. Yet, regardless of its true nature, he firmly believed that all those secrets and truths locked within the myths would be revealed soon.

After a while, a subtle shift occurred in Rafaelzo's mind, as if a severed connection had been restored. He blinked in surprise, even though he had been waiting for this moment for hours.

"Our enemies are now on the move," he announced abruptly, startling the others. "They are moving slowly, but towards the destination I predicted."

Gloria's eyes gleamed with anticipation, and she pressed her hands down on the table as she stood up. "Are you absolutely certain?"

"Very certain," he replied firmly. "There is no mistaking it."

"Then what are we waiting for?" she demanded, her impatience surpassing even that of Jeremia. "We must go immediately and take them down!"

"Stay calm, Gloria. They haven't resurfaced yet," he cautioned, raising a hand to temper her eagerness. "Besides, we need the Son of Chaos to fight alongside us."

"The enemies won't wait for us to stop them committing dreadful acts." Her jaw tightened, but she reluctantly sat back down. "If he doesn't return on time, I say we strike down our enemies regardless."

"Agreed, but there's no harm in us going to a nearby spot to stand by."

As they made preparations to depart, Jeremia stretched his body, his mind consumed by a flurry of questions. Curiosity burned brightly in his eyes. "Chief Elder Rafaelzo, why did

Solarades select that particular location? I thought his goal was to destroy the Throne of Immortality or something more iconic. This seems… random. What are they really planning?"

"I have an idea," Rafaelzo answered with an obvious sense of bother, "but it's only a guess."

"Please go on."

"Perhaps, well, he may want to remind me of a mistake I made a long time ago, one that had significant repercussions for the Auras us and the Earthlings."

13 Aqual, W.D. 471
Starfall Tomb of Mateek, Teddix

Despite being trapped and abandoned, Mu Mann refused to give up hope. She valiantly fought against her negative emotions, determined to find a way out.

"Let me out!" she shouted, uncertain if anyone would hear her cries. "I said, let me out!"

She punched the transparent wall once again, even though she knew she didn't possess the same power as Huxtin or any other powerful being to shatter the cell into fragments.

"Human... can you please be quiet for a moment? Just one moment?"

Mann turned around and noticed that the floating Star Soul of Mateek still emitted a soft indigo light. She found herself irritated by the complaint. Nonetheless, she welcomed the opportunity for conversation. "Well, besides screaming and shouting, what else can I do?" she began, unable to think of a better opening remark.

"Sit down, meditate, and contemplate your life," Mateek coolly responded. "Just... be quiet."

"I need to escape from here. Will you help me?" Mann disregarded the directive from the Children of God. "I have to stop Huxtin from carrying out his foolish plans before it's too late. He must be stopped!"

"I cannot," Mateek simply rejected. "I am currently under the command of the Son of Chaos, and he will not allow me to free you until the appointed time."

"What time?"

"The appointed time. And I will not repeat myself. You must wait."

"No, I can't wait!" Memories of terrifying scenes kept replaying in Mann's mind—the gruesome images, the twisted thoughts, the clash of darkness and light, the unstoppable collapse. Her heart ached, and tears welled up in her eyes as her limbs grew weak. "You don't understand. If I hadn't encountered Huxtin in Bagoland back then... if I hadn't tried to stop him... he... he might have—"

"Do you truly believe you can change his mind?" Mateek quickly interjected, expressing doubt. "The fact is, you didn't prevent him from killing his own son, nor did you prevent him from ending his own life. He is immune to his own power, and if there were a slim chance to make him perish in this universe, it wouldn't be by his own hands. So, tell me again, what is it that you truly believe you stopped him from doing? Nothing! You stopped nothing, and you didn't have any power in here, human."

"You knew what happened in Bagoland... Of course, because you're a Children of God."

"I may not be physically present, but my soul encompasses one-twelfth of the universe. I am forced to overhear a lot, and I have a general understanding of things I'd rather not know."

Perhaps Mateek and Mann shared the same memories, centred around the events that unfolded over four years ago when Huxtin's uncontrollable rage altered the course of the universe. However, Mateek possessed deeper knowledge of the aftermath: the Elementro energies protecting Celestiloo had weakened, and the Umbras resurfaced in Timeloss, a continent on Celestiloo that was particularly vulnerable to evil forces. The darkness had been quietly preparing to rise once more with the assistance of the Fallens, aiming to repeat the tragic history, and this time they might succeed.

Where there was a hint of trouble, there was usually a deeper problem. Huxtin's rebellious son, Huringo, had been designated as a key figure in their plan, and it couldn't be dismissed that he was being manipulated by the Umbras and the Fallens. Mateek had once been used by Huringo, but he didn't stop the evil scheme, feeling that he no longer had the authority and qualification to change anything, considering himself a failed warrior of ancient times.

"The choice between 'Good Deeds' and 'Bad Deeds' cannot be overlooked. If the Son of Chaos refuses to make a choice, driven by his own will, when he encounters illusions, hears clamour, smells death, tastes blood, feels pain, and becomes entangled in the cycle of love and hatred of his past, his stimulated soul will make the decision for the universe, but the Son of Chaos will never regain consciousness or sanity ever again."

While Mateek questioned himself, wondering if he had revealed too much about matters that a human shouldn't know, he couldn't help but divulge more truths—perhaps out of pity for the doomed fate of Huxtin and Mann, or out of shame for himself.

"This is the extent of my knowledge regarding the power of Chaos," he continued. "It may not be entirely accurate, but the Umbras firmly believe in it. They plan to forcefully summon the power of Chaos, manipulating their pawns to gradually push the Son of Chaos into the abyss. By doing so, they hope to overturn the order and create a new era solely under their control.

Human, the Son of Chaos is approaching a critical juncture in his fate. Who will reign, who will perish, who will emerge unscathed, and who will lose their sanity forever—all of it hinges on the final battle between the wielders of the power of Chaos. However, your safety is assured, for now."

"Damn it! He didn't tell me everything! He isn't battling just his inner emotions... He is resisting a predestination..." Mann suddenly realised the interconnectedness between the Bagoland incident, the Battle of Sun and Moon, and the recent attack on Teddix Castle, having a clear idea of the requiem playing out in her mind. She continued to rub her sweaty palms, her fingers clenching into wrinkled folds. "That's why he wants to... He's going to... Mateek, do you know where he is now?"

"Don't do this anymore. You don't have the power," Mateek urged her to stop as he observed her readiness for another attempt. "Don't make a fuss."

"But I want to make a fuss!" Mann's fist collided with the wall, turning red and swollen, yet remaining unbroken and bloodless. Although pain surged through her flesh and bones, she could continue trying; she had to let the godly figure understand that the endurance and perseverance of humans mustn't be underestimated. "I want to escape from here... I want to see that fool... I want to stop him!"

"Why do you insist on staying by his side? He chose to lock you up here precisely because he wants to sever all ties with you. This is the only way."

"The only way for what? For keeping me safe? His thoughts are his own business!" Shrugging her shoulders, wiping the sweat from her body, Mann gritted her teeth and clung to her own will. "I am very clear about my own thoughts! I also have my own wishes to fulfill!

Mann awakened a waltz of Mateek's love for Kristalanna, the Children of God who commanded crystal Elementro but was forever absent from the universe. In Mateek's eyes, Mann seemed to be the reincarnation of Kristalanna—a courageous woman with a distinct and straightforward character. Although she lacked Kristalanna's physical lineage and intelligence, their spirits and souls were equally beautiful. As he pondered the relationship between Huxtin and Mann, pity started to transform into envy within him.

"You love him?" he asked, as the Star Soul flickered.

"Yes, I love him."

Upon hearing the definitive response, Mateek's half-body illusion reappeared, and the metal Elementro particles scattered like an indigo sea of flowers, blooming beneath a magnificent scene where the sun and moon gazed at each other.

"Has he ever told you the story of my Magic Mirror?" Despite his seemingly emotionless appearance and the absence of a physical heart, the Children of God also possessed genuine emotions, and his mind was now inundated with his tragic love story between him and Kristalanna.

"Yeah, I know about it. Not every detail, but I've been given the general idea." Mann nodded in response, her gaze fixed on the shield created by Magic Mirror of Mateek. It still stood steadfastly in front of the treasure box at the end of the room, reflecting the solitary shadow of the long-lived being. There was no despair in her clear eyes, only hope.

"To fall in love with a man she shouldn't have loved, that woman had to pay a price. I am a traitor, a man who betrayed my brothers and sisters but ultimately failed. I am not worthy of anyone's love. If Kristalanna had chosen Flammando instead of me, she would have lived," Mateek reminisced with a sigh, his right hand instinctively moving to cover his chest as if to protect an imagined physical heart that was no longer there. "There's nothing left inside me except an empty promise…"

"It's better than having no promises at all. And yours is not an empty promise. You have been trying very hard to keep it!"

Mann's words resonated deeply within Mateek, moving him time and time again. He now believed that the course of the universe might have an opportunity to be altered again if she stood by the Son of Chaos.

"Human, your fists cannot break through the cell," he said, gathering the indigo Elementro particles around his fists, which swarmed and transformed into two enormous hammers. "Step aside."

With a powerful swing of his hammers, he easily shattered the golden-coloured sphere. The wall rained down to the ground, only to disintegrate into particles that quickly vanished. Mann was released earlier than planned, and Mateek affirmed that he could reclaim his faith in the universe through his free will. He wanted this human woman to pursue her ideals freely, without regrets, and create a future filled with limitless possibilities.

In the ancient era, when the Children of God were entrusted with guarding Celestiloo under the command of The Creator, Mateek defied his duty and aligned himself with the Umbras in an attempt to free the Auras who had devolved into human beings. Unaware that he was being manipulated by the Umbras, he engaged in a fateful battle against Flammando in Timeloss. Tragically, it was during this battle that his beloved Kristalanna lost her life while he tried to strike a final blow against Flammando. He admitted defeat and surrendered, failing to protect the woman he loved and accepting the judgment and punishment he deserved at the end of the war.

He crafted the Star Souls, the Throne of Immortality, Silverlight Overflow, and more for the Auras. Afterward, he and his siblings relinquished their physical bodies to save the universe. Mateek constructed his own Starfall Tomb, but he was swiftly exiled alongside Litorio by the order of the Auras. Since then, he had become enslaved by his sins, forsaking his concern for the universe and denying his core belief that there could always be a different path leading to a better universe.

Regardless of the ultimate fate of the universe, there was one being who would never bear witness to its conclusion— Kristalanna. Her complete soul had been broken and lost, forever separated from her beloved.

13 Aqual, W.D. 471
Kuna Plains

The doors of the transport docks remained tightly shut, intensifying the Earthlings' anxiety as nightfall descended upon them.

"Come on, people! We need a solution here!" Mark Carlo barked at his subordinates. However, his attention kept getting diverted as his gaze repeatedly returned to his ex-wife, who stood on the sidelines, her eyes darting around as if expecting something to happen.

Without warning, a Binary of Teleportation appeared above one of the transport docks, Noira. Solarades and Huringo materialised on top of it, peering down at the bewildered Earthlings below. The crowd gasped collectively—all but Sheung Oren, who seemed to recognise the culprit responsible for the Bagoland incident. Carlo, despite his fear, clenched his fists and assumed a posture of leadership. He just couldn't afford to show weakness at this critical moment.

"Earthlings! Degenerated life forms from the Auras!" Solarades began, his voice echoing through the night. "We are here to liberate all of you, to cleanse the sins committed by my people, of which you might not have had previous knowledge, but soon will."

Everyone stared up at the strangely dressed man in white, confusion and fear etched on their faces. What did this supposed liberation entail? The word had often been associated with negative connotations in the context of the Earth Alliance.

"Leave us alone!" Carlo mustered all his courage and took a forceful step forward. "We will find our own way... and we won't be needing your help! You have no place here!"

For a brief moment, Oren watched Carlo with admiration, her heart swelling with pride for the man she had once loved. However, her feet rooted to the spot, unwilling to let herself be fooled by a single act of courage. There were too many abominable memories that she needed to hold tightly in her mind, serving as a constant reminder that love could be elusive and extremely destructive.

On the other hand, Solarades tilted his head, studying Carlo with interest. As he gazed into those ordinary eyes, he discerned not only the will to survive but also a deep sense of ambition, sparking his contemplation about the potential future of Celestiloo and Earth under Carlo's leadership, should this human ascend to the pinnacle of the power hierarchy.

"Have no fear," Solarades reassured, though Huringo beside him seemed annoyed by the statement. "We do not intend to harm you; rather, we aim to help you."

Carlo found himself caught in a dilemma, torn between mistrust and curiosity, as Oren maintained her silence, carefully weighing her options and considering the potential consequences of her actions. The other T.P.S.E. soldiers stared wide-eyed at Solarades and Huringo, their breaths catching in their throats. But before anyone could take another single step, the four Auras arrived on the scene. Gloria took action first, launching a bolt of lightning from the sky, aimed squarely at the duo. With uncanny reflexes, they evaded the electrifying attack, leaping in opposite directions. The lightning struck the transport dock instead, tearing a gaping hole through its roof and showering sparks like a deadly fireworks display. Remezo followed up with a massive circular shield that enveloped the damaged transport dock, trapping his enemies inside.

"Everyone, head to Hanmuk! Go! It's time to leave!" Oren suddenly shouted, her voice reaching a volume higher than the Elementro power display, as the Earthlings scrambled for cover. Amidst the chaos, she wasted no time in contacting the person she needed help from via her communicator. "Unlock Hanmuk's door right away!"

Upon hearing their vice commander's order, some Earthlings promptly complied, rushing towards the nearby transport dock with whatever equipment and resources they could carry. While a few seemed hesitant to move at first, Carlo, having finally understood Oren's intentions, exerted his influence to ensure their compliance.

At that moment, Rafaelzo stepped forward among his fellow

Auras and called out to Solarades, "Surrender now, and we can still talk this out. There must be another way!"

"There is no other way," Solarades spat contemptuously, his voice dripping with disdain. "You have lied countless times, Rafaelzo, and you are the least trustworthy person I know in this entire universe."

Guilt and regret masked Rafaelzo's expression. "I admit I've made mistakes and failed to keep promises, it's true. But I never had any intention to cause harm. I'm doing my best for everyone here."

"Your incompetence is a crime in itself. Trying to please everyone is the stupidest thing I've ever heard," Solarades sneered before turning his gaze towards Carlo, their intense stares creating a strange and unsettling atmosphere. "I apologise that I can no longer liberate you today, Earthlings. Perhaps I never will be able to. But remember, this universe requires constant change to move forward. Leave the past behind and push onward as far as you can!"

As if to prevent Solarades from unleashing his manipulative words on the Earthlings, Rafaelzo transformed into a swirling mass of colourful marbles and floated upward towards the evil duo. He passed effortlessly through Remezo's shield, and together with Solarades and Huringo, they leaped into the hole created by the lightning bolt. After cancelling the shield, Remezo and his companions also transformed into their respective disguise forms to join in the fight.

Meanwhile, the Earthlings regained their resolve and began boarding Hanmuk. When everyone else had boarded, except for Sheung Oren and Mark Carlo, the two of them stood alone, facing each other. They both understood that it was time to move forward and embrace the unknown future that lay before them but in separate way.

"Leave, and never come back." The raw emotion in Oren's words struck deep, unearthing tender memories of a love that had once burned brighter than any star.

"Oren... I love you." And without saying goodbye, Carlo removed the wedding ring from his finger—the ring that had caused him so much struggle and confusion—and threw it to the ground. He then joined his fellow Earthlings who were heading northwest, never looking back.

Soon after, the deafening roar of Hanmuk's engines reverberated through the air, signalling the commencement of a new chapter for the stranded Earthlings on Celestiloo. As the transport dock shrank to a mere speck against the darkened sky, Oren stood in sorrow, bathed in the faint glow of the makeshift light stands around. Her ex-husband's wedding ring lay on the ground, tears glistening upon it, evoking a sense of pity. She carefully picked it up, gently wiping away the settled dust, and cradled it in the warmth of her palm.

"Did I make the right choice..." she whispered, lost in her thoughts, oblivious to her surroundings, until she barely noticed Huxtin approaching, standing almost next to her.

"Is everything settled? Huxtin asked, his voice devoid of any hint of the emotions churning inside him, and when Oren turned around, she saw two identical swords held ready in his hands, the star on his armour shining with a frightful brightness. Her admiration for him dwindled, replaced by uncertainty in her reddened eyes. Her belief was being pelted off, layer by layer, questioning what really allured her to stay on this alien planet. Was it Huxtin alone? Or was there something else?

"Yes," she replied, attempting to appear emotionless just like Huxtin, though her blinking eyes betrayed her. "Lokiata is ready in the command centre."

"Good," Huxtin said, his tone cold but not fierce. "You should go. Join him. Lingering here is dangerous."

"Understood."

As Oren quickly turned to leave, Huxtin unexpectedly called out her name, his voice softening just a fraction, "Oren, thank you. Thank you for everything you've done for me."

Stunned, an additional layer of misfortune blurred her vision. "It was my... pleasure," she choked out, then hurried away, desperate not to let him see her vulnerability.

On her way back to the Earthling facility in Teddix, she couldn't help but wonder once more if she was truly making the right choice by confining herself in Paralloy Teddix. What was her purpose in this doomed kingdom? And most importantly,

who would continue to be her support in this realm far from
her own people?

13 Aqual, W.D. 471
Noira

In the grand hall of Noira, the four Auras engaged in a ferocious battle against Solarades and Huringo. Gloria's lightning Elementro powered up the area, revealing the intricate devices and unused leisure facilities that had been dormant for years, along with the emergence of Solarades and Huringo's wings. Each of them bore half of the energies of Wings of Sunlight in the form of a pair plus an additional single wing— the left side on Huringo, the right side on Solarades—as they wielded identical copies of the Blazing Sun in their hands.

Despite the united efforts of the Auras quartet, they found themselves struggling to make any significant progress against the strongest Aura in the room and the young man infused with the blood of the Son of Chaos.

"Prepare yourselves!" Huringo roared, his arrogance and devilish flair on display. "Your defeat is imminent!"

Solarades added, a dark smile playing on his lips, "This ends now."

The duo charged forward, their combined power surging forth to strike Gloria and Jeremia. The impact was immense, sending the two Auras careening across the room. Rafaelzo and Remezo narrowly avoided being knocked down, though Remezo winced as the residual energies grazed him, leaving him weakened.

"Are you alright?" Rafaelzo expressed his concern. "Can you still get up?"

"I can!" Remezo gritted out between laboured breaths. "We can't let them win!"

Next, Solarades and Huringo raised their swords high, transforming them into pure flows of energies. They twisted the flows together, creating a light column reminiscent of the one that had destroyed the protective dome of Wings of Moonlight above Teddix Castle—albeit somewhat weaker.

"Defend!" Rafaelzo yelled, and together with Remezo, they

quickly conjured a shield to block the incoming attack. But their integrated defence proved insufficient; they struggled to maintain their footing, and the compound shield turned opaque and gradually crumbled under the onslaught.

"Is this all you have?" Huringo mocked. "I expected more from the chief elder of the Auras!"

In the final second, Huxtin appeared, his dual swords catching the light as he lunged forward to intercept Solarades and Huringo's attack. The sudden interruption caused the duo to halt, momentarily caught off guard.

"Father!" Huringo's wicked smile stretched even wider upon seeing Huxtin. "Welcome to the ultimate game!"

Huxtin had no interest in engaging in conversation, but Solarades, who hadn't encountered Huxtin in thousands of days, interjected, his tone mocking yet solemn, "History repeats itself, the Son of Chaos. Do you remember what I told you when we first met?"

There was an extremely weird sensation surrounding Solarades, evident in his expression, physique, and the core of his life force. Huxtin suspected that trouble was brewing, recalling the conversation with Solarades, together with Wyach, during their initial encounter in Poona, where Solarades declared:

"I do not wish for my power to be taken by someone who is more deserving of wielding it. Instead, I would prefer it to be bestowed upon someone who truly desires to utilise its full potential, exploring every possibility it holds."

As the playback of his memory ceased, Huxtin felt a rush of the power of Chaos—not from within himself, but from his son, who was draining the essence of life along with the unique Elementro power from Solarades. Turning to face Huringo, he discovered that his son's outstretched left arm was adorned with six Rings of Chaos, each one absorbing the vibrant energies of brown and green, intermingled with the swirling and shimmering particles of black and white.

Once the process reached its climax, Solarades's drained body silently collapsed to the ground. His figure failed to emit even the slightest vestiges of magical radiance before his soul shards returned to their rightful place, as his energies had already been completely depleted. Huringo, discarding his black cloak, revealed the original white outfit with its origins in the Auras. Although his overall appearance remained unchanged after absorbing Solarades's energies, he now assumed the mantle of one of the strongest Auras, compensating for his previous weakness in the lack of Elementro transformability.

Determined to confront his son alone, Huxtin commanded the Auras without even casting a glance at them, saying, "Leave us. Take the dying Aura with you."

Rafaelzo's eyes flicked from Huxtin to Huringo and the fallen Solarades, and then back again. He knew all too well that he had to honour his promise to Huxtin, which meant allowing Huxtin to begin the battle between father and son. He then moved to lift Solarades, cocooning the bleak body within a protective sphere formed by his colourful marbles.

"We'll keep a close watch from outside of this carrier," he whispered to Huxtin before leaping into the air, disappearing through the hole on the ceiling. He was closely followed by Remezo, Gloria, and Jeremia who managed to stand on their own. They transformed, their silhouettes fading into the depths of the night sky.

With a deliberate, deep breath, Huxtin prepared himself for the inevitable confrontation with his son. Their swords clashed with a resounding clang, sparks flying as metal met pure, volatile Elementro energies. Each strike was fuelled by years of unspoken resentment and great pain.

In that pivotal moment of their duel, Huxtin could only hold onto hope, praying that his decision would ultimately pave the way for peace—for himself, for his son, and for the countless lives ensnared in the crossfire of their convoluted destinies. The clock was ticking, and his chaotic mind now overflowed with love and hatred, which would eventually determine his life and death, both substantively and symbolically.

CHAPTER 32

WHEN COMPARED TO THE MEANING OF LIFE, DEATH IS
ALWAYS A MORE OBSCURE SUBJECT

32:1

13 Aqual, W.D. 471
Kuna Plains

Returning to the gathering place of the evacuated Earthlings, Rafaelzo carefully laid Solarades's body on the ground before reverting back to his human form. Solarades now lay beneath the star-filled sky, surrounded by makeshift light stands, as if he had been granted a stage spotlight for the final moments of his life.

As his breaths became more laboured, he whispered faintly to his old friend, "My mission as an Aura on Celestiloo is finally complete... I will depart, knowing that the universe will make some progress."

Rafaelzo knelt beside Solarades, his heart burdened with conflicting emotions. "You still believe you were doing the right thing?" he asked softly. "You resorted to such a destructive method just to urge us forward?"

"Yes, my friend. Otherwise... what's the point of regressing?"

"But the consequences are too great, even for the Auras to bear. The humans on Celestiloo have no means to defend themselves against the Umbras..."

Standing nearby, Remezo, Gloria, and Jeremia listened to their conversation, each displaying their own distinct reactions. Remezo appeared to understand the depth of mercy emanating from his chief elder, while Jeremia maintained his carefree demeanour. Gloria, however, revealed her discontent with a wooden expression and crossed arms.

"I still have trouble accepting what you've done, but I now realise that I've made a grave mistake in casting the humans out," Rafaelzo continued, considering Solarades's words and actions. "I have witnessed their capabilities. I know that it was futile to prevent them from developing their true selves. We should have never oppressed them in the first place. They will only grow stronger and find ways to overcome their obstacles. But how can I make every Aura understand all of this? It seems impossible."

A weak smile flickered across Solarades's face, his eyes reflecting the glint of the stars. "The fact that you're willing to acknowledge your mistake is a significant fulfilment of my wish, Rafaelzo. Lead by example. Help them understand the importance of embracing change and growth, rather than fearing it... Just look at yourself. You have already taken a great step by not being afraid to show yourself to the humans. That's precisely what Lunarcaria wanted for all of us."

"Lunarcaria also reminded us of the importance of protecting our people." Rafaelzo took hold of Solarades's hands and placed them on the fading body's chest. "I will forever follow her spirit and continue in that direction."

"We were always destined to follow different paths, but in the end, we shared the same vision for the future... From this point onward, you will have to make difficult choices, one wave at a time. Chaos exists in this universe to remind us that we cannot simply be observers, but must strive to make the universe an ideal sanctuary."

As his life ebbed away, Solarades's physical form began to disintegrate into stardust, gently carried away by a breeze.

"You still have time to think it over, Rafaelzo... It's not too late to choose a different path than aligning with Novaubri."

With Solarades gone, Rafaelzo stood up, his gaze scanning the starry sky for traces of his old friend. The other Auras present pondered Solarades's final words. They had been presented with a choice: to continue living as detached observers or to embrace the chaos.

Shifting his attention to Noira, Rafaelzo no longer cared to speculate on who would emerge as the victor in the clash between Huxtin and Huringo. Regardless of who stepped out of the Earthling carrier, there were more pressing matters for him and his companions to address.

His eyes then turned to Gloria, whose irritation and bewilderment were evident in response to Solarades's wishes. He knew all too well that the already volatile situation was about to escalate further. Once she obtained the answer she desperately sought, the thunderstorm would undoubtedly transform into a full-scale calamity.

13 Aqual, W.D. 471
Noira

Huxtin was an anomaly. From the moment of his birth, with his innate ability, he was destined to disrupt the world, and perhaps even the universe. As he matured, his comprehension deepened, and he grew increasingly skeptical of his own existence, gradually distancing himself from ordinary people. He feared others, but what he feared most was himself.

There was a time when he attempted to open his mind, believing that he could free himself for the remainder of his life. However, those days belonged to the past, and his fears crawled back deeper into the core of his soul. It seemed as though there was no elixir in the universe capable of erasing his nightmares

The ordinary rules of survival dictated a cycle of birth, ageing, illness, and death, but they didn't apply to Huxtin. He wanted to embark on an eccentric and extraordinary dream in which he had a mission. As long as he fulfilled all the requirements, he would be granted a wish—a death wish. But what experiences awaited him upon awakening? Could it be another dream? The end of one dream connecting to the beginning of the next, an old door closing and a new one opening—a realm of infinite possibilities.

Yes, within the overlapping equilibrium of time and space, dreams were infinite, everything was fictitious and magical. One stage smashed, and in another stage, actors and scenes presented themselves one by one. Whether he encountered good or bad people in the dream, whom he befriended, whom he fought against, with whom he had an ambiguous connection, and those he merely brushed past; the assets and treasures he possessed; the hardships he endured; the wrong decisions he committed to; how he clung to fleeting moments of happiness while time slipped away unnoticed; how many souls he hurt; how many times he wept in despair, letting go, and missing out on love…

He had tried, dream after dream, mission after mission, yet it hadn't reached perfection. In his next dream, maybe he could start anew, finally obtaining what he had desired the most all along.

However, he pondered, would it be appropriate to remain in an eternal slumber?

"Tsk…"

"Father, don't daydream during the battle! Haven't I warned you about this before?"

Snapped out of his indulgence in dreams and destinies, Huxtin's nerves trembled in response to the dancing blades and flashing sparks. He almost forgot that he was engaged in a duel with his son. Being not particularly adept at wielding two swords in both hands, he often lost focus on how to swing the weapons simultaneously. However, this might be his only chance to keep up with his son's nearly perfect swordplay

"Why don't you just give up and surrender to your destiny?" Huringo's impatience didn't affect his offensiveness at all; in fact, he even accelerated the pace of his subsequent attacks. "Why do you keep wasting time on those meaningless pursuits? Why don't you…"

The battle between father and son lacked excitement as the son dominated for most of the time. In contrast, the father held back, constantly restraining himself, seemingly unable to unleash his full power. It appeared as though his indecisive heart was weighing him down and hindering his true potential.

"Why don't you just make up your damn mind!" Huringo continued to apply pressure to his father. "And kill me again… I know you want to. What are you waiting for?"

The Blazing Sun was on the verge of sweeping across Huxtin's lower leg, and finally, for the first time in this fight, Huringo felt the real force of resistance. Three swords intersected above their heads, tracing opposing arcs. Huxtin's expressions became terrifying, his blue eyes wide open, and the texture of his muscles and tiny blood vessels appeared exaggerated, as if magnified hundreds of times. With all his strength, he forcefully pushed his son to the ground.

"I hate being asked the same question again, again and again!

Why do you keep hurting me, hurting your brother..." he accused, "and hurting our family!"

As he spoke, several familiar figures flashed through his mind —roaring flames, raging lightning, and the constantly shifting interplay of light and shadow. Then, the respective Star Souls materialised, circling around him. They weren't physically present but only manifestations of energies drawn from the mutual cognitive space between him and every Star Soul he had gained recognition from. The turbine devices on both swords absorbed the Elementro energies, causing the swords to emit mystical colours, taking the form of a flying flame dragon and an agile electrifying leopard, hurtling straight towards Huringo.

Rather than standing up to dodge or block the attack, Huringo embraced it and allowed himself to be engulfed by the beasts. Next, he stood up unharmed and spread his wings of arrogance. The power of Wings of Sunlight granted him the supreme ability to regenerate at a speed beyond measure. This was precisely the moment to demonstrate why he hungered for such power.

"This is what I desire, Father," he finally revealed. "I want you to kill me. Not with the power of the Children of God, but with your true power... I am invincible now, and the only way you can inflict damage on me and take my life is by unleashing your power of Chaos."

There was no visible wound on him, but there was a cost: he had to endure the pain of the injury each time, even though it lasted no longer than a second. Huxtin observed the transformation Huringo had undergone after dismissing the power borrowed from the Star Souls, realising that a simple fight couldn't satisfy his son's twisted mentality. His heart throbbed with pain, about to explode.

"Perhaps you don't know what I desire either..." Suddenly, tears welled up in his shining gems, and the colour of the gems flickered from navy blue to bloody red. "This is the end, my son...

He had tried desperately to suppress the demons living in his heart, but now he had to admit that there was no peaceful way to settle the matters between him and Huringo, or between him and the universe, if he continued to reject the offers from the demons. He once hoped his story would conclude with a reunion with his son, but there were debts of sins to be paid. The murderer had to take responsibility for Hurian's death. The traitor had to face judgments from the Teddixian royal family. The sinner had to be erased from the universe.

"Answer the summon from Chaos... and become the king of the universe! I have been waiting for this moment for so long... and I can't wait any longer!" Huringo, with his eeriness, observed the abnormal expression on his father's face. He indulged in his own monologue, like a puppet on strings, moving his limbs and smirking face, his crazed muscles twitching perfectly. He probably knew what was inside his father's head right now—the whirring of an electric drill hitting metal walls, the roaring of tires skidding, the shattering of glass hitting the ground...

Blood was coursing through the veins at an astonishing pace. The scent of it was reaching the taste buds, dissipating on the tongue. The consciousness was fading, until the path of the future had been forged.

"Where is your anger? Where is your discontent? You should now feel the same fury that I felt when you took the throne from me and made my brother king instead of me! And the same heartache that I experienced when you killed me in Bagoland... No... But I didn't harbour a vengeful heart. I didn't. I'm not returning for revenge. I'm returning for a sacred mission. It's true, Father. I didn't seek revenge. I seek power, and with power... I can finally become the most deserving person standing on your right."

32:3

Unknown
Unknown

In the final moments before complete silence, Huxtin heard the familiar melodies that held a special place within his heart. Soon after, a familiar voice initiated a conversation.

"Welcome back."

"It's you... You are my own voice."

"Go. Go and take the power you desire. And then..."

"Then what?"

"Release... me."

Huxtin awoke, finding himself lying on the familiar sea of blood, tears streaming down his cheeks. He quickly rose to his feet, recognising the withered trees drained of all vitality. The gruesome surroundings remained unchanged, as did the scar and the crescent moon in the purple sky. However, this time he spawned much closer to the astronomical clock, its mysterious pendulum swinging louder and louder. The sound of the pendulum overwhelmed his senses, shattering his beliefs with each swing.

In this place, time existed in an ambiguous state, and the astronomical clock beckoned his soul to return to an unknown realm brimming with infinite possibilities. Suddenly, the stellar activity intensified, captivating his attention as he admired the meteor shower. It triggered a realisation that there was more to the myth of the Dolphin, the Human, and the Creator:

"Just before the rebirth of the world, the Human underwent a division. One portion was drawn into a colossal vortex, accompanied by a swirling entourage of

fragmented stars, destined to become the building blocks of the reconstructed realm. The other portion found itself imprisoned within the final teardrop shed by the Dolphin. Among the Messengers, who were all assigned new roles and bestowed with fresh purposes, the Dolphin stood apart as an exception, cherished and favoured by the Creator.

Jealousy permeated the ranks of the Messengers, for the transgressions of the 'Emperor' were consistently pardoned, while the betrayer trapped within the tear incessantly pleaded with a futile phrase, 'please forgive me,' desperate for the Dolphin's forgiveness. Nevertheless, the Creator refused to respond to the voices of jealousy, and the Dolphin was shielded from the disturbance, carrying on with the eternal slumber.

The reason why the sole remnant from the old world, which transitioned from bloody red to navy blue, became entwined with love and hatred, was due to the preservation and transfer of half of the Human's body, memories, and soul to the brand new world."

Was it a blessing? Was it a curse? Huxtin remained uncertain. Perhaps there were fragments of the myth that eluded his recollection, leaving the truth incomplete.

"Huxtin, have you forsaken the love for our son?"

Another voice resonated, its beauty and melodiousness familiar, yet laden with layers of worry and heartbreak.
"No, I haven't... I do love him. Why should I hate him? How can a man call himself a father if he hates his son?"

"Is this really your decision?"

"It's the only way."

"What happened to the promise you made to me?"

"I'm sorry... Just... allow me to go... Let us go..."

"Huxtin."

"Huxtin..."

"Huxtin!"

As Huxtin's right hand submerged into the intangible clock, followed by his left hand, left foot, until his whole body was engulfed within the box, the grand finale was about to begin. He dared not open his eyes on the other side, thus missing his chance to witness the sea of Star Shards, shattering, merging, shattering, merging... The process went on and on, nonstop, creating a magnificent spectacle bursting with unique and vibrant energies coming from the Primary Fruit—Elementro, giving birth to all forms of life which would soon travel to random places in the universe.

With the soul of the Son of Chaos drifted further into the core of the universe, his physical body and the tears he shed stayed in the tumultuous darkness—reality. In that reality, he had a mission: to slay his own firstborn, Huringo.

13 Aqual, W.D. 471
Noira

Resembling a fluorescent red cocoon, the power of Chaos enveloped Huxtin, looking static but vigorous in truth. Remarkably, this cocoon originated from his very blood, revealing one of the secrets of the nature of such power. Huringo silently observed his father, his aggressive flair fading away. With no need to maintain pretences, he became rarely calm, knowing there was no audience left to appreciate his previous play of madness.

Suddenly, the transport dock jolted and ascended into the sky, causing a slight tremor. The reddened liquefied Thunderites coursing through the network of transparent tubes within intensified the atmosphere. Huringo's gaze shifted towards the opening in the ceiling for a brief moment, but it didn't faze him. In fact, nothing could bother him anymore, for he was now prepared to accept his fate.

"This is the true essence of who you are," he said, securing twelve Rings of Chaos around his forearms, wrists, thighs, calves, ankles, waist, and neck. "And I am the one who made this happen. Only I possess the capability to bring this about, you see, Father. So go ahead and do as you please."

A tingling sensation crawled up his scalp, akin to a child unable to defy the authority of a father. He stood frozen in a corner, trembling not from the fear of danger, but from the fear of losing parental love. His mind began to recollect memories of his past interactions with his family, acknowledging that he had always been the rebellious prince, unlike his younger brother who dutifully adhered to their father's desires. It was his way, his unique style—a means to affirm his existence and maintain his position within the family. It became a habit, a scripted set of actions to project the image he and others believed him to be.

But who was he truly, deep down?

His father approached him with an unmistakable aura of

merciless intent, but Huringo just wanted to enjoy the final song of the battle. Therefore, he violently clashed his jaws, gathering his last remaining willpower to fight. "Now is the time! Show me your final score in the game, Father!"

Though they shared the same power, Huxtin served as the original source, far more powerful and far more destructive. Huringo, as a successor, could only access limited features of the power, but he didn't need to bear the side effects of it, such as the loss of senses—smell, touch, hearing, taste, sight, and extrasensory perception. He might be the first to manage to control the power at will, but what he could do with it was like an egg facing off against a great wall, incomparable to Huxtin's full potential.

13 Aqual, W.D. 471
From Teddix City to T.P.S.E. Command Centre

Fifteen minutes before midnight, Mu Mann rode the night breeze, traversing the smaller hills near Teddix City, Kousou in her right hand, indigo light slipping from her fingers. She floated and glided through the air, propelled by the magnetic fields generated by the Children of God who had defied the Son of Chaos's orders. Eventually, she descended upon a green slope in front of the city's eastern entrance.

"You better not cause any trouble," she murmured, surveying the deserted city in the darkness. It was unexpectedly desolate and unsettling, considering it had been the busiest area in the kingdom just days ago. "Where are you, Wood..."

Deciding against heading to Teddix Castle, as she could observe its quiescence from her vantage point in mid-air, she opted to go to the command centre of T.P.S.E. She believed she could find some Earthlings she knew there who might provide information. Her intuition proved correct when she spotted Sheung Oren standing near the structure on the surface, gazing up at the starry sky above the Kuna Plains. One of their transport docks hovered hundreds of meters above the ground, while the other was missing, already far away from the core area of Teddix.

With haste, Mann landed on the ground near Oren. "Sheung Oren!" she called out, struggling a bit to regain her balance. "Where is Huxtin? You have to tell me what the hell is going on!"

Oren turned around, utterly astonished, beholding Mann's arrival with the magical orb clutched in her hand, its indigo light never diminishing. "Why are you here..."

"Answer me," Mann pleaded, gripping the sleeve of Oren's military uniform with her left hand. "Is he on the transport dock? Noira? Hanmuk? What is he planning?"

The realisation struck Oren that Huxtin had intended to imprison Mann somewhere. Mann must have summoned her utmost determination in pursuit of her love. A pang of guilt washed over Oren as she confronted her own helplessness in the situation. For a moment, she was at a loss for words, unable to articulate her thoughts.

"Say something!" Mann urged.

And Oren finally replied, attempting to shake off Mann's hand but finding herself firmly restrained, "He doesn't explain his plan to you because he doesn't want you to stop him, don't you understand?"

"I understand!"

"Then why are you still so stubborn, pursuing a dream that will never come true?"

Initially, Mann refused to let go, and she noticed a diamond ring adorning Oren's right ring finger. It was the same ring that belonged to Mark Carlo, she believed, recalling that the lady's ring had been discarded and left buried in a scrapyard on Earth long ago. Deciphering the intricacies of Oren's relationship with Carlo, however, wasn't her point of interest, as she understood the importance of guiding Oren to prioritise the future over dwelling on the past.

"Oren, I should have been honest with you from the beginning, about my true feelings for Huxtin... Trust me, it was complicated," she stressed. "But we still have time to fix this! I don't know what stupid plan Huxtin has in his mind, but I know you also disagree with him, so help me stop him, please!"

She finally released her grip, anger welling up inside her, not directed at Oren but at Huxtin. While Oren hadn't yet succeeded in dismantling her own icy shield against the woman she once called sister, her haughtiness halting her from doing so, she had to admit that their care for each other still existed. Besides, Mann's bravery fundamentally moved her. It would turn her into somewhat of a villain if she ignored the request.

In a deliberate move, she covered the ring on her finger before offering to help. "Follow me... Lokiata is in the commander's tower."

13 Aqual, W.D. 471
T.P.S.E. Command Centre, Teddix

Three minutes before everything was set in stone, Sheung Oren led Mu Mann to their destination. Along the way, Oren briefed Mann on every detail she needed to know, leaving no time to waste in stopping Lokiata Kee from activating a bomb covertly installed in every transport dock under a confidential protocol—Protocol 1W—within the Earth Alliance.

As Mann entered through the opened door, her eyes immediately fell upon Kee. To her surprise, Kayley Mien was present, guarding the device that held control over Noira.

"Stop! Don't activate it!" she exclaimed nervously, rushing towards the device and forcefully pushing Kee aside. She frantically detached the keyboard and threw it away, leaving Kee and Mien startled by her actions.

"Kid, there's nothing you can do..." Kee's expression turned helpless. "The self-destruct procedure has already begun. There's no stop button, and the clock is ticking. It's best if you don't look at that screen. You wouldn't want to—"

"No way!" Mann shouted, realising that her nightmare had become a reality, her hands shaking. She let the Star Soul slip to the floor with a crisp sound of collision, its impact echoing the weight on her heart, and the indigo radiance finally extinguished. "There must be some way to stop him!"

"Accept the reality. This is Huxtin's will." Kee didn't look at Mann but instead stared at the screen of the device, where the red square above the name of the transport dock was flashing continuously. "He wants to sacrifice for the universe... and for you.

"Don't romanticise it! He just wants to die!" Not satisfied with Kee's response, Mann instead turned to Oren, who stood still near the entrance. "Get on the Hokan! Get him out of the dock!

However, Oren coldly rejected Mann's plea. "Impossible. Only Huxtin has the password to activate the operating system. Mann, you… just get over it."

With that, Mann fell speechless. Her face hardened, her lips turning try and pale, and her fingers ceased their movement, uncertain of where to hold onto. Perplexed, she glanced at Kee, who cared only about the completion of his task, then at Oren, who refused to look at anyone or anything, and finally at Mien, who shouldn't have been involved in their affairs. She had no idea why there wasn't anyone, including herself, shedding at least one tear in this very moment. Maybe they had all become numb to sadness, or perhaps they weren't sad at all but furious, feeling the wrath of understanding how insignificant they were in this hostile universe.

Thirty seconds before the arrival of a new day, the melodies that Huxtin used to hum and that Mann overheard on the day of their encounter orchestrated in Mann's heart. Back when she hadn't yet figured out what her future would hold during her extended stay in this alien world, she found the tune peculiar. However, as she continued to overhear him humming it on multiple occasions, she came to appreciate its true elegance. It felt as though he was using the music to convey a message, substituting the words they both lacked the courage to utter.

14 Aqual, W.D. 471
Noira

As the new day dawned, Huxtin's consciousness mysteriously returned to his body. He found himself lying on the floor, the power of Chaos that had cocooned him dissipated. His body convulsed involuntarily, his face pale, and his lips quivering. His eyes returned to normal, but they were filled with blinking sorrow, avoiding the pool of blood and the gruesome sight that had become unbearable to witness.

Having participated in countless battles, Huxtin should have developed immunity to the horrifying scenes of bodies and severed limbs. However, when it came to the victim being his own son, it was an entirely different scenario.

The self-destruct procedure of Noira was primed. The tubes transferring liquefied Thunderites glowed brighter than ever, the carrier expelled cold air through its ventilation fans, and the red alarm lights flashed incessantly, marking the countdown to the ultimate explosion. As Huxtin prepared to face the consequences of every perceived sin he had committed, Hurian materialised before him, enveloped in the usual elusive dark purple fog.

"Do you hate me?" he asked, looking up at his deceased wife, who was dressed in the attire she had worn on the very day they first met. "Will you forgive me?"

He received no answer, and whether this Hurain was a ghost or any form of hallucination, it no longer mattered. Before he died, he had his lover by his side, which could be considered a small comfort in his tragic existence in this universe.

Then, a cloud of hot red flames emerged from the encompassing fog, consuming both the fog and Hurain. The fire burned fiercely, spreading rapidly throughout the surroundings. Huxtin felt the flames drawing nearer, experiencing the agonising pain of his entire body being engulfed in searing heat. Nonetheless, amidst the torment, he also felt a profound sense of relief. He believed this would be the end of his tragedy, sabotaging the delusions of the Umbras, awakening the Auras from their corruption, and eradicating the beings that had only brought harm and tears to those around them

In the inferno, his skin turned red, his blood leaking and vaporising. Strangely, his armour remained intact, as if only his flesh accepted the damage. Simultaneously, the transport dock violently shook. Tears could no longer escape Huxtin's body, and his disintegrating form offered no more resistance, as the Elementro particles that composed him detached from his physical appearance.

With one final breath, he whispered, his voice feeble as the dying star at the precise moment it transformed into a mere residue of ash. "I... finally tried... letting... go."

"Come home, return to my side. Allow me to reveal the truth of this universe to you once again. Share with me your desires."

One minute past twelve, the transport dock detonated, but the fragmented debris didn't contaminate the land on the Kuna Plains. All the shattered metals, smoke, and ashes expelled from the explosion were drawn towards a core resembling a black hole, moving at supersonic speed. Until that core shrank into an invisible dot, it quietly disappeared, ensuring that nobody would discover there was once an explosion unless they had witnessed the firework show from beginning to end.

Everything proceeded in particular tranquility, except for the pair of the Key of Create and Destroy that had survived the explosion. Both silver-white swords earned a place in reality, tearing through the black sky and plummeting to the plains, producing a sound louder than the silent obliteration of the transport dock. Perhaps their survival held bigger secrets that couldn't be explained by the knowledge of this universe.

"Now, ask me the question, Father."

CHAPTER 33

THE SOUL, THOUGH NEW,
IS INUNDATED WITH ANCIENT THOUGHTS

33:1

"Mann, just like the entrance to the temple, the words on this letter will only be revealed to you. The first thing I want to say to you is sorry, and thank you for everything you have done for me over these years. I wouldn't have been able to reach this point without you by my side, but I also know that I have become a tremendous burden to you, and it always makes me feel sad. When you read this letter, it should signify that I have already departed quietly, and we are both stepping onto the path of true happiness. It's what I want, and it's the only way to free us from our troubles.

Maybe you are right about me. Maybe I am a good person after all. I wanted to be, and I have tried to be, but whenever I found myself overwhelmed by darkness, I did entertain thoughts of dragging the whole world into its embrace with me. I contemplated becoming the worst being in the universe, using my destructive power to feed my anguish and selfishness. I even fantasised about building a new kingdom from the ashes, where I could live with and protect my beloved. But I also felt shame and guilt for harbouring such horrible desires. Is it worth it? Do I really have to sacrifice the entire universe just to save nine, or maybe ten people? Or perhaps, deep down, I only want to save myself?

Mann, if you were me, what would you do? I am sure you would loudly say, 'Don't be stupid. Don't even think about doing something wrong.' But what defines wisdom or foolishness? What defines right and wrong? You often ask me to return to the Huxtin I used to be. You have never encountered that version of me, and my understanding of that version and the events that transpired has become increasingly blurred. Honestly, no one understands me better than you, and because of you, I tried to piece together fragments of my past and follow your lead, being shaped by your guidance. But sometimes, it just doesn't work out.

Who am I? Is the version of me you always speak of merely a figment of imagination?

I wish our lives were scripted, so that I could find a way to rewrite them, so that I wouldn't be entangled in the war between the Auras and the Umbras. Or, at the very least, I could write you out of my story, so that we never met in Bagoland, so that your people could survive the explosion, so that you never witnessed what I did to my son and myself. It was a total disaster, wasn't it? If I could, I would even make you an ordinary person, not a commander of an army, and you would live a peaceful life with your sister on Earth. From beginning to end, you would never leave Earth, and you would never come to Celestiloo.

But let's consider the situation from a different perspective. If you hadn't found me and stopped me back then, Celestiloo might have already turned into a living hell, and I would be the murderer that everyone feared or sought to exterminate, assuming there were still people left alive. You saved me. You saved Celestiloo, and even the universe, and you should be proud of yourself.

If everything was merely a dream, then I wouldn't have to endure the fear of losing you one day, and the same goes for you. As for my dream, it is nearing its end. I won't tell you to leave Paralloy Teddix. I believe you don't want to, so stay as you wish, but if that is your decision, I have no choice but to entrust the task of protecting the Stars of Teddix to you. Don't worry. You won't face the dangers alone. I have already made arrangements, and my most trusted allies will protect you along the way. I dare to ask for help because I know you want to continue your adventure on Celestiloo, don't you?

Mann, take care. Perhaps you will see me again in your dreams. And if miracles exist, I hope to meet you again, someday, somewhere—not in dreams, but in the destination we both yearn to reach.

Goodbye."

"What a nonsensical joke. On what basis do you think I have the ability to shape your life? It's the other way around, Wood. It always has been…"

Mu Mann held the letter from Huxtin, written on high-quality paper bearing the royal family crest of Teddix, in her hands from dawn until an hour before dusk. This was the fifth time she had read it today, and she knew every word by heart. She sat atop a small green slope near Teddix City, finding nothing amiss except for the radiant sun, the billowing white clouds, and the sky animals flying freely without apprehension. With a serious expression on her face and her long brown hair tangled, she had her military uniform donned with the jacket zipped up, knowing it was more appropriate for the challenges ahead.

"And how can you be so certain that I won't leave Paralloy Teddix? What can I do with only my bravery and without you by my side?" Carefully folding the letter, she placed it inside her tool pocket hanging from her waist. Looking out over the abandoned city, she couldn't help but wonder aloud, "Am I still in a dream? Are you in my dream?"

Beside her rested one half of the pair of the Key of Create and Destroy. As a human being, she lacked inherent abilities, making her battles against enemies with mere flesh and blood like striking a metal robot with a wooden stick. However, the sword left by Huxtin served as a symbol representing the authority of the master of all Star Souls. She needed it to press onward, resembling a tireless guardian of the sword, never able to rest even for a moment. It was her only choice.

Her gaze then shifted to the ark of the Auras, still connected to the magnificent ice bridges on the cliff's edge in the Shell Valley. Huxtin had highlighted that it wasn't merely a colossal weapon or mass carrier; it possessed a spirituality akin to a Star Soul but with aspects of what Earthlings called artificial intelligence. It breathed, listened, and patiently awaited completion of its internal repairs.

Currently, Silverlight Overflow could only remain silent by the side of the Throne of Immortality. The true nature of the beast was kept as a mystery, and no one could predict its actions if it were to awaken from its prolonged slumber.

Suddenly, a sense of sinister presence loomed. Unusual black shadows lingered just above the Kuna Plains, beneath the clouds. The nerves within Mann's being teetered on the edge of a massive explosion, provoking an overwhelming tension she had never experienced before.

"Okay, Mu Mann... calm down," she whispered to herself. Gripping her sword, she rose to her feet. "I know you have expectations of me, but it's not an easy mission. Give me a moment to gather my thoughts..."

The number of distant shadows multiplied rapidly, causing her to feel like her blood was boiling throughout her body. However, within seconds, she regained composure and reviewed the mental images taking shape in her mind, ultimately making a crucial decision. "Alright... I will go into battle, and I will not freak out. Breathe."

Just as she prepared to set off towards the Kuna Plains, a signal crackled through her earpiece. Pressing it, she heard urgent news from her ally.

"Kid! They're here!" Lokiata Kee's voice rang out. "Come to where I'm stationed! Hurry!"

"Understood, Uncle Kee," Mann replied, her voice steady. "Hang in there."

Scenes of various disasters replayed in her mind—tornado, earthquake, tsunami, thunderstorm... but she refused to be consumed by fear. She didn't seek to be a hero; her goal was to honour Huxtin's legacy—to gather the Star Souls, seal away the Umbras, and protect the Stars of Teddix.

"It's time," she reassured herself before officially accepting the most difficult challenge she had ever faced. "I am ready, Huxtin."

16 Aqual, W.D. 471
Teddix Castle, Teddix

Teddix Castle and Teddix City, once thriving and prosperous, now appeared like two dying stars that awaited reduction into stardust. The inhabitants had been forced to migrate eastward, leaving behind the very essence that had nourished their national spirit. This wasn't the first time such a migration had occurred; history had a way of repeating itself, turning a golden age into an abrupt shadowiness. However, it didn't mean that a dignified return was impossible. As long as there were people standing against the forces of evil, there was always hope for a resurgence and the reclamation of the lost land. However, the precise timing and circumstances—the specific year and day, the leadership role—all depended on the decisions and subsequent actions of the present fighters.

In the merciless rain that heavily hit the castle grounds, Huricane stood alone in the garden, looking at all the withered flowers and smelling the sourness emanating from the soil. He engaged in a deep prayer, hoping that the rainfall could breathe new life into the diverse ecologies that once thrived there. But despite his efforts, the rain couldn't save the Icrings, nor could it revive the precious memories that he shared with his late mother.

"My King, please come indoors. I fear you will fall ill standing out here."

Huricane remained silent, lost in his self-proclaimed spiritual cleansing, seemingly oblivious to Wyach's voice of concern. Rainwater trickled down his face, mingling with tears. His regal attire became drenched, reflecting the uncertainty of whether it symbolised the destruction of a majestic kingdom or the emergence of new life within its hallowed grounds. There was a sense that he was intentionally inflicting pain upon himself, seeking catharsis through physical suffering.

The rainwater continued to pour over him, forming a harmony as if his body communicated silently with nature.

Would it show the path he should tread in the future? Would it disclose the whereabouts of his father's soul, whether it resided in heaven or perhaps in hell? Would it foretell his inevitable death due to his perceived failure?

Unexpectedly, the rainwater above him diverted its course. "I thought the Earthlings had removed everything... Wyach," he mumbled, raising his gaze to behold a transparent canopy shielding him from the downpour.

"I borrowed it from a new friend," Wyach replied, "but borrowed things must be returned. However, My King, this kingdom belongs to you. It is a commitment for a lifetime."

Huricane turned around and took note of Wyach's attire in shades of black and grey. The unexpected sight added to the disarray in his already confused thoughts, oscillating between moments of vibrant colours and moments of emptiness.

"My father is dead. Paralloy Teddix is in chaos. What can I rely on to survive?" His words dripped with a tone of despair, matching the oppressive humidity brought by the rain. "Are there any options for me, apart from summoning courage, standing up, and fighting back? Is there another path I can choose?"

"The answer is very simple, My King. Live or die." Wyach's response was straightforward, her voice steady. "Please, find the answer within your own heart. You are not doing this for anyone else in the world. You are not doing this for seeking heroism or to be hailed as the greatest king in history. You are doing this for yourself. If you choose to fight alongside me, it would be an honour. But regardless, I have your back, and I am willing to sacrifice my life if needed."

As their brief conversation concluded, Wyach inspected the unusually gloomy sky, detecting a stirring of powerful evils within the clouds, while Huricane lowered his head, observing his own spiritless reflection in the cracked ceramic floor, where accumulated water formed a small mirror-like surface. He could barely recognise the face staring back at him. The decision to live or die hadn't yet been made, but he also sensed the approaching danger through his primal instincts.

Water possessed a mystical quality of communication. While

wind could be blocked by obstacles and electromagnetic waves could be disrupted by interference, water carried messages without interruption. It spanned across distant worlds and unforeseen realms, its eternal tension and adaptability serving as conduits for hidden codes.

Wyach felt a subtle calling from the rainwater as she monitored the transparent jewels falling onto the umbrella, converging into streams and branching off into infinite smaller streams, perpetually circulating. She believed that there were encoded messages within the droplets, and she earnestly hoped that the sender of those messages was precisely the one she had always placed her faith in.

16 Aqual, W.D. 471
Kuna Plains

On the Kuna Plains, battles had already erupted. The Auras, Rafaelzo, Gloria, Remezo, and Jeramia channeled their powers, unleashing the fullest extent of their distinct Elementro energies to confront the oncoming enemies from the north. Meanwhile, Lokiata Kee and Mu Mann arrived at the entrance of the plains, only to be intercepted by the intruders of the kingdom. In a moment of carelessness, Mann was struck by a smoke bomb. Instead of a physical projectile, the bomb released a short-range diffusion of odourless and tasteless purple smoke, designed not only to disrupt sight but also to conceal a hidden danger, lingering and firmly rooted in the ground.

"Get away from the smoke! It's corrosive!"

A warning could be heard from the other side of the smoke. Without hesitation, Kee ventured into the smoke, reaching out to help Mann escape. Although the smoke seemed to have no immediate effect on human flesh, it was clear that they needed to avoid it. Thus, Kee drew his laser gun and aimed at the bomb, destroying it and halting the release of the harmful gas.

Mann, lacking expertise in swordsmanship, ironically relied on Huxtin's sword to protect herself. As more smoke bombs descended, she attempted to slash them, hitting some while others evaded her blade, with Kee lending his assistance to eliminate the missed targets and ensure their safety.

As the situation became direr, a terrifying ash-grey creature resembling a giant hawk with two pair of feathered wings and four strong legs emerged before Kee and Mann. Its body was covered in hardened scales, each scale acting as a deadly bomb capable of stunning and melting its prey. As the vacant spaces on the creature's body refilled with bubbling black slime, expanding and forming new scales, the human fighters grew increasingly vigilant.

Luckily, their saviour arrived on the scene. The monstrous Umbra let out a high-pitched scream, which initially seemed like a provocation but turned out to be a cry of agony. The fisherman skilfully manoeuvred his fishing rod and hooked the creature's head, decapitating it with a brutal force. All scales instantly disintegrated into black slime, dissolving the creature's entire body with its own weapons, ultimately leaving behind a pool of rotten ash-grey liquid.

"Hey! Miss me? Mu… Moon? Mon?" The fisherman, who had traveled all the way from Auta Rex to the Kuna Plains, burst into laughter. "Oh gosh, how impolite I am. I should have remembered your name, hahaha!"

But Mann only felt a great relief upon seeing Huxtin's old friend. The arrival of Autaming, orchestrated by Huxtin before his death, brought a wave of added confidence and latent power rising to the surface for her journey ahead.

"It's Mu Mann, you little brain," she responded to Autaming with a smile, but her expression quickly changed as they heard a nearby explosion. "What's happening? Are there others fighting the Umbras? It has to be the Auras, right?"

"Yeah, but there's also a guy fighting alone. He's not with me," Autaming replied, still wearing a joyful mask on his face. "I don't think he belongs to those living gods wearing white either."

"So, are we back as a team?" Kee interjected, impressed by the fisherman's ability to match supernatural powers. "Shall we hunt down these evil creatures together?"

"I thought you would say, 'Let's be real friends this time' or something similar," Autaming teased.

"I thought you hated the idea of making new friends," Kee jokingly countered. "No wonder they said I shouldn't trust every word that comes out of your mouth."

"Well, I may desperately need a few new friends now… Wait. Excuse me? Who are the "they" you were referring to?"

Simultaneously, another explosion occurred, and columns of roaring fire shot up into the sky. Autaming, now dressed as an ordinary citizen of Paralloy Teddix rather than a seasoned fisherman, wearing a khaki T-shirt, olive green shorts, and an unbuttoned darker green vest, firmly held his fishing rod and pointed towards the burning flames. "Follow me," he said cryptically. "You might find something interesting there, Lokia... Kay?"

"Alright... Whatever." Kee sighed inwardly, reminiscing about the annoyance of dealing with the talkative fisherman. Little did he know that even more complex troubles awaited him. "This is so brilliant."

In the absence of Huxtin, a group of human adventurers, including the former T.P.S.E. commander, the stranded Cosmo Scavenger, and the seasoned fisherman who had battled against waves and winds throughout his life, prepared to undertake a mission that exceeded the capabilities of ordinary humans. Hence, it was evident that they needed a touch of divine power and a greater number of companions to proceed with certainty.

Led by Autaming, Lokiata Kee and Mu Mann arrived at the site of the explosions. Dozens of hawk-headed crawlers, the very same Umbras they had fought moments ago, scurried about with noticeable activity. Amidst the smoke-filled air, a broad dark green sword glimmered with a holy light. It swung through the air, accompanied by scorching flames, effortlessly dispatching several monsters in a single fluid motion. Following this display of prowess, a pair of majestic fire dragons and a duo of phoenixes took to the sky, their ethereal claws and teeth extended, incinerating the purple smoke released by the bombs until nothing remained.

"Kid... Lokiata," Mann uttered in disbelief, her vision filled with afterimages from the flames. "You've returned... It's been a good while."

Lokiata Zen, who had vanished alongside Huxtin in Cape Nameless, now stood before them, bearing the same appearance and attire, albeit worn and stained. In just a few weeks of absence, his once youthful and innocent face had acquired traces of time and cunning. His disheveled hair and stubble hinted at the fatigue and hardships of his solitariness, or perhaps it was a deliberate portrayal of decadence and detachment.

"Mu... Mann..." Zen's voice trembled as he looked at Mann with astonishment, never expecting to encounter his former army superior again. The presence of two unfamiliar individuals by her side further puzzled him. "I... I'm glad that I... see you again."

"He's... my brother's son," Kee whispered to Mann, taken aback by his initial impression of Zen and the conflicting emotions stirring within him. "Is he?"

"Yes, he is," Mann responded simply. "Lokiata Zen."

"What a terrible arrangement by the universe, damn it..." The familiarity in posture, facial features, and even aura struck Kee, causing a flare of pain on the scar on his chin, though it could have been a mere placebo effect. He absentmindedly traced his scar, grumbling inwardly at Huxtin for never informing him about the possibility of encountering Lokiata Edward and May Dori's only child. His heartbeat quickened, and his thoughts jumped chaotically within his mind.

On the other hand, Zen couldn't believe there was another human seemingly from Earth apart from his fellows in the army, yet he sensed some intricate connections between himself and the stranger. However, it wasn't just his concern.

"Where is Huxtin?" he blurted out, voicing the burning question that fuelled his desire to fight. "I don't see him around the battlefield. I need to meet him right now."

"Huxtin no longer exists in this world, kid," Mann responded with the authoritative air that she had been deprived of but always possessed. "Perhaps you can tell me where Miria is instead?"

She closely studied Zen, noting the tension in his facial muscles, the omission of any smile, and the deep, shining eyes filled with animosity. She had encountered similar gazes in the past and understood their implications: forsaking the ethos of protection and embracing the path of destruction, eliminating any obstacle, whether friend or foe. With Miria not within her sight and the young man's abnormal spirit, she sensed a terrible omen.

"Ho-how is that possible? How could the Son of Chaos..." Zen hesitated, caught between belief and doubt, deliberately avoiding Mann's question. "I refuse to believe he perished so easily."

"Trust me. He is dead. He disappeared along with Noira,

killed by an explosion." Mann's voice remained resolute, but a tinge of depression permeated her words as she recounted the moments when Huxtin repeatedly distanced himself from her life. "And I don't wish to say those words again."

Zen still clung to disbelief. However, he couldn't overlook the fact that Mann now wielded Huxtin's Revenging Shard without any other reasonable explanation. Unbeknownst to the human alliance before him, he had embarked on a treacherous journey back home. He had escaped the hunting of the Umbras in Timeloss, traversed the desert of Dakadan with its coloured sand of fluctuated temperature, navigated the intertwined peaks of the Betwanry that formed a natural cross shape, and finally returned to the continent of Paralloy.

Sadly, the place that he could finally regard as his comfortable home had undergone a dramatic transformation. The T.P.S.E. command centre had been emptied, and nearly all Earthlings had departed Paralloy Teddix abroad Hanmuk, their destination unknown.

Temporarily setting aside the unpleasant memories, his gaze shifted towards Mann's left, where a tall and sturdy man stood, always wearing a cheerful smile and holding a fishing rod. "Would you mind telling me who you are?"

"Autaming," the fisherman proactively replied, introducing himself. "Just a regular human with no extraordinary powers. Nice to meet you. You're welcome."

Zen then focused on Mann's right, strengthening his suspicion of the unspoken connection. "And as for you..."

"Kay. Just call me Kay. I'm also nobody special," Kee lied, glancing at Mann and signalling for her to keep his secrets before returning his gaze to Zen. "I came from Earth, but you don't have to doubt my intentions of being with them. You can trust me."

"No problem... Pleased to meet you, Kay."

The atmosphere couldn't be lightened during their introductions because Mann was still deeply concerned about an important matter. "Hey, you haven't answered my question yet," she interjected, her attention briefly drawn away by the intense exchange of light and darkness in the nearby battlefield between the Auras and the Umbras.

Realising that the flame of truth was on the verge of bursting out, Zen reluctantly let his guard down. Similar to Mann's approach to Huxtin's death, he had also been avoiding an emotional outburst. However, he lacked any skill in the art of deception.

"Miria..." He turned his head, looking up at the shadowy clouds, habitually scratching his hair. "She is in there."

The Umbras, born from the so-called "Bad Deeds" within the souls of the Auras, had formed an army and returned to Celestiloo with one of their ancient leaders, determined to eradicate any living being clinging to "Good Deeds". The war had already begun.

APPENDICES

Appendix III - the clans of the Auras and the Trinity of Twelfianity

Every Aura belonged to a specific clan, distinguished by the Elementro attributes they could wield. Some Auras possessed the ability to harness multiple types of Elementro, and exceptionally rare were those who could command all twelve. However, being a multi-Elementro user didn't automatically confer greater power upon an Aura. The dynamics and interplay between the twelve Elementro dictated the upper limits of each clan's abilities, with level ten being the pinnacle of achievement.

There were a total of twenty-three clans in the Auras society, namely: the Solitary Mind (mind), the Solitary Illusion (illusion), the Solitary Blink (sun), the Solitary Silence (moon), the Enchanting Fairy (mind, illusion), the Undying Binary (sun, moon), the Major Spirit (mind, illusion, sun, moon), the Quaking Field (rock), the Undulating Stream (water), the Melting Heat (fire), the Chasing Howl (air), the Horizon (rock, air), the Opposition (water, fire), the Bloom Blossoming (rock, water, bio), the Thunder Rising (fire, air, lightning), the Glacier Calving (water, air, crystal), the Molecule Switching (rock, fire, metal), the Ninja (rock, water, air, bio, crystal), the Kaseki (rock, water, fire, bio, metal), the Soltisite (water, fire, air, lightning, crystal), the Superconductor (rock, fire, air, lightning, metal), the Sennin (rock, water, fire, air, bio, lightning, crystal, metal), and the Twelfianity (all twelve Elementro).

Additionally, there were three types of special Elementro users who didn't belong to any of the aforementioned clans of the Auras. The wielders of Wings of Sunlight (sun, moon, rock, bio), Wings of Moonlight (mind, illusion, water, crystal), and Wings of Starlight (fire, air, lightning, metal) formed the Trinity of Twelfianity, representing the three most powerful legendary Auras. It was said that in the universe, there were only three Auras who possessed one of the unique Elementro powers each time. When any of them perished, the power would be reincarnated in the next newly born Aura or absorbed by another host.

In terms of their abilities, Wings of Sunlight enabled energy

278

neutralisation, Wings of Moonlight generated absolute defence, and Wings of Starlight unleashed lethal attacks, contributing to the Trinity of Twelfianity's unparalleled power. Moreover, the interplay of the three special Elementro powers restrained each other. Wings of Sunlight could neutralise Wings of Moonlight, Wings of Moonlight could defend against Wings of Starlight, while Wings of Starlight could penetrate Wings of Sunlight, ensuring a dynamic and ever-shifting balance of power within.

Considering the interrelationships among the twelve Elementro, apart from the Auras from the Twelfianity, no Aura could simultaneously harness both bio and lightning Elementro or both crystal and metal Elementro. Furthermore, Auras that harnessed basic and compound Elementro (rock, water, fire, air, bio, lightning, crystal, metal) couldn't harness advanced Elementro (mind, illusion, sun, moon), and vice versa.

About the Author

JAY CLIFFIX

Jay Cliffix is an author and entertainment industry professional based in Hong Kong. He published his debut novel, 光影星碎, in 2012 and has since worked as a movie journalist, columnist, and critic.

Currently, Jay Cliffix is immersed in creating a sequel to his online episodic novella, 麻將大激鬥, which was published between 2019 and 2022. Additionally, he is exploring the fantastical realm of Celestiloo and the Earth Alliance, which he established twenty-five years ago, through his writing of fantasy adventure stories.

THE PROVIDENCE OF
CREATION/ANNIHILATION

The **Umbras** arrived in **Paralloy Teddix**, accompanied by two familiar faces. One had transcended humanity, harnessing the awakened power of **Elementro**, while the other had been consumed by total darkness, her once silvery radiance extinguished. With **Huxtin** absent, **Mu Mann** took the lead, fighting alongside **Rafaelzo** and their allies. Their mission to collect the twelve **Star Souls** and seal the existence of the Umbras pressed on, forging a second alliance in **Celestiloo**'s history, unexpectedly uniting human beings and the Auras.

In the face of the kingdom's impending demise, **Huricane** grappled with his own depression, striving to rise again and uncertain if he could unleash the full extent of his power to protect what he held dear. As one of the successors of the power of **Chaos**, he remained a target for both the Auras and the Umbras. His own fate hung in the balance, yet a dormant soul was about to stir, bringing forth boundless possibilities for the ultimate battle.

Unspoken secrets lingered, shrouding the story of the **Son of Chaos**. How did Huxtin navigate his powers of Elementro and **Six Xenxes** in the past? What path did he tread to ascend as the king of the **Teddix Empire**? Who was the Aura named **Lunarcaria**, and what transpired in **Bagoland**? Amid their most challenging mission, Mu Mann prepared to unravel the intricacies of Huxtin's life, eagerly anticipating their reunion, if it were to come to pass…

Made in the USA
Monee, IL
23 April 2024